The South Wind Blew Softly

Ruth Livingston Hill

HARVEST HOUSE PUBLISHERS
Eugene, Oregon 97402

"And when the south wind blew softly, supposing
that they had obtained their purpose loosing
thence they sailed . . . But not long after
there arose . . . a tempestuous wind."

Acts 27:13, 14

one

The lawyer's office was bare. Its starkness was appalling to
Nancy. In spite of the fact that she was reasonably sure that
she was her uncle's only heir, she felt apprehensive.

She suppressed a shudder and took a deep breath when the
iron-gray man appeared and solemnly took a seat at his mas-
sive desk.

"Miss Lansing," he began in a subdued voice befitting one
who was about to read to a near relative the will of a dear
deceased, "I sent for you so that I might communicate to you
personally the content of your uncle's will. He was one of my
most esteemed clients."

With considerable ceremony he drew out of a long envelope
a single sheet.

"I shall read it now." He cleared his throat. "I might say
that your uncle made a somewhat unusual stipulation regarding the bestowal of his effects. You may prepare yourself to
make a decision." He peered grimly over the top of the paper
at the pretty young girl before him as if he were warning her
of approaching doom. Apparently he was not at all impressed
by her fresh loveliness, her shining dark eyes and short, short

dark curls crowned with a perky little upturned bit of red straw, as pert as the tip of her little nose.

Nancy's mind was suddenly in such a whirl that she scarcely heard the legal terminology of the introductory sentences. Then the words "my entire estate, amounting to approximately twenty-five thousand dollars" startled her into alertness.

" 'On condition' "—the lawyer paused exasperatingly and glanced up at her again.

" 'On condition,' " he repeated, " 'that my niece reside continuously in the town of Pine City, Florida, for at least six months, beginning not later than six weeks after my demise. Should she decide against this condition, the entire estate shall go to my sister Beatrice, and at her death, to the Westside Community Church of Pine City of which my sister is at present a member.' That is all." The man glared at Nancy.

She stared back at him a moment, her pretty mouth half open, trying to size up the situation. Then she smiled brightly and spoke, in short, jerky, excited phrases.

"Oh-h! I think—I understand. I believe I know why Uncle Harry made such a—a *crazy* condition. His sister, my Aunt Bea, lives in Pine City. He has always said he wished I were more like her. She's very—very—religious, you see. And I guess he thought that if I lived with her awhile it might—rub off on me!" She finished rather breathlessly, half indignant and half amused.

"Your inference is astonishingly accurate," Mr. Laidlaw announced. "Your uncle discussed the matter with me more than once." He frowned at Nancy.

"As if he thought I was a hussy," flared Nancy as she reviewed the conference to her friend, Rose Trask, on the way home. "Self-righteous prig! I'm not so sure I want that money.

8

If Uncle Harry thought he could make me into a holy roller, he and his money can go hang."

"Not really!" exclaimed Rose. "You wouldn't turn down twenty-five thousand!"

"Well," amended Nancy, "at least, I'll sleep over it. Yikes! I wish I knew Aunt Bea. She must be deadly. I wonder if I could stand it for six months. But twenty-five thousand. That's a pleasant wad. What couldn't I do with it!"

The two girls gaily fell to making all sorts of fabulous plans.

"It's sort of like the fairy tale dreams I used to have," said Nancy. "I've always longed for scads and scads of money. It's just the string to it that bothers me. It was hateful of Uncle Harry to do it to me. It makes me mad."

"Don't you know your aunt at all?" Rose was obviously impressed at being right next door as it were to a mystery story legacy.

"Never saw her. She was a missionary in India most of her life. She used to send me Indian dolls at Christmas, and she still sends a greeting card from Florida which I duly answer with another. That's all. She's rather antique, and impossibly religious, I've been told."

"I wouldn't care," asserted Rose. "I'd be ever so religious for twenty-five thousand. After all, it couldn't be too bad, for only six months."

"Oh, I suppose I'll do it. But I dread it. Six months can be horribly long under certain circumstances. I wonder what my folks will think of the deal. I know what Mother will say: 'Take it.' She wouldn't pass up money anywhere. Dad will shy away from the religion angle. Parents are funny, aren't they? It's so easy to see through them."

"At least you have some. And they don't quarrel all the time. Whenever mine were home at all, they were at each other's throats—until Dad left. Then Mother moped till this

9

new man turned up. I still don't see much of her. We pass in the front hall occasionally. Say, what do you think Hank will say to your going to Florida?"

Nancy shrugged. "I don't know; it doesn't matter. He can come down if he wants to—*if* I go. It's a good way to find out how much a fellow thinks of you. I am certainly not going to stay home on his account. I'm through with men, anyway. He's gone off somewhere himself now, hasn't he? I don't really care whether he comes down or not, except that I may die of boredom if somebody doesn't. You'll have to come and visit me. If I need rescuing I'll send for you."

"All right, but don't expect me to join in prayer with you. *I'm* not getting twenty-five thousand."

The girls laughed mockingly, and Rose got out at her own home.

Nancy drove on, a puzzled thoughtful frown and a little impish grin vying for first place on her pretty features.

It was characteristic of Nancy that she waited until dessert was served that evening before she mentioned the will. She had lived a rather independent existence since she left home for college when she was seventeen.

"Let her make it on her own," had always been her father's admonition when her mother would have tried to shield her. "If she's smart enough to finish high school she ought to be able to take college in stride, and all that goes with it." Nancy respected her father tremendously, and loved him, although there had never been much outward manifestation of it; she tacitly understood that Mrs. Lansing's cold conventionality would not have countenanced much show of affection.

Nancy announced the terms of her uncle's will and then smiled to herself when both parents reacted exactly as she had predicted.

She brushed aside her mother's immediate desire to talk

Florida wardrobe, and gave concerned attention to her father's cautious dictum.

"I never knew your Aunt Bea well," he said thoughtfully. "She was twelve years older than I, and she went off to some kind of training school when I was only a small boy. Then she set sail for India as a missionary and broke Mother's heart. I never could fathom just what she did to my brother Harry. He went out to India to visit her and stayed two years. He slid off the deep end in religion after that. Gave more than half his income to some South Sea Island mission or other and lived like a pauper although his business still made plenty." He shook his head. "It never made sense to me. I've had to struggle like a fool for the little I got. But—go down there if you want to. Heaven forbid that you turn out like that, though." He lit his pipe and sauntered from the table into the living room.

Nancy gazed after him, the little frown dominant again. Then her mother began to chatter about clothes for her trip. The decision seemed to have been made, in her mother's mind.

Nancy lay awake a long time that night; her parents were discussing the matter in their own room.

"Well, George, I think this Florida trip for Nancy is simply providential. It will take her mind off the memory of all the horrible things of last winter. Honestly, I've been afraid for her mind sometimes. I often come on her in her room tramping up and down, her eyes just smoldering. She could go off the beam at any time."

"Nonsense. Nancy will keep her balance."

"George, you don't see her as I do. Most girls would have gone completely berserk. I'd like to see that fellow Worth strung up and tortured. I never did trust him. How he could throw over a girl like Nancy for the wretch he ran off with!"

George Lansing halted at the top button of his pajamas and stared at his wife. "Now why do you say that? You were one hundred per cent sold on Worth. You practically threw them at each other."

"I never did!" His wife raged in a sort of hushed scream.

"Oh, yes you did. Why don't you admit you were wrong?"

"I wasn't wrong. I never did. I wasn't wrong. I was right. He was a fine-looking fellow, with scads of money. He seemed perfectly ideal for Nancy."

"At least stick to one side for two sentences in a row," flung back George dryly. "But that's over with now. The point you were making, I believe, was that Nancy would be benefited by going to Florida. What would the benefits be, in your mind? Twenty-five thousand dollars, plus—what?"

"Why, twenty-five thousand dollars plus all the peace and sunshine of Florida living. It's restful and healthy. She could make new friends and forget all about Worth."

"Rest and peace and Florida sun. How about rest and peace and California sun?" He whirled on her. "Why not admit it, Frances? Money is all you ever care about. California, or any other place, doesn't offer twenty-five thousand dollars!"

"Well, no, of course it doesn't. Then, why *not* have her go to Florida?"

George threw up his hands. "I'm not going to *have* her go anywhere and neither are you. She's going to do what she pleases! Good night!"

When Nancy came down to breakfast the next morning her parents were glad to see that instead of the haunted look she had worn lately, there was an assured lift to her chin and a determined new sparkle to her dark eyes. She picked up the phone and called the lawyer.

"Mr. Laidlaw?" Her voice was poised and cool. "Nancy Lansing. I've decided to take the dare."

"Uh—I beg your pardon, Miss Lansing?"

"I'll go to Florida. I shall be leaving the end of next week. Did I understand you to say that you would notify my aunt? Thank you. And I shall write her also. Good bye."

The next few days were busy ones. Nancy was popular among her crowd and there was much mourning and ado about her "interment" as her friends called it. They wrote epitaphs to be read at the farewell parties they gave her; they bought sympathy cards to go with her bon voyage flowers and gifts.

"If you only weren't going to a little jerk dump in the sticks! And with an octogenarian fanatic at that!" they wailed. "If it were Palm Beach or Miami, it wouldn't be so completely stinkaroo. But Pine City! It sounds like a hole."

Nevertheless, Nancy rollicked through the days and danced through the nights until it was time to leave. Having made up her mind, she was not one to let apprehension dog her.

"You might think I was the first space traveler," she flung at them laughingly when they assembled at the airport to bid her good bye. "I'll make it. You'll see."

By the time the plane took off, on a bright Saturday morning in June, she actually had herself persuaded that she was looking forward to a balmy six-month vacation in Florida.

two

"You understand, gentlemen, that I cannot vouch for my nephew on the basis of any personal contact with him. I have not seen him since he was a boy. He must be around twenty-eight now."

T. Dunn Cash waved his small soft hand as if to dispel responsibility, and glanced confidently about at the gathering. It was a warm evening, even for Florida; summer seemed to be impatient to begin. The deacons of Westside Community Church mopped beneath double chins, and shifted to find cool spots in their chairs.

Cash went on, savoring the mastery he held over the circle of attentive men seated around the big polished table. "I do know that Jack graduated with high honors. I saw a picture of him in his cap and gown—good-looking kid—didn't take after his uncle! He's a big strapping fellow with dark hair, hands like hams, and a good smile; carries one shoulder high like so many baseball players do. He was called straightaway to what was then a small country church in New Jersey. I thought he could have done better for himself, but it proved to be the making of him. He went on and got his theological degree while he was preaching. He built up the church, and town, too, in five years. I guess he must have the Cash drive, even though his mother, my twin sister, was always a mousy little girl." He chuckled. That chuckle often came in handy to counteract any unpleasant impression that might be created by his twisted nose and his harelip.

"His doctrine's okay, I'm sure," he continued. "Only one thing wrong with Jack from our point of view." Attention tightened. Mr. Cash was a slight, frail-looking man to command such a distinguished-looking group. But he seemed to expect it as his prerogative, and somehow he managed to maintain the fine line between self-assertiveness and instinctive leadership. He grinned at their obvious relief when he added, "He's a widower; has two kids. He married while he was still in college."

"That's okay," put in Chuck Immerman, round-faced, youngish and well-heeled. "We'll soon fix him up. How about Winnie? My brother Nick would be willin' to let him have

14

her." He guffawed. Several others with difficulty pinched back tentative grimaces from the corners of their mouths, waiting to see how Flemming Elder would react to Chuck's pleasantry. Elder's white hair, thinning now, and his long sober face, often proscribed some bit of hilarity that threatened to break out at the deacons' meetings. But he seemed not to be listening, so the propensity of Winifred Windom for wealthy unattached gentlemen was bandied about good-humoredly.

"I doubt if Jack is wealthy," said his uncle. "He would be likely to think money was a sign of unspirituality, if he's anything like his mother. In fact, if we start him out a thousand less than old Dr. Glasser was getting, he won't mind. We can save a little that way. After all, he's young. He shouldn't expect too much."

At that, Flemming Elder spoke up in trembling, measured tones. "He sounds like the kind we want, I should think. When I was young it wasn't considered the thing for a minister of the gospel to have very much of this world's goods." He shook his head slowly. "We are living in careless times. Too much carnality everywhere, even in pulpits." He raised his long hand with two fingers extended as he continued to shake his white head mournfully. His thin white eyebrows and lack of any lashes at all gave him a cadaverous look.

"Let's be realistic in this," spoke up a stout middle-aged man. He amply filled his wooden chair, which was a little out of line with the others on his side of the table. Robert P. Manton was a banker. He talked rarely, but always to the point. "When can this man candidate for us?"

Dunn Cash responded instantly. "I'll write him tonight if you all agree, gentlemen. In fact, if Edna is still in the office, I'll give her the letter now."

"She's gone," put in Chuck. "I heard the outside door close ten minutes ago. She sure puts in long hours extra. By the way, what are we going to do for a church secretary when she gets married? Here we thought we were all set for years to come. Who'd ever have thought of a confirmed old maid like Edna going to the altar and setting out for Indonesia, of all places!" He wagged his head wonderingly.

Cash laughed. "She's not so old, really. Early thirties, maybe. And she'll be a good missionary, all right. Somebody else will turn up. I can let my secretary help out a little with letters and that sort of thing for a while. I'm sure some of the rest of you can help, too, that way?" Cash looked about expectantly; there were reluctant murmurs of assent and vague noddings. "Could be we might save the church exchequer a little that way, just for a time, you know, till somebody turns up. Or if your own business is slack, it might help to have the church paying your secretary!" He grimaced, just in case anyone was inclined to take his pleasantry unfavorably. "Well, I'll get the letters off to Jack first thing tomorrow morning." He rose and then paused, looking sober, and sat down again. "Maybe we ought to close this meeting with prayer. Brother Manton, will you ask the Lord's blessing on what we are doing?"

Manton addressed the Lord rapidly and rather formally and the gathering broke up. A general sense of satisfaction prevailed.

Dunn Cash smiled carelessly at a tall, plump man in brown-rimmed glasses who had had almost nothing to say during the discussion. He seemed to lack the personality polish of the others. He was aware that he was sometimes dubbed "a diamond in the rough." He took that in stride as he did many other thrusts, up to a point.

"Good meeting, eh, Blount?" remarked Cash, just for a pleasant bit to say. Dunn Cash always spoke the name as it was spelled although he knew that the man himself pronounced it "Blunt."

Richard Blount put one hand nervously into his coat pocket,

16

then took it out and smoothed down the flap. Before he knew it the hand went in again as he answered, "Yes, Mr. Cash. I—I was just wondering—uh—you know Harvey Donaldson was not here tonight. I suppose you have talked it all over with him?" Blount kept nodding his head, as if he was quite sure that all things must be in order if Cash had handled them.

Cash shrugged. "Well, as a matter of fact, I haven't. Too bad he's laid up so long. But I'm sure it will be all right with him. Have you ever noticed that he always says, 'Anything is all right with me'? I'll call him, though, the first thing in the morning. After all, we haven't issued a formal call to Jack. It will be only an invitation to preach for us. We can drop it afterwards if we don't like him. I remember in my own ministerial career that I preached for a good many churches as candidate and then never heard from them again. It's usual." Cash chuckled contentedly.

Blount agreed, but he still wore a troubled look as he passed out of the building, holding the door deferentially for the smaller man.

There were several late-model pastel-colored chariots in the church parking lot. Only one car, Richard Blount's four-year-old black sedan, seemed to be in keeping with the plain frame structure that presided over the pleasant, rather unkempt grounds.

"Good nights" zigzagged through the quiet neighborhood; the chariots purred off into the night; Blount's car barked a time or two and then it, too, chugged away leaving the place to the night creatures and the moonlight sauntering among the palms.

On the edge of town, in one of the choicest residential areas, Dunn Cash turned his car into the drive and got out to open the garage door. He stood a moment taking in with satisfaction his spacious moonlit lawn sloping down to a quiet bayou. The shadowy draperies of flexuous cocos plumosa palms swayed gently in rhythm with the idle rocking of a snug little white yacht at his dock. The mild southern zephyrs seemed to be whispering sweet promises of long lovely lazy days ahead.

Dunn Cash raised his eyes to the heavens as if worshiping. But amid all that quiet grandeur the slight little man seemed very small, and he wore a tense, anxious expression as he touched the fingertip control that opened the big doors. His frown deepened when he saw that the other half of the garage space was still empty. By the time he had driven in, shut off his motor and closed the doors again, his face was twisted and knotted in distress.

He fairly yanked the kitchen door open in his irritation. He strode to the bedroom where his wife lay reading under a frilly bed lamp. She glanced up patiently, recognized his mood and closed her book.

"Church squabble?" she asked. She had learned that her husband expected to have his annoyances drawn out of him rather than to state the trouble openly.

"No."

Alice pushed back the silky, stringy, unwaved hair that clung about her face and waited, scanning in her mind the list of her husband's usual grievances. Then she tried again.

"Meta and Bob Manton are out with the crowd at the young people's fellowship sing," she offered.

Dunn's manner relaxed. "Good," he said, as if everything had been all right all the time. "I hope she steers clear of that Valentino fellow. He's going to be a ne'er-do-well. Never made more than a dime a day in his life. He'll have spent what his father left him before he's twenty-five."

Alice suppressed a knowing smile and opened her book again. "I told Meta to be in by eleven-thirty. Bob couldn't have the car tonight, so I let her take mine. Bob's very dependable."

Dunn agreed and went into the bathroom for his hot bath. He always hoped it would help him to sleep well, but he generally had to resort to pills anyway.

It was just as he was stepping into bed that the telephone rang.

"It's for you, Alice. From the hospital. What now?"

Possibilities dashed their anxious way through Alice's mind as she took the receiver.

"This is Lakeview Hospital calling. A Miss Beatrice Lansing wishes me to let you know that she has had an accident. She says that she was expecting a guest tomorrow morning to arrive on the eleven o'clock plane from New York. She asks that you look after her."

"Tell her we will be glad to do it. Thank you for calling. Is Miss Lansing's condition serious?"

"I have no report on her as yet."

Alice Cash hung up with a troubled look. "Poor Bea. I wonder what happened. Well, I guess that means we have company tomorrow. I know she was expecting her niece. Can you meet her, honey?"

"Sure. Is she a blonde?"

"Oh, don't be foolish! She's Bea's younger brother's child. We can put her in with Meta for a few days; that is, if Meta takes a notion to her."

"Better give her the guest room. She's liable to be a stuffy old maid. Leave Meta to herself. It's tough for poor old Bea. I'm glad we can help her. Bea's a fine old soldier. Good night, Alice. Let me sleep late. I'm bushed. If I don't make it to the plane, send Bert."

three

Nancy did not expect to be met at her destination. Her plan had been to take the airport limousine to her aunt's address.

So when a tall, well-groomed young man in a wildly flowered sport shirt began to eye her familiarly, she tried to shake him.

But Elbert Cash was not easily shaken. In fact, he had friends who took vicious pleasure in calling him Fuller Brush Cash. He did have a friendly manner, almost too smooth, and he obviously counted a great deal on flashing his smile here and there. His face was a slick oval and his sandy hair was plastered flat. He was not overweight but what flesh he had was soft.

Whichever way Nancy turned, there he was. He flashed the Cash smile on her.

"Welcome to Florida! You *are* Nancy Lansing, aren't you?" He laughed at her astonishment. "I knew you had to be. It's your name, you know; it's so rhythmic. It fits your walk and—well, everything about you. There couldn't be two like you on the same plane."

His tone remained carefully respectful. Nancy smiled coolly, feeling her way.

"And you?" she asked with a dignified lift to her pretty chin.

"Just Bert Cash. Cash, you know—what we all like to have around all the time." He chuckled. "My family are friends of your aunt. Don't be afraid of me. You have your baggage checks? Just come this way. We'll soon have your things and be on our way."

In a few minutes they were seated in Bert's convertible. Nancy's heart sank as they left the airport and the landscape presented what seemed like hundreds of miles of desert scrub. She lit a cigarette and offered one to her companion.

"No, thanks," he said blankly. She threw a sidelong glance at him, then bravely began to ask about Pine City, when Elbert interrupted her.

"I guess now is as good a time as any to let you know that there is not very good news awaiting you."

Soberly he told her, "Your aunt, Miss Lansing, is quite a friend of our family, and that is how I happen to be here. The fact is," he hesitated, trying to put off the telling until his guest could adjust herself, "she was in an automobile accident last night, and was taken to the hospital. She is in pretty serious condition. Did you know your aunt well?"

"I never knew her at all." Nancy gave a flippant, indifferent little shrug.

"Then it will not be too hard on you to know that the doctors do not expect her to live the day out."

Nancy caught her breath. Never before had death dared to intrude so boldly into her life. When Uncle Harry died, she had been too far away to go to the funeral. But it came over her that here she was, the only one of the family in Pine City, and she would be expected to carry on as a relative. She resented the responsibility.

What effect would this development have upon her six months' stay in Florida? Could she avoid that? From the dreary looks of the landscape, she sincerely hoped so.

Elbert Cash watched her closely, but he could not decide just how shocked she was over the information he had given.

"If it's all right with you," he said tentatively, "we will go straight to the hospital. It may be the only chance you will have to talk to her before she goes."

"Yikes!" she ejaculated, aghast. "Is she—conscious?"

"They said so. At times, at least. But they told me to get you there as quickly as possible. Do you mind my speeding up a little?"

Nancy tried to pull herself together. "Help yourself," she agreed with tremulous gaiety. "The sound barrier's the limit. But don't get me wrong. If I never get there it's all right with me."

Almost imperceptibly the big motor lengthened its stride. In a few minutes houses and trees appeared in the distance. With relief Nancy saw that Pine City was actually a beautiful town, gracious with palms and dotted with a gleaming lake here and there.

"Oh, lovely!" she exclaimed. "It's not so— I mean—" She stopped, realizing that her tone of voice had betrayed her.

Bert Cash laughed. "I admit it's bare out in the sticks. But towns in Florida are nothing short of paradisiacal. You've never been down before?"

"No." She was still blushing in embarrassment.

"I shall enjoy showing you the sights. Here we are."

A strange trembling seized the girl as she entered the modernistic white building, where Death lay in wait around every corner. She wanted to hold back, to fight it off as an enemy.

Nancy had always made it a point never to shrink from meeting any issue. But Death! That was different. How should one greet Death? What was the proper thing to say? Nancy wished desperately that her father were there.

There was a sign on the room door: NO VISITORS. She knew what that meant. She shuddered.

Bert identified her and the nurse led her in.

"She's been waiting for you," whispered the nurse, gently.

Nancy forced her eyes toward the bed; it was one of the hardest things she had ever tried to do. She scarcely knew what she expected to find. What she saw was almost as startling as if she had seen an actual death's head.

22

On the pillow lay the sweetest, most peaceful little person Nancy had ever seen. She was so white and so delicate that Nancy stopped and gazed in wonder. Because of the radiance of that little personality, even the room itself was not the dim, sorrowful, frightening place that she had imagined. The soft Florida sun was fairly dancing over the little lady's gray curls; a small bouquet of yellow flowers on a stand nearby gave Nancy the fanciful impression that she was standing knee deep in buttercups and daisies.

As she watched, her aunt opened her eyes and saw her. A light of welcome shone there before her weak lids closed again. She tried to raise a fragile hand. Then Nancy saw her lips move. Instinctively the girl bent down to hear.

"I hope—you enjoy it here—in Florida. I—can't—stay— it's so—beautiful—over there. But I love you. Do come— sometime. I'll tell Him—about you." The breathing was more and more labored. Nancy felt as if she were on the very threshold of another world.

Then all at once a brilliant smile lit up the gentle face. With amazement the sick woman exclaimed in delight, "Why— Harry!"

The nurse swiftly put her finger on the woman's wrist, then looked up with sympathy. Her eyes told them that she was gone.

For the first time in years Nancy wanted to cry. She didn't know why. The tears she shed seemed to be tears of relief. Relief from what? Could it be that dying was always like that?

Bert Cash led her away. His mother was just coming down the hall. He nodded his head to warn her.

"She's gone," he said. "Mother, this is her niece, Nancy Lansing."

"Oh, my dear!" exclaimed Alice Cash. She took Nancy's cold little hand warmly in both of hers.

Then they stood there, mute. Nobody knew what to say.

Nurses hurried by. The intern came. Everybody was busy here and there.

"Is there anything you would like me to do?" asked Mrs. Cash feebly. It was as if she were the young thing who didn't know which way to turn.

"I guess, if somebody would wire my folks—" suggested Nancy. She was more shaken than she wanted to admit.

"I'll do it," offered Bert. He rushed off with the address Nancy gave him, glad to be occupied. A telegram soon started on its way.

"Suppose you come on home with us now and get a bite of lunch and rest up," said Mrs. Cash, steering Nancy out to her own car.

In New York, Mrs. Lansing was just about to enjoy a second cup of coffee with her cinnamon bun for lunch, when the telephone rang. She still held the steaming cup in one hand as she reached for the receiver.

"This is Western Union. We have a telegram for Mr. or Mrs. George Lansing. Is this Mrs. Lansing?"

"Y-yes, this is she." Frances Lansing had never got over feeling a twinge of terror at the possibilities behind a Western Union call. She set her cup down carefully with trembling hand and picked up a pencil. Suppose something had happened to Nancy's plane?

She listened in growing horror.

"Oh-h. Please read it again . . . . Thank you."

Mrs. Lansing put down the receiver, breathless. Then she frantically dialed her husband's office.

"George!" she screamed. "Your sister Beatrice is *dead!* Now what will Nancy do?"

24

four

There was a moment of astonished silence at the other end of the wire. How characteristic of Frances, her husband was thinking, that she made no attempt to soften the news about his sister. She thought only of what might affect herself or her child.

"Don't go into a tailspin, Frances." Irritation was carefully erased from her husband's voice. "Tell me what happened. How do you know?"

"A telegram just came from some friends of hers. Wait. I'll read it. It's from Pine City."

" 'Beatrice Lansing in accident last night. Died this morning. We are her friends. Have met your daughter and will keep her with us until you come. Wire instructions. Mr. and Mrs. T. Dunn Cash.' "

"Oh, George! I just knew she oughtn't to go down to that godforsaken place."

"You didn't know anything of the kind, Frances. You urged her to go. It seems to me that everything is being taken care of very well. I suppose I'll have to fly down, though. It's just as well. I'll have a chance to see what Nancy is in for."

"She won't have to *stay* to get the money, now that Beatrice is gone, will she?"

"I don't know. I'll call Laidlaw. But I doubt if this will make any difference. It all depends on the terms of the will and how they are stated. Pack my things. I'll see about reservations."

Nancy, having weathered the first shock over the change in

25

circumstances, had graciously accepted the Cash hospitality for the time being, so that when her father arrived late that afternoon, she was bathed, fed, and napped, and was enjoying an iced drink with Elbert on the Cashes' spacious patio overlooking the bayou. The languorous air and the atmosphere of luxury were obviously very much to her taste.

"Oh, Daddy! It's fabulous here!" she breathed when they were finally alone a few minutes after all the correct things had been said.

The Cashes had insisted on putting him up in the guest room. Meta, they said, could "move over" for the time being. There was a refreshing informality about their hospitality that finally made him capitulate, although he had held out for a motel at first.

"Tell me," Nancy demanded, "what the lawyer said. Do I stay? I'm glad!" she squealed as he nodded. "I'd like to live right here with these people.

"Daddy, this is just the sort of house I shall buy for us all, if you will sell out and come down here to live. I simply adore it! Just look at that view! And the glass walls! These gorgeous tropical trees, growing right in the house! And the weather's just like this, they say, all year long. They have a little cruiser, too, Daddy. Think of it. Couldn't we move down here?"

He smiled. "Calm yourself, Nan, and get your sights lower. This house would never be bought for your twenty-five thousand. Nearer fifty, is my guess."

Nancy tossed her dark head. "Oh, well, it wouldn't have to be this big, not for only the three of us. But oh, I just love what money will do. I intend to find some really rich guy down here and marry him as fast as I can."

"Take it easy, Nanny. Look him over well. Money isn't everything."

"Maybe not, Dad, but it's nine tenths of everything."

He raised his eyebrows and did not answer, for Mrs. Cash

in red shorts, red sandals, and red-framed sun glasses appeared just then. Her straight hair was pulled back tightly from her rather plain pale face and done in a round knot like a doorknob at the back of her head. Little wisps slid down onto her neck from behind her ears. She kept adjusting her glasses constantly.

Mr. Lansing observed her intently, a puzzled expression on his handsome face. He was immaculate himself; his silver-rimmed glasses were always spotless and shining; his little black mustache was clipped just right to enhance the shape of his rather small mouth. He considered impeccable grooming essential to any degree of culture.

Mrs. Cash was hospitable, and seemed sincerely glad to have them there. She evidently considered herself a very close friend of his sister Bea. So he watched and wondered. Would she wear well for Nancy during six long months?

Mr. Cash had disappeared almost immediately after Lansing's arrival, to go about his own business. At dinner that evening, however, the whole family were gathered.

Both Nancy and her father had expected a high degree of formality at the evening meal, in accordance with the luxury of the house, but aside from the fact that a colored maid served them, there was the same easy atmosphere that had been the persuasive factor in Lansing's decision to accept their hospitality.

The two guests were a little taken aback at the beginning of the meal when Dunn Cash glanced pleasantly around the table and then bowed his head.

"Gracious God," he said, "we are grateful for all of Thy mercies to us. Especially bless these friends whom Thou hast sent to be with us tonight. For this food we thank Thee, and ask that it may be used to strengthen us that we may the better serve Thee. In the name of our blessed Lord Jesus Christ, Thy Son, we pray. Amen."

Dunn Cash looked up smiling and said, "We surely are glad to make your acquaintance, Mr. Lansing. I'm only sorry it has to be under such circumstances. But—as a matter of fact, as well as we knew your sister, we are quite sure that her going could have been only a joy to her. It is we who shall miss her."

Suddenly Nancy remembered those remarkable few minutes with her aunt. But for the first time in years George Lansing was at a loss for words. He stammered and coughed into his napkin. He tried to look bereaved and then he was ashamed of himself, for he had always prided himself on being a sincere person, and he knew that he did not feel the loss of his sister. He was there only to make the funeral arrangements as quickly and simply as possible and get back to his business.

The embarrassing moment was interrupted by Ellenelle, the Cashes' spindly little ten-year-old. She was seated in a chair higher than the rest, for she was tiny, and wore a heavy brace on her leg. She had a fluff of reddish-blond hair and a gentle, wistful smile.

"I was just thinking, Daddy," she spoke up softly, "I wonder what Miss Bea is having for dinner tonight with Jesus. Do you suppose it's manna? I'll bet it's awfully good." She sighed pensively. "I wish I could be there."

Dunn Cash gave her an indulgent nod and agreed that it surely would be something very good. Mrs. Cash's yearning look lingered on her little daughter, but Elbert glanced at Nancy to see if she was laughing.

She wasn't, but her eyes were big with astonishment.

Meta, the elder Cash daughter, seemed not to have heard at all, for her expression was utterly blank.

By the time Mr. Lansing found his voice and explained to his host that he really had never known his sister very well, as she was considerably older than he, and out of the country for years, the incident had passed. But Nancy remembered it. It seemed to fit into what Aunt Bea had said to her just before she died. Sometime she would take those two things out and look at them together.

The men discussed business, especially Florida business; and Elbert, sitting across from Nancy, discussed boat trips, especially the Florida boat trip he was planning for her. Meanwhile, Meta made it her business to examine every detail of Nancy's clothing and coiffure, her New York accent, and her manners.

After dinner they went out on the porch and the subject of Nancy's stay in Florida came up.

"My daughter seems to have fallen quite in love with your Florida." Mr. Lansing smiled.

"As far as I can tell, it's mutual," teased Mr. Cash, with a wink toward his son. "Well, she was planning to make her aunt quite a visit, I understand. Is there any reason why she shouldn't transfer it to us? I could do very well with another daughter as good looking as she."

Nancy dimpled, Meta sniffed, and the rest laughed; then the conversation drifted to other things.

But the next day Nancy took opportunity to bring it up again.

"I really do like it down here, Mr. Cash, and I'd love to stay, at least for six months or so. But I'd have to find myself a job. You don't know of any for me, do you?" She smiled prettily in a businesslike way. "I may as well tell you why I'm here. It's all right to tell, isn't it, Daddy?" She glanced at her father for confirmation.

"Oh yes, if you like. I wouldn't want to broadcast the story, but your hosts may as well know."

Nancy told him about the will. Mr. Cash raised his thin eyebrows and twisted his mouth in appreciation. "Hum-m. Nice little legacy. And you want to work until you get it?" Mr. Cash thought a moment. "What sort of work can you do?" he asked.

"Well, I majored in childhood education in college, but I

don't suppose I could walk into anything like that for only six months. I can type, and keep books, of course. I'm a little rusty on shorthand. I suppose I could at least get a receptionist's job." She made a wry face.

Mr. Cash turned and looked full at her for a long minute, as if he were evaluating her whole personality. Then he said, "I do know of a job that will be open in three weeks, if you can wait that long. I don't know whether you would like it or not. If you are anything like your Aunt Beatrice, you can hold it down."

Nancy brightened. This was better than she had hoped. It was not easy to step into anything in a strange town.

"I don't know that I'm like Aunt Bea," she said dubiously. "I saw her only a few minutes, you know." She spoke with a tenderness that made her father look at her in surprise.

"Well," Cash spoke hesitantly, "our church secretary is getting married and leaving for the mission field in the Far East. We'll need somebody, at least temporarily, to take her place." He watched Nancy keenly as he talked. She showed no sign of emotion, favorable or unfavorable.

"I suppose I could do that," she answered evenly. "Just what would I be expected to do, other than write letters and answer the telephone?"

"That's about it," replied Cash. "Of course in a church of six hundred members, that's no simple job. But you could probably handle it. There's only one thing that might make you ineligible."

"Yes?" Nancy waited.

"Smoking. It just couldn't be known that the church secretary smoked."

"Oh." She paused. "You mean not on the church grounds, I suppose?"

"No, I mean not at all. If it got about, your goose would be cooked. It would make a lot of talk. This church doesn't approve of smoking, or drinking either, of course."

"Oh?" There was a shade of dignified withdrawal in Nancy's voice. "I can understand the drinking, I suppose, but smoking! I—I should think that would be a personal matter, outside of working hours."

"No. The people wouldn't go for a secretary who smokes. Of course, we aren't accustomed to having it here in our house, either."

At that Mr. Lansing made haste to rub out his cigar at a convenient place on the concrete railing. "I beg your pardon, Mr. Cash," he said nervously. But Nancy held her cigarette and simply looked at it, meditatively.

"No offense, Mr. Lansing," went on Cash. "I know most people don't think anything of it at all. But, well, we are pretty narrow-minded, I suppose, in the eyes of the world. We just don't feel that it's a thing pleasing to the Lord. Most of our important church people feel that way."

Nancy was nonplused. A silence fell. Then she said, "Well, Mr. Cash, I would have liked a job such as that, I believe, but I enjoy a smoke now and then. Maybe only two or three a day, but I'm not ready to pass that up. I guess I'll have to find other work." Her voice was cool.

"Well, now, Miss Nancy, please don't feel that I'm condemning you for a cigarette or two. I used to smoke a lot, myself, when I was a boy. And after all, if that's all you use them, I don't see that there would be any objection to your smoking in your own room—now and then, you know. Personally, I don't think we have any right to lay down rules for somebody else. It's just the public opinion of the church. You see, don't you?" He fidgeted, and bit his harelip.

Nancy shrugged. "Oh, well, if that's all, I suppose I can keep it to myself."

"All right, if you're willing to do it that way. Fine. You can consider yourself hired." He looked down at his feet.

"But don't I have to be passed on by some board or committee of the church? How do they know they want me?"

Cash laughed confidently. "Oh, I'll give you a build-up. They will take my word for it."

Then Mr. Lansing spoke up. "What about living expenses? Are they high here, Mr. Cash?"

"Fairly so. Especially for tourists. We have to get all we can out of them, you know." He chuckled jocosely. "But seriously, I'll tell you what we'll do. I'll make you an offer, Miss Nancy. I usually give a considerable amount anyway to the church, of course. How would it be if you take part of your salary as room and board here with us? I know Mrs. Cash would enjoy having you here, and certainly the young folks would like it. Let's see, you wouldn't be able to get a nice room under ten dollars a week, and then your food would be—uh—well, how about your room and board and a hundred a month? Would that sound good to you?"

Nancy turned the proposition over in her mind. At last she said hesitantly, "Okay with me. You're sure that it wouldn't be a burden on you all to have me here always in the way?"

Then Elbert spoke up in his best Fuller Brush manner. "When were roses and violets ever in the way?"

Nancy dimpled and blushed. Her father looked pleased and Mr. Cash patted his son on the shoulder. "Well said, young man. You're going to make your father proud of you some day."

Little Ellenelle struggled up from where she was playing and, clanking across the terrazzo floor, sidled up to Nancy and whispered, "I'll be so glad. I like you."

Nancy looked down at her in amazement. Then impulsively she put a loving arm about her shoulders and kissed her.

Meta's approval of the plan would have to wait, for she had slid out of the room unobtrusively a few minutes before. Mrs. Cash was just coming in. "Dinner is on now in the Florida room. Come on, folks."

On the same night that the deacons of Westside Community Church were meeting in Pine City, Florida, another meeting was scheduled in the New Jersey church of which Dunn Cash's nephew Jack was pastor. Jack had been unusually silent at the dinner table, and he was still preoccupied as he read the evening paper after dinner. At last, however, the insect-like insistence of his young son gained his attention.

"No. No more candy, Teddy boy. You know what the dentist said. We don't want any more holes in your teeth." Jack Warder's voice was firm.

"But Daddy, I didn't have as many pieces as Cindy had. She had four big ones and I had only three little ones. Just *one* more, Daddy?" The big dark eyes, replicas of his father's, pleaded wistfully over the upper edge of the newspaper which the big man lowered to speak to his little son.

Jack shook his head lovingly. "I said no, Ted. Don't ask again."

The three-year-old gave an angry growl and kicked his father's shins. "Well, Gran'ma will give it to me."

Down went the newspaper. Jack arose and grasped his son's arm.

"That will be *all*, Ted. It's bed for you now."

Paying no attention to the howl of frustrated fury that drowned even the Mickey Mouse story that was enthralling his five-year-old girl, Jack lifted Teddy off his feet and bore him to the bathroom. The cries were soon stilled, one way or another, and before long Jack reappeared, looking worn but manfully determined. He sat down and took up his paper once more. But he was fully aware of the bitter, antagonistic attitude of his mother-in-law, knitting in suppressed rage on the opposite side of the room.

He read on as if she were not there.

The program was over at last, and the TV turned off according to Jack's orders. Cindy sat with gleaming eyes, looking from her father to her grandmother and back again. At last she stole up and whispered in her father's ear.

"Gran'ma will give Teddy some candy later, won't she, Daddy? She always does." Then she looked wickedly over at her grandmother.

Jack choked back his exasperation and picked up his little daughter.

"Time for shut-eye for you, too, baby." He smiled, holding her high above his head.

She laughed with glee, but as he let her down she shook her curls proudly and scoffed.

"I'm *not* a baby any more. Gran'ma says I'm a little lady."

With an effort Jack ignored the small provocation and agreed, "We hope you will be a real lady, sugar. Come on now, we'll ask Jesus to make you what He wants you to be, before you snuggle into bed."

He put her down and her hand stole happily into his as she started off beside him in her little pink nightclothes.

"Go kiss Grandma good night," exhorted her father.

"Okay. Goo' night, Gran'ma." She planted a wet kiss near her grandmother's ear. "You *will* give us some more candy tomorrow, won't you?" she murmured just loud enough for her father to hear.

"You precious little darling. Of course I will. I'll give you anything you want. *Oh*, you're so sweet!" Grandma gave one last squeeze before she let the child go and took up her knitting again. Her fingers worked fast and jerkily for some time. Now and again she glanced up swiftly as if expecting to see the man of the house return to his armchair and newspaper. But minutes passed and he did not come back. Her lips grew tighter and her well-coiffed head tossed resentfully. At last she gathered up her yarn and the little sweater she was knitting for Teddy and marched noisily and obviously into her own room and shut the door hard.

A half hour later, Jack came out, immaculate and bearing himself very straight. An expression of determination made his already firm chin more noticeable. He glanced into the empty living room, then retraced his steps and tapped softly on the door of his mother-in-law's bedroom.

"I'm off to the church board meeting, Mother," he told her. "It may be quite a long session. I'll be late."

An indecipherable sound came from within. He waited a moment, then he took his hat and went out.

At eleven o'clock that evening he was still in the church study. Most of the deacons had gone; only one middle-aged man, straight-backed, gray-tinged, prosperous-looking, was seated on the opposite side of Jack's desk studying the young minister.

"Are you sure you don't want to reconsider this resignation, Jack?"

"Absolutely sure." Jack's lips set thinly.

"And it's not more money you want?"

"It has nothing to do with money."

"But Jack, don't you realize that you could be a power for the Lord here in this city? It is growing fast. You need a wider vision. Can't you see what this church could be in another five years? It could double its membership and triple its Sunday school. Just think of reaching that many—close to five thousand—besides the transients who visit occasionally."

"I don't think service to the Lord can ever be measured in numbers. You know I've said that many times, Mr. Hethering. I believe that there is only one place of service where I can be of the greatest usefulness, and that is wherever the Lord puts me."

"But Florida, Jack! Of all places! You will bury yourself. Jack, you have terrific talents; admit it. It is only fair to the Lord to put them to work where they will count the most for Him. There are only two types of people in Florida. I know; I toured the state a few years ago. There are ignorant crackers, and there are playboys. That's all, except of course, the mass of octogenarians who are not worth working with anyway; they have no time left to amount to anything. You could be a great success here. You are near centers of culture. Think of your children. There are unlimited opportunities for them here. What would you find down there?"

"Just a minute, Mr. Hethering. I never said I was going to Florida. It's just that the thought keeps recurring. I don't know why. It may be Kamchatka for all I know. But I'm sure of this, that I'm through here."

"How do you know?"

Jack hesitated. "It's not anything I can put into definite words. I've felt it coming for a long time—months. I've been more and more aware that the church here, much as I love it, can get along without me now. It's on a good solid footing. I have taught you all as much as I can. I need to learn more."

"Well, why not take some refresher courses here at the university?"

"It's not that kind of learning that I mean. It's a deeper knowledge of the Lord. You get that only by stepping out by faith wherever He says to go. It's the same with these people. They are depending on me too much. They expect me to do their praying and their Bible reading as well as their marrying and burying. That's no good. I've tried my best to get them to see that they won't grow if they don't exercise—get out and win souls. They think that's just the preacher's work. It's not. The people ought to be doing it as well. The time is past

36

when unbelievers will come into a church to hear the truth. It's the individual's business to win his own friends and neighbors and bring them into the church to be fed. I've failed to make our people see this. All they want is to sit back and 'enjoy' a sermon on Sunday. As if a sermon was meant to be *enjoyed!*"

"But Jack, suppose I put it up to them; I'll tell them about this talk. I think it will mean enough to them to keep you, so that they will do what you ask."

Jack turned on him almost savagely. "It's *not* what *I* ask, sir. I consider this my failure as well as theirs. We are at a standstill. And I am content in my own mind that this is a step the Lord would have me take. He never intended His people to depend on mere man, not after they have been taught enough to know the difference. No, my decision is final."

After a minute of emotion-filled silence, Jack added:

"Don't think I'm not as sorry about this as you are, sir. I love this church, and I love the people. But when the Lord says 'Go!' I go."

"But where? It's not practical to cut loose from one place before you have plans for another."

"I suppose not. It was not practical for Abraham to go out, not knowing whither he went, but the Lord was pleased." Jack spoke musingly, humbly.

The deacon made a sound of disgust. "Well, you're hopeless!" Then he took his hat and went out.

The next morning Jack, according to his usual custom, was up a couple of hours before the rest of the family. When Grandma called them all to breakfast he had both children washed and dressed ready to start out with him as soon as they should finish their meal.

"Well, this is the first day of Bible school." He smiled. "You're both going with me today." The children exclaimed with glee but their grandmother looked shocked.

"Not Teddy!" she cried. "He's entirely too young to go. What would he get out of it?"

"Oh, I want to go, too. I'm free years old. I will, too, go to school."

"Yes, you may go, Ted. Well," he turned to his mother-in-law, "we'll be moving to a new town soon. I've turned in my resignation at the church."

"Jack! If you feel that you can't trust the children with me any longer, if you think I'm not *capable* of bringing them up right—" Her voice shook, her nostrils were quivering and her big placid blue eyes were filling with tears. "You are just trying to keep the children away from *me*."

"Now, Mother," he began, "don't go getting ideas! You know I've been considering this move and praying over it a long time. I don't care to go into all the angles of it here and now, but the church is well on its feet, and I feel that the people are beginning to depend on me too much. Another man in here now would keep the church healthy."

"That's ridiculous. If *I'm* in the *way* here, I can go back to Mary's. She *needs* me, with her six. I just wanted to be where I could be of help to Lucy's children." Each word overflowed with self-pity.

"Mother!" remonstrated Jack gently.

"Well, I know you've gone and taken this crazy step on my account. Where will you go? Do you have another call?"

"No, but I'm sure it's the right move. The Lord will show me the next step."

"Meanwhile, you will sit and starve. All because you want to put me in the wrong."

"Now look here, Mother," Jack blazed up, "there's no sense in your getting touchy. I appreciate all your help and you know it. But if you're referring to last night's little episode, you know I don't like it when you work behind my back and give the children things I have said they can't have."

The woman's big blue eyes grew bigger with righteous indignation. "I never—" she began.

Jack stopped her. "Oh yes, you have, and you know it. But it's just a failing of yours, like blowing up is a failing of mine. I know I should keep my temper. I don't want to hurt you, but I have my own youngsters to consider."

"Everything I ever do is for them," blubbered their grandmother. "You are too hard on them. If you think *you* are setting them a good Christian example by trying to put their own grandmother in a bad light before them . . . Oh-h, if their mother had lived it would be different." She burst into sobs.

By this time Cindy was in her grandmother's arms, trying to comfort her, or be comforted, and Teddy was howling in sympathy.

Jack, in desperation, extracted Teddy and took him in to his own room and set him down firmly in his crib.

In a low determined tone that the boy well knew meant business, Jack told him, "Either you stop crying instantly or you stay home from Bible school."

Another, more frantic howl.

"I mean it. Which is it?"

"I—I—I'll be good."

"All right. That's fine. Now you come into the bathroom and we'll clean you up again."

As Jack gave a quick wash to the teary countenance, he glanced at his watch. Five minutes to get to the church. And he had promised to be early to help get things organized!

Calmly he took his subdued son by the hand and marched toward the front door. Without a word to Cindy or her grandmother, he went out to the car.

"Daddy! Daddy! Take me. I'm coming too!" screamed the child, rushing toward the car.

Jack looked stern. "Not unless you can behave yourself. And look! You're all mussed up, and your face is dirty again. You may go but you will have to get cleaned up when you get there. Come now." He lifted her gently in and started off.

Nothing was said for several minutes. Then Cindy glanced sidewise at him tentatively.

"Daddy, when we get mad at Gran'ma you make us apologize. Are *you* going to?"

Torn between humiliation and laughter, Jack thought quickly.

"Yes, I am, Cindy, because I did get angry. But there are times when I have to say and do some things that you may not understand. I have to because you are my children and I love you. God expects me to train you to be the right kind of people, for Him. And if I know that some things, like too much candy, are not good for you, I have to keep them from you, even if it means hurting somebody's feelings. Do you see?"

"Why, of course, Daddy. You didn't have to tell me that. I *knew* all *that*."

Jack threw his daughter a grim look. How far could he trust this too-wise child of his? She was so like her mother. Inwardly he was praying, "Oh, Lord! How am I going to handle these two?"

It was some time before Bible school activities simmered down enough for Jack to settle to work in his study.

He opened his mail first. There was the usual collection of bills, ads, begging letters, and prayer requests; then he came upon an air mail letter from Florida.

Well, I wonder what my unknown wealthy relatives want now? Maybe someone has died, or they're coming to visit. He opened it without undue interest.

"Dear Jack:
You won't remember me from your childhood when we visited your mother, but I remember you very well. I have followed your career with interest and considerable pride to think that such a successful young fellow was really my nephew.

40

My present reason for writing is to request you to come to Florida at our expense, at your earliest convenience, to candidate for our church. I enclose a check for transportation, and a church bulletin that you may get some idea of what we are like. We have about six hundred members, most of whom, I believe, are true born-again Christians. Naturally, we are strong on the fundamentals of the faith. Knowing the seminary from which you were graduated, I assume that you are, also.

This is a worthwhile field, as the city is growing fast. The present salary is six thousand. You could easily increase that, if you produce the same results that I hear of in your present church.

Right now, at least, we are not in any church broils, and hope not to be. The former pastor died rather suddenly two months ago, and yours truly has been filling in, so make it snappy! As you probably know, I gave up the active ministry several years ago on account of my health.

Think it over and let us know. We need you.

Yours,
Uncle Dunn Cash

Jack read the letter three times. Then he spoke softly. "Well, Lord, you knew all about this all the time!"

Cindy and Teddy chattered constantly on the way back. But Jack scarcely heard them. He drove slowly. The Florida invitation looked good. Also, he was certain that, much as his mother-in-law loved Cindy and Ted, she would never leave the town where her other children and grandchildren were. Well, it couldn't do any harm to go down to Florida and look the situation over.

five

"So you see, Daddy, this hole is simply impossible. I hate it. There is slimy gruel for breakfast; the kids are all a bunch

41

of squares; the beds are granite, and the classes are strictly for the birds. Honestly, as revolting as housework is to me, I'd rather come home and *cook!*

If I don't hear from you by the end of the week, you may as well have my room ready, because I'm coming home anyway.
                                    Love ya. Be seein' ya soon."

There was a determined pout to JoAnne's full red lips as she signed her name. She gave her coppery head an assured little shake, thrust her tongue along the edge of the envelope and pounded her letter shut with a firm, plump little fist. Then she dashed off the address in bold script:

Dr. Harvey Donaldson, Pine City, Florida.

The letter, arrived at its destination, fairly shouted its defiant lines at the man who sat staring down at it.

He was a rather handsome man. Prematurely gray, he had what Victorian novels would have called a "patrician face." His gold-framed glasses became him and brightened up his somewhat serious expression.

It was late morning but, bathrobed and slippered, he sat with unhurried ease in an armchair. At his elbow was a small table on which lay some books—among them a well-used Bible; a pen and writing pad; a thermos bottle, and a box of capsules. On the lower shelf of the table was a tray of sandwiches neatly wrapped, and a cluster of grapes.

After he had read the letter twice he reached across to the thermos bottle, suppressing a spasm of pain, and poured himself a cup of hot coffee. He sipped it slowly while he read the letter through again.

At last he set down the cup and sighed.

Just then there came the sound of the front door gong, soft footsteps, and a moment later a tap on his room door. He called eagerly, "Come in."

The door opened a crack and a spiky red feather appeared. It stemmed rakishly from a shiny black straw hat, as round as a button. Underneath it sparkled the vivacious face of a woman of about forty. Short, but very smartly dressed, she just missed being dumpy. A cloud of smoky black hair held the little hat up from her head lightly. The woman was not exactly pretty, but she possessed a certain youthful charm, an air of being completely enthusiastic about living.

She spoke rapidly, with a strong southern accent.

"Harvey-y!" she cried eagerly, almost running across the room toward the easy chair. "Are you glad to see me, Harvey?"

Harvey Donaldson's somber expression melted into a warm welcome. "I hoped you'd come," he admitted. He started to lay aside the letter that had so absorbed his attention, then he thought better of it and held it out to his visitor.

"Here's what the postman brought me this morning. Now what would *you* do with a girl like that? This problem is too much for an old, dried-up college professor. I need a woman's viewpoint." He let his look linger on her adoringly while she read.

Swiftly she took in the contents and then glanced up brightly.

"Why, that's no problem," she said. "Let her come home. She's not going to learn anything with an attitude like that. She'd only get into trouble. Dismiss Emma and let her do exactly as she suggested. She's already finished high school, hasn't she?"

"No, she has one more year. She's sixteen."

"Well, give her the job of cooking and scrubbing and all the rest. It may develop her to give her real responsibility. She might turn out to be a good housekeeper, who knows? It will keep her busy this summer. Then I'll take over."

Harvey looked skeptical. "You don't think that would be spoiling her, Eva, to give in? That is a good Christian camp, where she is. I thought she'd be sure to get some good training."

43

Evelyn Constant gazed back smilingly at him as if he were a small ignorant boy. "Oh, no!" she stated conclusively. "If she is spoiled, you did it long ago. If she isn't, you won't spoil her now by letting her make her own decisions. Make her try out housekeeping for three months. Keep her to it. Then if she doesn't learn to like it, let her train for anything she chooses, whether it's aviation or feeding the animals in a zoo."

Donaldson gave a relieved sigh as of one who was glad to be conquered. He reached for her hand lovingly. "You always make everything seem so sensible and simple."

But she slowly shook her head. "No, I wish I did. Things aren't—not for me." Then she suddenly changed the subject. "When is the doctor going to let you go out for a ride?" She was all eagerness again.

"Tomorrow, I hope. He said that he wants me to get out among people as soon as possible. I guess he doesn't know that *some* nice people come in to see me." He threw her an affectionate glance. "I would, however, like very much to be able to get out to church a week from tomorrow. We will be having a young preacher from the north candidating. As I am on the board I'd like to hear him. He is a nephew of Dunn Cash."

Evelyn Constant raised her plucked black eyebrows just a fraction. She paused a long moment before she said, "You *should* be there. We'll just have to get you well enough. And we must ask God to send a minister who will be able to interest your daughter JoAnne. Oh, I wish my Henry would stay down here and get acquainted with the nice group of young folks here."

"Where did you say he is now?"

"In California with his other mother." A hard bitter look came into the woman's face. "What he sees in her! She must have done a lot of underhanded work on him when he first went to live there. I'm sure she told him a lot of lies about me.

44

He was there with them, you know, for nearly ten years, up until the time his father died. He's twenty-two now, and getting more wild every year." She sighed and wiped her eyes. "But if God could save me, He can save him, and JoAnne too. We must trust." Her face brightened. "Oh, it's all so new and wonderful to me yet. I wish I *knew* more, though. There is so much I don't understand."

Harvey patted her hand. "We'll read the Bible together, dear," he said. "Every day, after we're married."

She beamed and leaned over to kiss him.

Just then there was a solid, loud knock on the door. Harvey called, "Come in" and his visitor hastened to smooth her hair and adjust her hat.

A full-bosomed, full-hipped colored woman appeared in a big spotless white apron, a white cotton scarf tied about her head after the manner of an ancient Egyptian princess.

"Marse Donaldson," she announced in an accusing tone, "de man have brought Miss JoAnne's trunk. Whar mus' he put it?"

"Oh!—Oh, yes!" stammered Harvey. "I—ah—didn't tell you yet, did I? Miss JoAnne is coming back home, Emma."

A disapproving pause. "No sah. You didn't, sah."

"Have him put it in her room, Emma, until she gets it unpacked. Then we'll have to have a man come and take it up to the storeroom."

She rolled her eyes. "Yes, sah. But we don' need no man, sah. Ef Miss JoAnne cain't take her own little trunk up 'n one flight o' sta'rs, I can do it myself." She stamped flatfootedly away, muttering.

Evelyn Constant paused in arranging her hat and gave an irritated gasp of dismay.

"Well! Before I'd let a colored woman talk that way to me, I'd fire her. I know them! I used to have to keep them in order in my restaurant. What they would try to get away with! Give them an inch and they're impossible. It's *time* you let her go and let JoAnne do the work!"

Harvey smiled indulgently. "Oh, Emma's all right. She and I understand each other. She's a wonderful woman at heart, and really loves the Lord. I can tell you, she has been a comfort to me many a time when I've been lonely and in pain."

But Evelyn seemed not to hear. "Oh, don't try to tell me anything about them. The *times* I've had with help! Deliver me! I'd be a wealthy woman now if the help hadn't wasted so much and cheated me out of half my profits." Her voice rose tense and shrill.

Harvey looked distressed. "Come now, Eva," he said weakly, his breathing short. "You know we weren't going to go into all that again. That's over. You know you said you felt that the Lord had a reason for taking your money away."

Instantly she melted. "Oh, I know it. I'm sorry, Harvey." No voice could have been sweeter, or more humble. "I've made you feel bad again. I'm just a no-good worthless wretch. I just mustn't think about those old days and all I lost. But—" her voice began to sputter once more—"it's just that it's so *unfair!*" Then she stopped her tirade as suddenly as she had started. "I'm going now." She laughed a little at herself as she bent over to kiss him gently. "You're so good and wonderful. You will teach me, won't you? To be right, and a good Christian. It was *you* who led me to the Lord, and I do thank you so, and Him, too. Good bye, dear. See you tomorrow."

"Good bye, Eva, dear. Oh, on your way out, tell Emma to stop in. I want to talk to her."

He strained to listen, entranced, for her gay quick step, fading now down the hallway; then the eager light slowly died from his eyes and grayness overcame his features once more.

In a few minutes he heard Emma's heavy tread. He took a deep breath.

Unsmilingly the faithful woman stood before her employer, waiting for him to speak.

"Emma," he began gingerly, "I've made a decision about my daughter, and I want to talk it over with you."

She said nothing.

"She has written me several times since she was at camp that she was very unhappy. She said she would rather do housework than stay there, so I've made up my mind to let her do just that. Now Emma, after all the help you have been to me, I'm not going to let you suffer by having no work. You stay on—won't you?—for a week or so after JoAnne comes, until she gets onto things; then I will pay you regularly as if you were here, until you find other work."

Emma stood with her hands on her big supporting hips, staring at the pitiful figure in the armchair. Then she spoke.

"Marse Donaldson, whut y'all decide and whut I decides am two diffrunt things. But befo' I tells you whut I decide, let me advise you that even though you think you have made up your mind, you ain't, at all. Miss JoAnne, she's the one. *She* makes up yo' mind jes' like I makes up a bed.

"Now, Marse Donal'son, I surely does thank yo' for thinking kindly o' me, but I intends to take pay for whut I does, not for whut I does not do. As for stayin' on here, I'll *try* to teach Miss JoAnne whut I can, effen y'all gives me the right o' way. 'Thout it, I cain't do nuthin'.

"But I might as well tell you now as any time, that I was agoin' to give you notice soon. I ain't blind, an' I kin' tell how the wind blows. I ain't stayin' on *nohow* to work for Mis' Constant when she gits to be Mis' Donal'son. An' that's that. I don' want you to take any bad feelin's from whut I say, but I think the Lawd gives each one of us sense to run our own lives the way He wants 'em an' if we miss it, it's our own fault. I've know'd fer some time that He don' want me here much longer. Thank you."

As if she had completed a difficult radio broadcast, Emma bowed slightly and swept out of the room leaving Harvey to solitude and his own thoughts.

six

The first two weeks of Nancy's stay at the Cashes' lovely home were a dream of delight. The water sports that she had always longed for were at the doorstep. Already a good swimmer, she swiftly picked up a degree of skill at water-skiing. Her quick gay wit captured the young crowd, and Elbert was her devoted attendant. If he was not taking her skiing, then Bob Manton or Chuck Immerman's brother Nick had her out somewhere. Nancy was puzzled, however, at Meta's aloofness. She thought back to the two nights she had spent in the twin bed in Meta's room when her father was there, and wondered whether she had committed some faux pas of which she was unaware. Meta had seemed friendly enough then, as much so as one would expect on first acquaintance. But she felt no closer to her now than she had then.

Meta was not exactly a pretty girl. She struggled hard to make the most of what she had: a slim figure, almost too slim; regular features; and ash-blond hair, which she wore in a pony tail. Nancy thought privately that it would have been much more becoming to her short, and flowing looser, with bangs, for her forehead was rather high, and her face was just a mite too thin. Her eyes seemed colorless. It was impossible ever to guess what she was really thinking. So far she had been unerringly polite to Nancy; that was all.

Nancy had been able to fit into the religious life of the Cash household without too much conflict within herself. She was annoyed at the prohibition about smoking. The family's attitude seemed inexcusably rude and inconsistent to her. But she did not violate the agreement. As for church going, her father had been there the first Sunday, of course, and they two had spent most of the morning at the undertaker's.

Nancy and her father had been somewhat at a loss to know what to do about Aunt Bea's funeral, since the old pastor she had loved was no longer living. Finally Mrs. Cash had solved that problem by suggesting that Flemming Elder, the senior deacon, share the service with her husband, who had been a minister. Mr. Lansing was quite agreeable, since he had no feeling in the matter whatever.

He had sat like a quiet image throughout, but it happened to be the first funeral service that Nancy had ever attended. She planned ahead of time to be indifferent, but she found herself wondering whether this part of death would prove as unfearsome as her aunt's actual decease had turned out to be. Actually she observed every detail of the service, with a sort of loathing, but with fascination, too.

Scores of people came. It seemed that Aunt Bea had been greatly beloved. There was some soft weeping. But on the whole, it was a sweet quiet time of meditation and worship. Much of the Bible reading was unfamiliar to Nancy. She thought it beautiful. Once she stole a glance at her father, but from his stony countenance she couldn't tell what he was thinking. Of course, she knew he was too well bred to sneer openly. But why should he? She was amazed to discover something in herself that was hoping he would not mock or even disapprove. Why did she care? Yet she did. Ever since she had met Aunt Bea, only two days before, and heard those few words just as she left for the other world, Nancy was less inclined to sneer. She looked back to the time before she had left New York, and the wisecracks she had made with her crowd about trying to be religious. They no longer seemed so funny to her. Why? She didn't know. Could it be because she enjoyed life at the Cashes' and did not want to find too much wrong with it? Maybe. Yet she had no use for what she termed "their brand of religion."

"What do you get out of all this church stuff?" she asked Elbert. That was the second Sunday morning. He was taking her in his own car; the others had already gone.

He gave her a sidelong look. "Hunh! *I* don't buy it," he muttered. "It pays to keep peace, though."

But that Sunday a missionary from Quito, Ecuador spoke. "Why, it was as fascinating as a travelogue!" Nancy expressed herself enthusiastically at dinner. "I had no idea missionaries could speak so well and knew so much! Why, that's a terrific idea, isn't it?—their making those little radios for the natives, that will tune in only their own station. It's a fabulous advertising stunt."

Mr. Cash grinned with appreciation. "Might try it myself," he said. Then he added with sudden seriousness, "Maybe the idea could be adapted somehow so that I could sell more washing machines."

Nancy glanced up at him, startled. She wished he hadn't said that. But again she didn't know why she wished it.

On the whole, she felt that she was making the grade religiously. It wasn't too bad at all so far. She was even getting used to having somebody pray before each meal.

And then Jack Warder came.

It was Saturday morning and Mrs. Cash had gone to meet him at the airport, since everyone else was occupied otherwise. They came in through the garage and Mrs. Cash stopped in the kitchen to speak to the maid about dinner, so he walked on through the house toward the patio.

Nancy was curled up in a corner of the glider, reading in the shade of a lovely blue-veiled jacaranda. She did not hear him coming.

"Well!" he exclaimed, coming toward her cordially, extending both hands as if she were a little girl. "At last I meet my young cousin!"

Nancy looked up in amazement. She had not been aware that a guest was expected. He was certainly no cousin of hers. Yet his merry brown eyes looked so straightforwardly at her that she could see that he was sincere and not merely fresh. Slowly, with only the least bit of reticence, she unwound her feet and stood up, shaking her head with a polite smile. Then she laughed bewitchingly at his look of astonishment, for petite though she was, dressed in crisp yellow bermudas, she was obviously no child-cousin.

"I don't think *I* have any cousin that could be *you*." She dimpled, leaving room for the implication that it would not have been amiss if she did.

"But surely I'm not in the wrong house? Mrs. Cash brought me in. Aren't you Meta? Certainly not Ellenelle. That's who I thought you must be at first."

Nancy laughed. "Nancy Lansing is the name, and I'm not one of the family. I'm just—just *here!*" she finished lamely. She had started to say, "I'm boarding," but that sounded odd without further explanation, as if the Cashes were taking in boarders.

"Well! I'm certainly glad you *are* here," said Jack, smiling. "That is, that you're not somewhere else." His smile lit up his face in a fascinating way, Nancy decided. It was a smile you couldn't help watching for.

In the middle of the smile, Meta's flat voice broke in.

"I see you have progressed with your usual speed," she remarked dryly to Nancy. "*I'm* your cousin Meta, Jack. Don't faint with chagrin."

Nancy froze inside. So *that* was why Meta had been so cold to her! Why had she not recognized before that Meta was shy and probably had an inferiority complex. The two mixed together generally did produce jealousy.

But Jack covered well. He was more cordial than ever. He took Meta's skinny hand in his big one and held it a long moment in a brotherly clasp. The atmosphere melted and the three sat down and chatted. Nancy, however, still felt as if she had been slapped in the face.

She thought swiftly through the register of young men who had been paying her attention. Surely Meta was not jealous of her brother Elbert's interest in her; there was not much love lost between those two. She ran through the others. Nick? Bob Manton! Several times Meta had dropped hints that might indicate that she and Bob used to go together. She puckered her brow. That's the one, she exclaimed to herself. But I'll bet it was Meta's concept, not Bob's.

That night a moonlight cruise was scheduled. Nancy expected that of course the newcomer would be along, but it appeared that he was staying at home to talk business with Mr. Cash. She was disappointed. Some time during dinner she discovered that Jack was a minister. Her heart sank and instantly she became critical of him.

But the next morning, half afraid and half eager to hear him preach, she dressed carefully, in white, crowning her short dark curls with a tiny cap of white velvet pansies. She was a little disappointed that she was assigned to go with Elbert again. She would have enjoyed being in the big car along with the rest, for she found Jack's conversation more stimulating than Elbert's. Preacher though he was, she had to admit that his rare smile fascinated her. She wondered whether Meta had had any hand in the seating arrangements.

During the service Nancy made little attempt to listen. She was completely taken up with watching Jack. She liked the line of his hair waving crisply back from his broad forehead. She read gentleness and mastery in the lines of his face, the set of his jaw, and even in the very way he held his Bible. She had never seen many men hold a Bible. This man took it up reverently, yet intimately, as if he loved it.

She noted the way one shoulder was slightly hunched up; it gave the impression that he might be ready at slight provocation to turn and swing an uppercut with that powerful fist of his. He might not do it, but at least he could! Altogether she decided that although she stood in awe of him, she admired this young man. She hoped sincerely that she would see more of him. If only he weren't religious!

She was not aware that Meta sat just to the left behind her and was taking note of every look and each change of expression that passed over her face.

The room was breathlessly rapt while Jack spoke. His sermon was short, and as soon as the last Amen was sung, the congregation crowded about him to shake his hand warmly and exclaim their pleasure.

Dunn Cash was at the front door to greet the people as they went out. He took occasion to observe the reactions of the more influential members.

"Isn't he just the best-looking thing this side of heaven?" exclaimed Winifred Windom in a tinkling treble that could easily be heard six pews away. She gave a drooping hand draped with soiled lace to Mr. Cash on the way out. "I could sit forever and listen to a minister like that."

"You picked a fine fellow this time, Cash," stated Bob Manton gruffly. His timid little wife nodded seriously.

Tom and Betty Martin were exuberant. "Oh, he is simply marvelous," she raved. "I can almost be glad now that dear old Dr. Glasser died. I thought nobody could ever take his place. Oh, Mr. Cash, if you all don't call this preacher, I'll never forgive you."

Dunn Cash smiled complacently. "My nephew, you know. He gets it from me." Then he laughed.

"Yes, but all kidding aside, Mr. Cash," urged Tom, "a spiritually minded man like that is just what we need. Don't wait a minute. Call him right away. Some other church will snap him up. I learned more this morning that I ever got in my old home church up north all my life."

"Our work's over, old boy," whispered Chuck Immerman in Cash's ear. With them all Cash beamed, and agreed.

As the assemblage streamed past, his attitude grew more and more assured, and when the majority had gone, he rumbled a triumphant aside to Manton who stood nearby. "Well, I guess it's in the bag."

Dick Blount went by and Cash stopped him.

"What do you say, Blount?"

"About Mr. Warder, sir? I really got a lot out of that sermon. There's much in it to think over. We all need that kind of preaching. It'll humble us. So far he looks like a good prospect. I'll want to hear him again tonight."

Cash and Manton raised eyebrows to each other after he had gone. "Not completely sold?" suggested Manton. "But he doesn't count much, does he?"

Cash shrugged. "Not too much. But he's the kind who will stick his neck out to make trouble if he thinks he should. I never know what to make of men like him. Won't go along with the crowd."

Harvey Donaldson was last out. He made his slow way down the empty aisle leaning heavily on a cane. Evelyn Constant was beside him, hovering.

"Brother Donaldson, it's good to see you out again," greeted Cash. "You're feeling much better?" Then in a lower tone, "What do you say to the preacher? Shall we call him?"

Harvey's long sober face gave meager assent. "Seems fine

to me, Brother Cash. Whatever you all decide is all right with me."

Dunn Cash's lip curled a little after the man had passed. He shrugged and nudged Manton, who had remained at his side. "No trouble with *him*," he said. "Well, how about dropping in for a while this afternoon, you and your wife? Along about five-thirty? Have a bite with us. You'll have a chance to see more of the boy then. But I've pumped him a lot already. He's sound as a nut."

Robert Manton thanked him. "No snags or peculiarities?"

"None so far. He'll have some, of course, but we can deal with those when we come to them. He's strong-minded, but I wouldn't give a rap for him if he weren't. You and I can keep him in line if he gets any wild ideas." The two men gave each other a knowing look.

"He preaches well," said Manton.

"Yes, that was good sound Bible teaching, the kind our people are used to. They'll keep coming. And they *give*, when they like the preacher. Well, see you this afternoon. So long."

Three days later, at the same moment when Jack, at home, was reading the letter which officially called him to the West-side church in Pine City, Dick Blount was saying to his fellow-deacon, Immerman, "Chuck, did you know that a letter calling Jack Warder was sent out before we had our meeting last night authorizing it?"

Chuck shrugged. "No, but I wouldn't be surprised. That's Cash. I know. I work for him. He's a high-handed skipper; sails pretty close to the wind sometimes, but he generally steers well because he knows which way the wind is blowing. I wouldn't worry too much."

Blount's solid heavy countenance showed his concern.

"It's not that it matters too much in this instance," he said in his slow dogged way. "I think everybody's in favor of Warder. It's just the principle of the thing. It might be all right in business to be high-handed, but this is the work of the Lord. *He* ought to be the one to run things, not some mere *man*."

Chuck laughed. "Why man, what do you expect? Are you looking for a hand to come down and write the new pastor's name on a clean sheet of paper? God has to work through men, doesn't He?"

"Yes, but we all ought to agree after prayer over things. Isn't that what it means in the Bible—'if two of you are found in agreement'? That's the way He works, isn't it?" he persisted.

"You start quoting scripture and you've got me. That's too deep for me." Chuck shook his head. "Where'd you hear this bit of gossip, anyway?"

"I don't know that it's gossip. Edna happened to mention to my wife last night something she liked about Warder's sermon Sunday, and said she was glad he was coming even though she was going. My wife asked if it was definite, and Edna just said she had written the letter, that's all. We didn't say a word to anyone else about it. And of course the meeting is over now and the news is out anyway. It's okay. I just wondered if you knew."

"No, but I wouldn't bother my head about it, if I were you. I imagine Cash has talked to most of the board individually. Anyway, I'd let sleeping dogs lie."

"Well," Blount persisted, "what do you know about the new secretary we all voted on so readily last night?"

Chuck shrugged. "Calm your ulcers, man. I don't know nuthin'. No more than you do. But Cash likes her, doesn't he? She lives there, doesn't she? He ought to know whether she'll do or not. And you know as well as I do that if he likes her she's in. If he doesn't, we don't keep her. So let down your blood pressure. Be seein' ya."

They parted, but Blount still looked serious.

seven

On the Wednesday after Jack had been there, Dunn Cash dropped Nancy off at the church to learn what she could from the retiring secretary.

It was a revelation to her. She had supposed that the work would consist of writing letters and addressing envelopes for church notices; making many calls on the telephone to this one and that one to take charge of committees, perhaps, or to substitute at a Sunday school class; or there might be sermons to type occasionally.

"Yes, there are all those," said Edna Forrest, a thin, calm young woman in her thirties, who wore her dark hair parted down the exact center, and never seemed ruffled by anything. Her face was too long to be pretty, but her eyes were lovely, deep and peaceful. Her gentle voice matched them. "But that kind of work is really the smallest part of it. Any stenographer could do that. The most difficult part is answering the scores of calls that come in on any and all conceivable matters, and knowing when to bother the pastor and when to try to solve the problems yourself."

Nancy gasped a little, but her eyes brightened. "That scares me to death, but it sounds much more interesting than the rest of it. I was afraid I'd be bored. I like *people*."

Edna laughed a cool, responsive laugh. "You will *never* be bored," she assured her. She studied Nancy a moment. "This may sound odd to you, but ever since I let the Lord run my life, I've never had a dull moment. That was ten years ago. When I was a teenager I used to think I would die of boredom." Sunlight seemed to reach the deep pools of her eyes and search out gold in them. Nancy decided that she liked Edna Forrest.

"I wish you were going to stay," she said fervently. "I'll never learn enough in three days."

"You wouldn't have a job if I did," reminded Edna with practical humor.

Nancy grinned.

"I'm not going to put you onto many of the old pastor's ways," said the older girl. "The new man may only change them. But you'll need to know the ropes, for you are likely to be here for a few weeks on your own before the new man comes, whether it's Mr. Warder or someone else."

Nancy gave a startled exclamation. Amid all the conversation the last two days she had never happened to hear the reason for Jack Warder's visit to Pine City. In her ignorance of church customs it had not occurred to her that he might be candidating, any more than the missionary from South America. But she covered her surprise with a little cough. After the thrust Meta had given her on Saturday she planned to be more cautious.

Her instructor paid no attention and went on. "I think it would be well if you would sit by and watch, and listen to the telephone calls. You can see what they are like. If you don't get the drift, I'll explain. But now let's begin with the files. I'll show you where everything is."

They had just opened the first filing cabinet when the telephone rang.

"It's begun," announced Edna, picking up the receiver. "Westside Community Church. . . . Yes, Mrs. Windom. Mr. Warder preached both morning and evening. Too bad you couldn't be here both times . . . Yes, everyone seemed to speak highly of him . . . His age? Well, that I wouldn't know, Mrs. Windom . . . Yes, I understand that she died a couple of years ago . . . Oh, I'm sure everyone is eager to see the right man come . . . It may be. Are you and your family going away this summer, Mrs. Windom? . . . Tomorrow? Well, I hope you have a pleasant trip. I won't keep you now. Good bye."

Edna Forrest studied Nancy a moment before she said, "I'm going to try to let you in on as much as I can of these conversations so that you will get to know the people. It won't take you long, I'm sure, to discover which ones really need attention and which ones are calling for mere gossip."

Nancy pursed up her lips in a wry grimace.

"This was in the latter class, I would say. I guessed what her questions were from your answers."

Edna closed her lips in a straight line. Then she said, "That's for you to discern. The greatest thing to learn in this job is to keep your mouth shut."

"I would think so," agreed Nancy.

They started once more on the files. Again the phone rang.

"Westside Community Church . . . Yes, Mrs. Buchanan. I think you will find that in First Thessalonians, the fourth chapter . . . There is another reference to it in First Corinthians toward the end of the fifteenth chapter . . . You're quite welcome. I'm glad I could help."

She turned and saw Nancy looking completely mystified.

"Yikes! What was that all about?"

"Just a dear old lady who didn't know where to look for the passage on the Rapture."

"The *what?*" Nancy ejaculated.

"The Rapture. The time when the Lord will come back to take believers up to heaven with Him."

"I never heard of it. What would *I* do in that case?"

"You mean in case He came now?"

"Yikes, no! In case I had to answer a call like that."

"Just tell them you're sorry, you don't know, and refer them to the pastor, or until there is a pastor, to—ah—well, Mr. Cash, or better, to Mr. Flemming Elder. He's the senior deacon and he practically knows the Bible by heart."

"Oh. I'm afraid this is getting to be too deep for me."

Edna smiled gently. "Do you think so? A lot will depend on whether you know the Lord. If you do, you can always look to Him for wisdom, you know."

"Oh." Nancy was still a long time. Then Edna looked up at her.

"You—*do* know Him?" she asked.

"I don't know. I don't suppose I do. In fact, I don't know exactly what you mean. I'm *not* religious, if that's it."

"No, it really hasn't anything to do with religion as such, any more than being an American has to do with knowing a friend of yours. You see—" Then the telephone rang again.

This time it was a personal message for Edna.

"Oh, *Mother!* No! All right, I'll be right home. Don't you try to lift him. Have you called the doctor? Yes, I can leave. There's someone here to help."

She put down the receiver quietly, but her face was very white.

"Mother thinks my father has broken his hip. I'll have to go home right away, for Mother isn't well herself."

She put out her hands pleadingly to Nancy.

"Do you think you could possibly carry on a little while for me? I'm sure the Lord sent you for just this time. Here, dear. Read this little booklet. It will tell you something of what I started to explain to you. Oh, thank you, so very much."

She was hastily gathering up her things, and she turned as she reached the office door to smile and say, "I'll be praying for you, dear."

After she left, Nancy stood utterly still. She felt as if the weight of all the burdens and problems of all the people since time began had suddenly fallen upon her shoulders. Never had she been so frightened in her life, not even the day two weeks ago when she first met Death in person.

Her first impulse was to run out of the office and slam the door and never come back, not even to Cashes' house or to Pine City forever. She had never backed away from anything before, not even the horrible publicity of her broken wedding plans last winter, but this time she was sorely tempted to. Yet her feet would not move.

She stood staring with wide terrified eyes at the door through which her new friend had disappeared. "No!" she muttered. "This *isn't* me. It can't be!" At last she slowly, very slowly turned her gaze around the room. There were the files. There was the typewriter. A page with carbon copy was already in it. A letter was started. Edna's shorthand book lay beside the machine. Nancy took a step toward it, hesitantly. At least she could read shorthand, and type. It might be a letter that should go out soon. She took a long deep breath and sat down gingerly. She found that her hands and even her knees were trembling. It felt good to be seated.

She picked up the notebook and compared it with the letter started in the typewriter. They were the same—a general letter announcing a coming meeting of the women of the church. She glanced through the shorthand. What careful neat notes Edna took. Would she ever be able to fill the place of a secretary such as this woman must be? Well, she couldn't let her down. At least she could stay there and answer the phone. She could tell everybody that Miss Forrest was out. Anything serious she would refer to Mr. Cash.

And so Nancy began her new job. For Edna Forrest never did come back except for a few minutes once or twice to find something for Nancy and to get her things.

A thousand miles away, the future pastor of the Westside Community Church of Pine City, Florida, was standing his ground again against his mother-in-law.

"Yes, I know that summer Bible school is over, Mother. But I still want to take the children with me."

"But I'm telling you, I won't be doing the wash this morning."

"Wash has nothing to do with it. I expect to do some calling and they can stay in the car and wait for me. Then I'm going to take them to the Feltons' for lunch and they will spend the afternoon there playing with Timmy Felton." His voice rose hotly.

"Well!" sniffed Grandma. "Why couldn't you have said so in the beginning?"

"Why should I have to go into detail about my own children? You'd be sure to disapprove, whatever I did."

"I'm sure I have *no* desire to interfere with your plans for them. I was only going to take them shopping and go to lunch at the Toyland Palace."

At that both children set up a wail. "We don't want to go to Felton's, Daddy. We'd rather go to Toyland."

"Of course," continued the grandmother with sharp insistence, "if you think the influence of that impossible Timmy Felton is better than that of their own grandmother, that is for you to decide."

Jack bit back more sharp words. "Look, Mother," he reasoned in what he tried to hope was a gentle tone, "I have been away and haven't seen the children much for four days. I want to tell them all about my trip."

"Oh. I suppose it *is* time they learned the geography of Florida, isn't it?" she responded scathingly. "I know. It all adds up to the fact that their own mother's mother is not good enough to take care of them." Her tears began to roll in large blobs down her cheeks. "I would have thought, after all I've done for them, and all the financial help I've given here, that I would at least be considered a little better than Timmy Felton! If that's what you call being a Christian—"

But Jack, tucking Ted under his arm and dragging Cindy by the hand, hustled them out to the car and away.

He drove with set jaw, silently. Teddy stood mutely on the seat beside him; Cindy sat next to the window complacently. She glanced at her father several times. At last she leaned forward and said with feigned sweetness, "Well, you did it again, didn't you, Daddy?"

"Did what?" he growled, not looking at her.

"Got angry at Gran'ma. But of course it's still morning. There's no danger yet of the sun going down on your wrath."

"Wherever did you get that?" he exploded.

"Oh, Gran'ma was reading us the stories they gave us at Bible school last week, and that verse was in it. She said you ought to learn it. So I 'membered it for you."

Jack glared at the road ahead.

eight

The first ring of the telephone sounded just as Nancy completed the letter that Edna Forrest had begun. She lifted the receiver gingerly as if it were a time bomb.

Her mind raced. What was it Edna had said when responding? Some kind of church. What *was* it? Something-side. North? No. Just before her hesitation became silence, she remembered.

She tried to enunciate it just the way Miss Forrest had said it. "Westside Church." There was some other word, but it wouldn't come back to her. Then her glance lit on the letter heading. Of course. Westside Community Church. Well, too late now. A man's pleasant voice was saying, "Miss Forrest, this is Tom Martin. I just called to say that if there is any question about the man who preached Sunday, I'm for him, a hundred per cent. Do you know whether any action has been taken yet? I know Cash quizzed everybody after the morning service pretty well. As far as I heard there wasn't a dissenting voice."

"I can't give you any information about it, Mr. Martin. Miss Forrest was called home unexpectedly this morning, and I'm just taking her place for a little while."

"Oh. Are you Barbara Jenkins?"

"Nancy Lansing is my name. I'm staying at Cashes'!"

"Well, well. Glad to make your acquaintance, Miss Lansing. I think I must have seen you Sunday with Mrs. Cash. I'm Tom Martin. My wife Betty and I will want to give you a welcome to Pine City some time. Did I hear that you are to take Miss Forrest's place when she goes?"

Nancy paused. "Well, I *thought* I was, but after this morning I don't know." She laughed deprecatingly.

"Why, what's the matter? Having a tough time?" He seemed like a friendly big brother.

"Not exactly, yet. But it was quite a plunge, and frankly, I'm scared."

"Oh, don't let it get you. From what I saw of you at a distance on Sunday, I'd say you look like the sort who could tackle anything. I tell you what. I'll send Betty over, if you like. She knows everybody in the church, and she's always into everything. She ought to be able to help. I'll call her right now."

Something inside Nancy warned her. Uncharted courses could be dangerous.

"Oh, no, Mr. Martin. I wouldn't let you do that. I'll have to learn to handle it myself. I might as well begin now. It was only that Miss Forrest was just starting to show me the ropes when she was called away."

"Well, Betty can tell you a lot, I'm sure. She may not know where letters are, and that sort of thing, but she can give you the lowdown on any people or problems that come up. She gets around."

At that the inner warning set up a clamor.

"Oh, but she will have her own plans for the day. Don't bother her, *please*, Mr. Martin. I'm doing all right."

"Nonsense. If she has plans she can change them. I'll tell her she has to. She'll love doing it, I know. She'll be over soon. Well, it's been nice talking to you. Hope I'll meet you soon. You must come over and have dinner with us sometime. So long."

Nancy laid the receiver back on its bracket with misgivings. Tom Martin had seemed so friendly. No doubt his wife would be, too. But it would really have been better to be left alone to work out her problems without other inspecting eyes. Well, if Betty Martin came, she came. It couldn't be helped now. But Nancy felt as if she had learned her first lesson already.

I'll never let on again that I need help. The plot thickens. I'd prefer it thin. She sat still and gazed around the office.

Its walls were rough plaster, of no particular color. One side was completely taken up with shelves on which were books and sorted papers. There was a table with neat piles of current religious magazines which did not look like attractive reading to Nancy. There were two leather-seated chairs, one each side of the table, and on another wall, a city map. That was all. No, not exactly all. Above the secretary's desk was a motto done in silver on midnight blue glass. It read: "Delight thyself also in the Lord; and he shall give thee the desires of thine heart." Nancy read it several times. What could it mean? Certainly not what it said, or religious people would be getting the desires of their hearts. As far as her experience of them went, nobody appeared to be satisfied. No doubt there was some symbolic meaning which some people attached to it, that rationalized it in their thinking. She sighed and began to look for stencil sheets. Six months in this hole? Impossible! That twenty-five thousand was dwindling. She started to make a stencil for the letter.

The phone rang again. The SPCA wanted a contribution. Nancy postponed them and went on with her work.

Then she saw a shadow pass the window; there was a timid knock on the screen door.

"Come in." She wheeled around in her chair. A thin man with pale hair and pale eyes set close together opened the door and instantly began to look straight at her, with a simpering smile. She noticed that his stringy tie was soiled and his fingernails were dirty.

"Good morning—" he lingered over the vowels—"young lady."

Nancy summoned her most aloof manner. "Good morning?"

"I would like to see the pastor," he said. He pronounced his nouns as if they were delicious. He never took his eyes from her. Looking at his incessant smile seemed to her like being fed syrup, sip after sip.

Nancy quickly decided to tell this visitor as little as possible.

"He is not in now."

"Oh-h." The response was like a caress. "Will he be in soon?"

"I don't know just when he will be in."

"I am anxious to see him. You see, I am a writer." The last statement was incongruous, Nancy thought. "I have just finished a masterpiece. I am about to let a publisher have it and I was sure that your wonderful pastor would like to have an opportunity to read it," he lowered his voice to a mysterious whisper, "in manuscript form. Before it goes to the public eye, you know. It is called 'The Art of Being Pleasant.' It sums up the best philosophies of all ages and all religions, and states the eternal verities in simple, euphonious epigrams. It is an epitome—of—"

"Yikes!" Nancy cut him short. "I doubt if the pastor could masticate that. You'd better scram."

Nancy arose swiftly and came toward him with such vigor that he staggered backward. She was ready with the screen door open, and practically shoved him through.

"Good bye!" she flung at him emphatically and shut the outside door.

She took a deep breath. Oh, for someone to laugh with!

The telephone rang. It was Elbert this time. She made sounds of relief.

"Why, what's the matter?" He chuckled. "Is the going rough? I hear you're all alone. More power to you. How about a little lunch with me at the Coffee Nook?"

"Wonderful! I didn't realize it was time yet."

"I'll be right there."

It was good to be able to speak to another congenial young person. At her recital of the last encounter, Elbert chortled with appreciation.

"That could have been none other than Pine City's famous celebrity, Arthur Pease. What a character! I'll tell Dad that one. He'll hold his sides. What I'd have given to see you give him the bum's rush! You're okay, Nan. If you can handle everybody that well, you'll soon have a raise."

"Oh, but suppose he had been an influential church member?" She shivered.

"There are some, even of those, who would benefit by that treatment, according to my estimation," he said with a sneer.

Their time together was short, but Nancy returned to her duties with a little more assurance.

She had been back only a few minutes when a bright-eyed

blue-eyed blonde with a confident little air of capability appeared at the door and walked in without knocking. She flung her purse on a table and sank into a chair.

"Well, I see you're still at it. I'm Betty Martin. Tom told me to patter over here pronto and give you a hand. I came as soon as I could get a baby-sitter. No, no, don't worry about me," she said hastily when Nancy raised a negative hand, "I'm delighted to help, I'm sure. As a matter of fact, I consider it a break to get away from my four precious brats. I never did like children, and why the Lord saw fit to load four of them onto me is more than I know. I try to do my duty by them, but when I have a good excuse to get away, I do. Now, what are you doing? Can I help? I saw you in church, and I liked you right away. I didn't know until this morning that you were going to take Edna's place. Dear fussy old Edna. Imagine *her* catching a man at her age. We were all flabbergasted. Sue Immerman said if she can get one anybody can. I mean, she's good, and correct, and all that sort of thing, but absolutely without looks, you know. Not a curve in a carload! Of course, Sue has nothing to brag about, if you ask me. She may have been sharp years ago, but I class her with Winnie Windom when it comes to sex appeal. All drip and drape, and no punch. But they both go after the men. You should see! What the males see in either one of them is more than I know. Still and all, at parties, where are they? Always sitting between two or more goofs with pants on. That's what the poor men act like when they're around either Winnie or Sue. Perfect nitwits. Well, I came to let you in on all the dope and I haven't told you a thing yet, have I?"

Yikes! thought Nancy. This I deserve?

Betty Martin rattled on. "Now, which do you want first, the dirt or the lowdown on who's who? I suppose you know that Meta Cash is fit to be tied because Bob Manton has been dating you. But her frenzy doesn't compare with Winnie's

68

frustration since Elbert has absolutely refused to look at her. She ignores the fact that she's twelve years older than he is. Dolores Vincent vows never to speak to Nick again since you came into the picture. All in all, you have really caused a stir in Pine City. Don't worry, though, for the girls really like you, and the men will all drop you as quickly as they dropped the others, as soon as a fresh daisy blooms. I don't blame you, really. If I were as young and sharp as you are I'd make the most of it. I'm just dying to see if you can catch the new minister. For cat's sake do it, and ward off Winnie Windom. He *might* fall for her. What a minister's wife *she'd* be. Some people criticize a Christian girl for showing any interest in men. But after all, God made sex, didn't He? I think we should be perfectly natural. Of course, when it comes to a woman as old as Winnie Windom—she's thirty-five if she's a day—I think it isn't even decent for her to try to cut out the younger ones. She has two children, too. She just never got over it that she once won a beauty contest in Paducah or Kalamazoo or somewhere. By the way, speaking of age, have you met all the deacons yet? It simply strangles me to think of old Deacon Donaldson falling for Evelyn Constant. And what does he know about her, anyway? I've heard that she has been married twice before and has a grown son. Well, it's the old deacon's funeral, not mine. I don't see how a cultured man like he is can fall for such a coarse person as she."

She paused for breath and the telephone rang. She sprang up to seize it. "I'll take it for you," she offered. "At least I can do that much."

But Nancy had quietly picked up the receiver.

"Westside Community Church." She had the name on her tongue now.

"Yes? . . . No, he is not . . . Would you like to leave a message? . . . I doubt it . . . Yes, I'll tell Mr. Cash. Good bye."

Nancy had decided after hearing Betty's comments that it would be wise neither to cater to her, nor to antagonize her. So she said, "Thanks for offering, but I'll have to learn sometime, and it might as well be now."

Betty tossed her head.

"Okay, whatever you like. I just thought I'd know the people better than you would, and I'd be able to tell them more about the church doings, you know."

"It's nice of you." Nancy smiled. "But really, I don't think you should take any more of your time on me. I'll manage." Nancy could appear quite mature and dignified when she chose.

"Oh, all right, if you really don't *want* me to help. I do have shopping I could do, and I think I'll look in on Sue Immerman. Have you met her yet? She's loads of fun. She's Chuck's wife, you know. Her baby is expected next month. We're going to give her a shower soon. Then I have to stop and get a pair of shoes fixed for Tom. We always take our work to Lou Johns. He has a tiny little shop down on Fourth Street. If you really want good, honest work done, go there. He's a saint." For the first time since she came in Betty seemed thoughtful. "Well, if I can't tell you anything about things or people, I'll go. Call me if you need me. 'Bye."

Nancy gazed a long time at the door Betty slammed.

At last she took a deep breath and turned to the filing cabinet and studied the headings, trying to become familiar with the various matters that might come up. The multiplicity of areas threatened to floor her.

Several unimportant calls came in.

Another shadow passed the window; another knock came on the door. She went herself to open it this time.

A thin wispy girl scarcely yet in early teens looked up at her with large sorrowful eyes; her skinny finger twisted a wet rag of a handkerchief.

"Oh." The child seemed disappointed.

Nancy smiled compassionately. "You wanted Miss Forrest, didn't you? She had to go home. Her father is sick."

"Well, yes, but I really wanted to know if there's a minister here yet. My grandfather is going to die soon." She sighed heavily and tears brimmed up. "He thought such a lot of the old minister, and I can't make him realize that he's dead. Seems as if everybody's dying. My mother died last year. And now Miss Lansing's gone too. She was awful nice. *Everybody's* dying." A great heaving sob seized her and she turned away to hide her grief.

Nancy was speechless. This sprig of a child, forced to face Death! She was aware of a cowardly desire to shut the door on the sight of her and run. That uncanny unknown darkness that surrounds all human consciousness threatened to close in on her. Yet for Aunt Bea the darkness had seemed light! How could that be?

The child had already started away, weeping. Nancy felt like a slacker. To meet the need of people like this was part of her job, apparently, at least until a pastor came. Somebody must look after such friendless persons. She called her. Hopelessly the girl turned back.

"You mentioned a Miss Lansing," said Nancy. "Could that be Beatrice Lansing?"

"Yes. Did you know her?" The big eyes brightened wistfully.

"Why, yes—a—a little."

"She was wonderful. She was so good to my mother. She came to see her every day all the months she was sick. She used to bring her nice things to eat, and then she would stay and read the Bible to her. Mother just loved her. Everybody loved Miss Lansing. Well, I must go back now."

"I'm sorry I can't help you."

"Oh, it's okay. I'll go to Lou Johns. He'll know how to help my grandfather."

Nancy couldn't think of any more to say. She had had some idea of telling the child her relationship to the other Miss Lansing but she was suddenly aware of the vast discrepancy between them. She knew that somebody ought to take over the responsibility for keeping light alive in this child's eyes, but it was beyond her. Miss Forrest had suggested calling Mr. Cash. Somehow she couldn't picture him providing whatever it was—love? sympathy?—that this bit of human flotsam needed. Maybe Lou Johns would do it, whoever he was. Strange, Betty Martin had mentioned him, too.

The little girl hurried down the walk and Nancy simply stood and looked after her. A helpless feeling of inadequacy seized her. She jerked herself back into the room. "He shall give thee the desires of thine heart." The motto greeted her accusingly. It seemed as if there was nothing else in the room.

"I'm *not* going on with this job!" she said vehemently, aloud.

"That ain't the way I heered it!" came a teasing voice from the corridor leading from the main auditorium.

Mr. Cash walked in, laughing. "Don't you dare to quit. You're doing a wonderful job."

"Why, what do you know about it?" cried Nancy.

"I get about. I hear things. Don't let a few rough places throw you. Aren't there always rough spots in every job? I'm sorry I let you go all day without a call. I got tied up and couldn't get away. It's about time for you to sign off. Lock up here and let's go home. Did anything come up that you want to ask about?"

It was pleasant to relax in the Cashes' patio. A shower and iced drinks faded the heat of the day into an almost forgotten dream. Florida had its good points. The soft gentle breeze was refreshing. A day at a time, and perhaps the twenty-five thousand was worth it.

nine

It was several nights later that the telephone beside Harvey Donaldson's bed began to ring wildly, persistently. He turned on the light and forced his eyes open. With a glance at the clock, he reached for the instrument. Who could be calling at one a. m.?

"Harvey! Harvey, *darling*. Please forgive me for disturbing you—" Mrs. Constant's voice was tense.

"What's the matter, Evelyn? What is it?" He was flustered and fearful.

"Don't be frightened. I'm all right. It's just that Henry has come home and I have no extra bed in this apartment. You know I didn't expect him. Do you think Emma could put him in your guest room, just for the night? He probably won't be here long."

"Of course, Evelyn," agreed Harvey, relieved.

"You are sure it won't put you out too much?"

"Evelyn dear! You know better. Anything's all right with me."

"Okay, darling. I'll ship him right over. You get back to sleep. He can manage by himself, if Emma will just show him his bed."

Harvey buzzed his housekeeper's room as he put back the telephone. That buzzer was a blessing.

Soon Emma appeared, in an immense floppy red wrapper.

"Sorry to waken you, Emma. I've just had word that a friend, a young man, is in town with no place to go. Is the guest room bed made up?"

"Yes, sah. I allus keeps it made up, sah."

"Well, he'll be right over. His name is Valentine. Henry Valentine. I don't think you'll have to wait up long for him. See that he has what he needs. You needn't bring him in tonight. I'm tired. Thank you, Emma."

"Yes, sah."

Emma flopped off down the hall and Harvey turned over, but he did not sleep. Apprehensions crowded his mind. His daughter JoAnne figured largely in his thoughts. In spite of the fact that her trunk had arrived ten days ago, she herself had not turned up. It was quite like her high-handed unstable ways. It would be not unexpected if after having written the letter complaining of the camp, she would about-face completely and stay all summer. But he was troubled about not hearing from her. He finally decided that if she did not appear tomorrow he would telephone the authorities at the camp. Probably she was still there, and would ask to have her trunk sent back again. He sighed. It had been difficult to manage a teenage daughter with no mother to help. A stepmother should be a break; Evelyn had good keen common sense. He wished for the hundredth time that she had come to Pine City long ago. In the three months he had known her she had proved stable and sympathetic. Of course, JoAnne had had little chance to get acquainted with her, but at least she had admitted that she liked the woman. The two of them had enjoyed the two weeks they had spent together shopping for JoAnne's camping trip. Things were sure to go better after the marriage was consummated. But what about Evelyn's son? He might pose a difficult problem. However, she had spoken as if he were only passing through Pine City. He never stayed long in any one place. A few days and he would be out of the way again. Quiet settled down. He fell asleep.

Emma waited, yawning, in the straight chair in the front hall, so as to hear the visitor's footsteps and open the door before he rang the bell and disturbed Dr. Donaldson. She was unfailingly thoughtful for the man she had served for seven years.

She dozed several times. The grandfather clock was striking three when she roused to footsteps on the porch.

Softly she turned the knob and ushered in a tall young man. He was handsome in a cinematic sort of way. He had black hair like his mother's, flashing black eyes, and a dashing air of being confident that he was welcome anywhere at any time.

"Oh. You!" he greeted Emma carelessly. "Man of the house asleep? Okay, just show me my room. I'll have a drink before I go to bed. That's all."

Her head held high, Emma wordlessly and disapprovingly brought a pitcher of ice water and set it on the dresser while Henry was splashing in the bathroom. Then she flapped out and up to her own room. Angrily she threw her wrapper off and eased her weight into bed again with a sniff and a snort. It was quite a long time, however, before she ceased to hear footsteps and movements about the house.

It was nearly noon before there was any sign of life from the guest room. Then Henry, immaculate and startling, in a vivid sport shirt and shorts, went out to his convertible which he had parked in front of the house. Without a word to host or servant he climbed in and drove off.

Emma, according to instructions, fixed a nice lunch. At one-thirty she slid the unclaimed food onto other plates and slammed them into the refrigerator.

At five o'clock Evelyn Constant called. She was just off work, she said. How were things going? Harvey was disturbed. He had called the camp and found that JoAnne had departed the day after she sent her trunk home. They thought she had bought a ticket for New York. That was something, but it was vague. He rather curtly told Evelyn that he had not seen Henry yet. She expressed concern for her son's manners.

75

"Oh, don't worry about that, dear," he reassured her. "In this day and age I'm not expecting much in the way of manners. Don't bother about me. I am troubled about JoAnne, though."

"Well, what do you always tell me, Harvey? We'll pray and ask the Lord to take care of her and bring her safely home."

Harvey almost purred his gratitude. "Of course. It's good to hear you say that, dear. We will. When are you coming to see me again?"

"I may drop in a few minutes tonight. I want to hunt up Henry and find out his plans if I can. Oh, what a nuisance to have him behave like this. But he always thinks he can just go and come as he pleases, without the slightest regard to whether he is inconveniencing anybody else. Sometimes I wish he didn't have all that income from his father. It would be so much better for him if he had to work. Here he is twenty-two and not settled down yet."

"I'll tell you what you just told me, shall I?" Harvey gently prodded.

Evelyn laughed. "I am trying to trust," she said meekly. "I'll see you later this evening."

That morning Nancy had lain in bed some time thinking over her new job. She had been on it nearly a week. Was it worth it to try to struggle on there for the measly salary she was getting? If she was going to have twenty-five thousand dollars before long, why should she kill herself working for a pittance now? Yet Nancy was of a practical turn of mind. She was aware that some slip might yet occur between the cup of Uncle Harry's will and her own lip. This work had practically fallen into her lap and in one sense it was not difficult. Perhaps, as Mr. Cash had told her on the way home the first day, she would soon get used to the questions and problems, and take the whole thing in stride.

At last she rose reluctantly and prepared for the day.

Meta glanced up at her as she took her place at the break-fast table. Nancy always looked like a fresh blown rose right out of the garden. Meta's own hair was still in bobby pins. Two strands had worked loose and were sticking out awkwardly. Her housecoat was mussed and a safety pin was substituting for a button. Meta's face hardened. She was sullen all through the meal.

Mr. Cash seemed preoccupied. He answered everyone abruptly. An early telephone call had upset him.

Chuck Immerman, up at dawn that morning, reading the newspaper, had phoned Cash, and got him out of bed long before breakfast.

"Did you see the paper?"

"No."

"Get it and look on page 12, section C, last column."

A long wait.

Chuck, in imagination, could see Dunn Cash's face twisting and his pale eyes narrowing in a sort of feverish thirst. He grinned to himself sardonically. How well he had learned to know his boss in the two years he had worked for him. Always plunging, always in hot water, always robbing Peter to pay Paul, and never learning to let well enough alone. Chuck shrugged. As long as the pay checks kept on for himself, he'd go it with him.

Cash wet his crooked upper lip. "The Worthington property, you mean?"

"Sure. It's a gold mine, for whoever gets it."

"You didn't know that I hold the option on that already?"

"You're kidding!"

"Not at all. You think I'm not on the ball on these matters?" He puffed out his chest jokingly.

"But it would take twenty-five thousand just to swing the deal and that means in cash."

"Yes." Cash wet his lips nervously again. "Yes, I know. I can get it."

"You mean—?"

"Yeah. A bank check on Cash Appliances. Nothing shaky about that. Good collateral."

"Oh? I—see." Chuck looked troubled. "Don't forget that's part my baby."

"No more than it's mine—not as much. I don't want to lose it either," retorted Cash, gaily defensive.

"Yeah. I know. But—"

"But nothin'. It'll be okay. Manton's order will take care of part of it. There will be at least sixty days, maybe ninety, before I'll need the rest. Sales will start by that time."

"But Manton hasn't signed yet."

"He will. Practically gave me his word last night."

"I thought you couldn't get the machines."

"Oh, shut your trap. Business is business. I've heard enough. Good bye." Cash slammed the receiver down.

During breakfast he snapped at his wife and roared at Elbert. Finally, after nothing but two cups of strong coffee and a couple of pills of some kind, he shoved back his chair and flung an ultimatum at Nancy.

"I've got to leave this minute. Can't wait all day. Are you ready to go to the office? If you can't come now you'll have to walk. Elbert's gone."

In hurt surprise Nancy patted her lips with her napkin and rose. Her purse lay on the hall table. She picked it up and walked out to the driveway.

Coolly she climbed in beside her host and they sped away. She did not pretend to make conversation. After a mile or so, he said sheepishly, "You'll have to forgive me if I was rude. I have a devilish headache this morning and I'm not responsible."

"It's quite all right," answered Nancy. She did not pursue it further. Neither spoke even when he let her off at the church. Cash started off, then backed up to call to her, "Call me at the office if you get into a jam."

She nodded and he drove away.

So God hates cigarettes, does He? she sneered as she unlocked her office door. But a brattish temper is okay. What a God! And I suppose Betty Martin with all her rotten gossip is His fair-haired darling because she goes to church regularly and says her prayers!

Her hostile eyes sought that paradoxical motto again. Humph! I'll bet old Cash never put that up. That must be Edna Forrest's. It fits *her*. Or does she go off the handle too, when she's off guard at home? Religion is putrid. I'm not going to keep this job!

Then the postman came, bringing a letter from her father. One sentence caused her to do some serious thinking.

"It's good you have a job, Nannie, because things haven't gone well for me. Three different deals have fallen through and that means I'll not be able to help you with any money for some time. I hope you'll make out all right."

Nancy spent the next hour in thought. She was still furious at Mr. Cash's inexcusable rudeness, but she was not quite as ready to quit her job.

No calls came in for a couple of hours. She was beginning to think that the work was not so difficult after all. Just then came a shadow past the glass in the window again. This time it was a tall shadow, that moved with easy assurance.

The screen door was yanked open.

"Well, how in hell did *you* land *here?*" cried a gay masculine voice.

Nancy paused a second to identify it. Then she whirled in amazement.

79

"Hank!" she fairly screamed. He seized her in his arms and planted a thorough kiss on her lips. Then he held her off and laughed at her astonishment.

"Am I glad to see somebody from home!" she exclaimed. "As to hell, I'm not sure yet whether this is it or not. Sometimes it seems like it, and other times it's been more like paradise." She took out a mirror and began to repair her face and hair.

Suddenly the door from the corridor opened and Betty Martin appeared.

She stood looking from one to the other for a long moment, a knowing smile on her face. Then she said to Nancy, "Well, introduce me to your friend from—Paradise, did you say?"

Nancy shot her a biting glance. Why did the woman have to act as if she had something on her? There was certainly nothing wrong in greeting an old friend as Hank had greeted her. Anyway, Betty had no business to come pussyfooting around like that without warning.

With coldest courtesy Nancy made the introduction. She called Hank "an old friend of mine from New York."

"From New York?" Betty raised her eyebrows and turned to Hank. "Haven't I seen you around before? I'm sure you are the one whom I saw at the golf links a couple of months or so ago with Meta Cash. And your mother lives here now? I think I saw her Sunday with a very fine gentleman, one of our deacons, to be exact."

"Not really?" It was Hank's turn to look surprised. "My mother with a *deacon*? It's time I checked up, I should say. That'll be the day, when *she* gets religion."

"Where are you staying? Surely not in your mother's apartment? She practically has to go out into the hall to change her mind, it's so small. The reason I know is that Sue and Chuck Immerman had it when they were first married. They gave it up because it was too small for the two of them, and now that the baby is coming it would be impossible. Are you at the Palm Garden Inn?"

Hank stared at the inquisitive girl before he answered haughtily, "No."

"There aren't many other nice places in town. Of course it's not as hard in summer to find a good motel room. Are you near your mother?"

Another pause. "No."

But Betty did not give up. "I think it's just fabulous that you two know each other. You know, Mr. Valentine, this gal has taken Pine City by storm. We are all crazy about her. I just got acquainted, a little, but we all love her. My husband had a mere telephone visit with her and he can't wait for me to invite her to dinner. Now don't you come down here and make her dissatisfied. We don't want her to tire of us and run back to New York. After all, Nancy, you have the new minister to hook, you know, to save us all from Winnie Windom's being the pastor's wife."

Nancy gazed at Betty in amazement. Did she mean all that? What reason would she have to say it? Nancy was glad to have the telephone interrupt the rapid conversation; its instability annoyed her.

After her routine "Yes" and "No" and "I'll leave him a note" was over, Hank started for the door. "Well, I'm going to toddle now. When do you finish here, Nan? Five? I'll pick you up. No, don't bother to dress. We'll go to dinner where it won't matter. See you."

Nancy accepted with apparent indifference. After he was gone Betty gave a little chuckle. "How they do swoon at your feet, darling. Well, have a good time. Don't mind what the church people say. Let me put you wise, though. Don't tell Cash who you're out with. He was fit to be tied when Meta used to date this fellow. But maybe you can get him saved. Where did you know him? Up north?"

"Yes, in New York. His father used to live there, and Hank spends most of his time there. He goes around a lot with our crowd up there."

"His father? I understood that his father was dead. His mother is Evelyn Constant, you know. She said that her husband had died just a few months before she came down here. Oh, but," she thought a minute—"of course that wouldn't have been this boy's father. Her name is Constant. She must have married again, after she was married to Valentine. Oh, brother! what a mix-up. And now I hear that Dr. Donaldson is going to marry her. At least that's the surmise, around the church. She got saved, you know, after she came down here. And she has no hesitation about testifying wherever she goes. I wonder what her son will say when he finds out she really is saved? I've heard that he drinks."

Nancy's rage began to rise again. Suddenly she turned on Betty.

"Well, if all you people who—" Then she stopped abruptly.

Betty scented battle. Her eyes gleamed. "What did you say?" she urged.

"Nothing. I've got to get a couple of letters out that Mr. Cash wanted done today. I'm sorry, Betty, but I'd better get to work."

Betty tossed her head. "Oh, all right. Far be it from me to hinder you. I really came over to help. But if you don't need me, I'll let you alone. Have a good time tonight on your date," she called as she went out the street door.

Nancy's nostrils quivered in fury and disgust.

Hypocrites. That's all they are. Stuffed shirts! Every one of them. Thank goodness Hank's turned up. He'll make sense. Her eye lit on the motto. "Delight thyself in the Lord." Delight thyself in gossip, I should say. "Saved!" Saved, my foot! They need to be saved from slander. Then she looked thoughtful. I wonder—I wish I'd had a chance to know Aunt Bea.

I wonder whether she was like that. Then she shook her head. I doubt if any of them are real.

She gave her paper a thrust into the typewriter and jerked the roller along. The keys sounded like machine gun bullets.

ten

JoAnne burst open the front door of her home, slid her overnight bag along the floor and flung her purse on the hall table.

Then she halted. Like a night creature aware of prey she cocked her ear. "There's a man in this house somewhere, and it isn't just my father," she whispered to herself.

She glanced at the grandfather clock. It was about to strike twelve. She tiptoed down the hall. The guest room door was slightly ajar. A dim light was burning. Ever so cautiously she pushed until she could poke her head around so that one eye had command of the room. The bed was turned back neatly; Emma's work. A pair of handsome mesh sandals pointed four different ways in the middle of the floor. A flamboyant sport shirt draped itself by one sleeve from the lamp fixture. The bathroom door stood open. No one was in sight anywhere.

She drew back. A muffled clatter sounded from the kitchen. Sliding out of her shoes, she padded softly down the hallway and pushed open the swinging door between the dining room and the kitchen.

Her eyes grew wide in pleased surprise. A very tall, decidedly dark and good-looking young man was helping himself to a glass of iced punch.

When he saw JoAnne he slowly set the glass down and stared in delight. In mock bewilderment he rubbed his eyes.

JoAnne pursed her full red lips into a slow, archly provocative smile. The encounter was to her delightfully like a romantic television drama.

After they had savored the situation for a full minute without a word, she spoke, saucily.

"Well, it's about time for the commercial now, isn't it?"

"Shouldn't station identification come first?" he parried.

She laughed a merry peal. Her black eyes became fascinating, sparkling crescents when she laughed, and a bevy of little dimples appeared in the curve of her cheeks. The smart line of her copper bangs added to the bewitching charm of her whole vivid personality.

"Station J-O-A-N-N-E Donaldson, Pine City, the only station in the south that springs a surprise with every program."

"And now, this message from our sponsor," he rejoined. " 'Each time you take an iced drink from the refrigerator, look for the pretty girl behind the door. Don't be satisfied with less.' I say, this is really jolly," he went on, pouring her a glass. "I shall stay tuned to this station for the second half of our drama, 'Caught in the Act.' "

They laughed and perched on high red stools beside the breakfast bar.

"But you haven't announced the name of the star," pouted JoAnne.

"Will Valentine do?" he offered.

Her eyes grew large. "Not *Jimmy* Valentine? Oh, to think we had no padlock on the refrigerator for you to pick."

He chuckled appreciatively. "I'm afraid it's only Hank this time. And I much prefer refrigerators that open with a touch."

"Oh, this is so super! I expected to come home and be bored

to annihilation. Would you mind telling me whence you come and why you're here? Are you a Lohengrin—or was it Lochinvar—that will vanish with the morning light?"

"Well, to tell you the truth, I don't know exactly why I'm here except that I, too, young lady, was bored everywhere else. I now assume that I came here to find you." He gave the last word a flattering little twist and looked impudently around his glass at her.

The dimples came again as he had hoped, and she returned the look.

"Seriously, I'm here to visit my mother, but she didn't have room for me; so, since she and your father seem to be rather warm friends, she called and asked hostelry here for me for the time being. It has begun to be very pleasant."

"Oh. Then your mother is Evelyn Constant. I like her," stated JoAnne. "She and I went shopping before I left for camp. We had a ball. She's purely a riot."

"She can be fun," agreed Hank, but with an unspoken reservation in his tone.

JoAnne caught it, for she said, "I know how stupid parents can be. They're of a past generation. It must have been absolutely putrid in those days." JoAnne tucked one plump bare foot up on a rung of the stool and let the other dangle its little painted toes back and forth. "Dad's a decent enough old fellow, though. He lets me make my own decisions. If he didn't, I would anyway."

"I'm glad you decided to come home. That was certainly a good decision."

She grinned. "I think so too, now."

"We can have fun."

"Yes," she agreed.

"How about a double date tomorrow night? Who do you know? I'm already dated, but it could be a foursome."

"I could call—Ted Martin. Do you know him?"

"Never heard of him. Or no, wait. I met a Betty Martin today."

"Her younger brother-in-law," said JoAnne.

"Okay. We'll have us a blast. Now I'd better let you get to bed or you won't wake up by tomorrow night."

He put out his arms. JoAnne slid into them for a long kiss. Then they turned out the lights and JoAnne stole upstairs to her room. Pine City had suddenly become an interesting town.

But JoAnne's reckoning was due the next day.

She slept until nearly noon. Then Emma came in and woke her.

"Miss Jo," she gently shook her, "yore daddy wants you should come to his room."

JoAnne struggled over on one side and yawned.

"Miss Jo!" Emma kept at her. "Miss Jo!"

A groan. "Yes, Emma, what's the matter? A burglar in the house? It's midnight, isn't it?"

Severely Emma persisted.

"Miss Jo, yore daddy wants you."

"Oh-kay," grumbled the girl. "Tell him to keep his shirt on. I'll be there eventually." Then she opened her eyes. "Hi, Em," she greeted the woman. "How's everything?"

"Yore daddy wants you, Miss Jo."

"Yes, I *know* it. You only said so about eight times. I'll get there. Scram."

Ten minutes later, after she heard her master's door open and close, Emma returned to JoAnne's room. She stood looking with disgust at the melee of bags, clothing and shoes.

She shook her head in disapproval. "Housekeeper! Huh! Housekeeper is the one thing she most ain't!"

She started to pick up the things systematically, then all at once she dropped them where they were.

"No sah! Not me! Ef'n her daddy wants her to learn, she gwine to learn. I gits back to mah own work."

She lumbered down to the kitchen. But she no sooner got there then Dr. Donaldson's buzzer sounded.

When she reached his door she could hear JoAnne's loud voice on the defensive.

"I *did* come right home, Dad. I just came by way of New York. What's wrong with that?"

Emma knocked and went in.

The elderly man was considerably disturbed. It was obvious that he did not know what to do with his recalcitrant daughter.

"Emma," he appealed to her, "you remember that I told you last week that Miss JoAnne was to come home, and at her own suggestion, would take over the housekeeping?"

"Yes, sah." There was finality in Emma's whole attitude.

"I would like you to give her instructions, for one week. By that time, I think she should be able to take over. This is not a large house. Now is that all right with you, JoAnne?"

"Jes' a minute, sah," Emma interrupted. "I wants to make one thing clear. Ef'n I takes the job fer a whole week of instructin' Miss Jo, I is de boss. It ain't gwine to be 'Does you like this, Miss Jo,' er 'Does you like dat, Miss Jo.' It's to be, 'Do it er else!'"

"Yes, yes, Emma. You should have full authority. I'll leave it entirely in your hands. Now, JoAnne, I expect you to cooperate, and to learn enough this week so that you can take entire charge when Emma goes. There will be nothing too hard for you to do, for there will be just you and me. Our young guest will surely be gone or make other arrangements in a day or two. He has been here so little he has made no trouble. I've scarcely seen him myself. Of course, I shouldn't care to have him here after Emma is gone."

JoAnne raised her crescent eyebrows and tossed her round cropped head, but said nothing.

"Is that all arranged now?" asked her father, that old placating tone in his voice again.

"Oh, I guess it's okay," replied JoAnne flippantly, twisting her overripe red lips.

Emma gave her a look which she didn't catch. The woman set her own lips in a determined line, and marched out. The interview was ended.

As her father seemed to be out of words for the time being, JoAnne flounced out of the room. She took a peek into Hank's empty room as she passed, then gave a little secretive laugh. So he'll be gone in a few days, will he? Ha! Leave that to little Jo. Sure, the arrangements are okay. Exit, Emma!

It was more than twenty-four hours later when Betty Martin poked her pretty blond head in at the screen door of the church office again. "Any news of your new boss yet? Oh, pardon *me!* I didn't know you had company."

Hank arose from his seat on Nancy's desk and greeted the visitor with perfect poise. But Nancy's eyes flashed.

Betty did not withdraw, in spite of her apology. Instead she came in, thirsty for crumbs of information.

"Well, Miss Lansing, *what* did your employer, Mr. Cash, say to your jamboree at the country club last night? I'm simply dying to know. I'll bet he blew a tonsil. Or did you manage to keep it from him? Of course, *I* won't tell him. I figure what people don't know won't hurt them."

Nancy stared her straight in the eye for a long moment. Then she said coolly, "I'm not attempting to hide anything. I have nothing to hide."

"No? Well, I think myself it's none of his business. But didn't JoAnne's father have kittens over her going with fellows so much older, and staying so late? I think it was three

a. m. before Tom's brother, Ted, came in." She turned to Hank inquiringly.

He spread his hands. "I wouldn't know," he said unconcernedly. "She wasn't up when I left."

Betty nodded. "No doubt. Or she never would have let you out of her sight to come over here where there was another girl. Oh, I know these young gals. They're out for big game. They hook all they can."

Hank and Nancy remained unresponsive.

"But you just wait, Mr. Valentine, until the new minister comes. I predict that within six months, with Nancy working here in his office—oh, don't leave us, Nancy," she cried teasingly. For Nancy had turned her back and, seizing a handful of papers, she slid out through the corridor door into the main church.

"I have to see to something that goes into the bulletins for Sunday," she flung back. But she slipped up into the dark choir loft and stood in the shadows, clenching her fists, and fighting back the angry tears.

I'll never even *speak* to the guy, she vowed. I won't look at him. I'll leave this putrid hole and never come back. I'd like to dig Uncle Harry out of his grave and *beat* on him till he can't sit up.

She heard a ringing laugh from Betty and growling rejoinders from Hank. No doubt they were laughing at her escape. After a while footsteps came, evidently in search of her, but she thrust her head down behind the choir seats, as if she were looking for a book, and in the dim light she was not noticed. The footsteps and the voices died away and then ceased. Hank must have gone out with Betty. He would follow any pretty woman. Nancy knew him of old. But Betty and all her talk of being "saved"! How disgusting.

I'll go out tomorrow and hunt another job, and another boarding place, she fumed. I'm sick of Mr. Cash's crankiness.

And as for the new minister, I wouldn't look at him now if he were the last man on earth. I hate him, already. He's probably just like all the rest. Religion is hogwash!

Nancy hammered at her work all day. There wasn't much to do, but she invented tasks. After lunch—she always took a sandwich and a thermos of coffee—she took out all the books from the shelves and dusted them and cleaned the shelves. She worked in nervous tense jerks. Few calls came in; no callers.

At last it was nearly time for Mr. Cash to stop for her. The work was finished and she was simply sitting, staring angrily at the wall, and that ubiquitous motto. Suddenly she jumped up in exasperation.

I've had enough of this. I'm *not* going home with that man again today and have him fret on my shoulder. I don't even like to ask him for a little favor any more. I'll take my shoes down to Lou Johns myself. I'll roast, walking downtown, but I can find the place, I'm sure, and the walk will work off a little of my own meanness, perhaps. *Let* Cash find out I left a half hour early; *let* him blow his top; *let* him fire me. He's not the only man in Pine City who can give me a job.

She seized her empty thermos bottle, her parcel of dancing slippers and her purse, locked the office door with a vengeful turn, and set off, walking very fast, her head held high.

It was a mile or more to the center of town where the old shoemaker had his shop. The sun was excessively hot. Nancy's speed began to wane before she had gone three blocks. Her head drooped. By the time she turned in at the tiny booth that was no more than a hole in the wall, she was exhausted and a little bit ashamed of herself. She was not used to such exercise in the heat of a Florida sun.

The inside of the shop seemed lost in darkness, contrasted with the glaring sunshine outside. Nancy pulled open the squeaky screen door; its upper half opened before the bottom half followed. The door was paintless; a tear in its wire was neatly darned with heavy black shoebuckle thread.

When her eyes became somewhat accustomed to the dimness, she saw that she stood in an area scarcely four feet wide and only twice that length. A worn wooden counter held the neutral ground between customers and shopkeeper.

Clean wooden shelves beyond the counter held row after neat row of mended shoes, awaiting their owners patiently, expectantly. Nancy studied them. That shoes had personalities had never before occurred to her. Not only each close snuggled pair, but each individual shoe proclaimed its owner's unique characteristics. There were blue brocade slippers, with sharp spike heels. They stood with their heels slightly apart, as if at odds. She pictured the girl who wore them as dainty, pretty, but very willful. Next was a stubby pair of tan and white saddle shoes, soiled and shabby. One turned its toe up defensively while the other held to its original shape with patrician pride. There were heavy work shoes, clodhoppers, riding boots, and dainty little-girl dancing pumps. Nancy smiled to herself trying to imagine their owners.

She was still smiling thoughtfully when she became aware of someone watching her. She had heard no sound of footsteps. She turned, and there behind the counter was a middle-aged man with a crown of short, wavy, silver hair. He was seated in a rubber-tired wheel chair. His legs stuck out like stumps, for they ended just above the knees. His benignant face and bright look belied so strangely the ghastly effect of his lower half that Nancy choked back a gasp.

She saw that he was smiling, quizzically, and he observed her closely while he waited for her to speak.

"Oh!" she exclaimed awkwardly. "I have some shoes here—"

She produced her parcel and unwrapped the little silver slippers. "This one needs a new lift on the heel."

She handed it to him and noticed with some embarrassment that he was still gazing at her with interest and a sort of yearning.

He took the shoe from her but still his eyes never left her face.

"And your name is—"

"Lansing," she replied.

"Yes!" he said, and breathed with great satisfaction. "Nancy."

Startled, she opened her mouth and stared at him.

"Why! How did you know?" She laughed in astonishment.

"I've been waiting for you. I hoped you would come soon."

"What do you mean? I've only been in town a few weeks." She began to think that here was a psychic medium of some kind. Yet his gray eyes were kind and his voice was strong and pleasant, not eerie as she had always imagined a mystery man's would be.

"I knew you were coming to Pine City. I have imagined many times what you would look like."

Nancy felt strangely drawn to the cripple. He spoke like a gentleman, with a courteous cultured accent.

"Well, do I fit?" she asked archly.

"Wonderfully!" he said with quiet satisfaction. "Except for one thing."

She raised her eyebrows and tilted her head to one side coquettishly. "One? Is that all?"

He laughed. "Some time I'll tell you about it. You have work you'd like done?" He reached for the shoes.

"Well, I guess I do. But you sort of put it out of my head. I don't really think I can sleep tonight unless you let me in on the mystery. Who told you about me?"

He was silent a long minute. Then he spoke as if he were in a holy place. "Your Aunt Beatrice."

"Oh, really? You knew her?"

"Yes. Yes, I—knew her." It was spoken not sadly, only reverently.

"I'm interested," urged Nancy, "because—well, I didn't really know her, but in a sense I feel as if I did know her very well. I saw her for the first time only minutes before she died. But she seemed to me like—like a most rare flower. I suppose that sounds silly. But actually, I have never been able to forget the sort of—*fragrance* that there was in her room that day, and the last words she said."

As Nancy was speaking, a great light of intense eagerness deepened in the man's eyes. He wheeled his chair as close to the counter as it would go.

"Yes?" he breathed as if impatient for her to continue. Then he sighed deeply, his gaze steadily upon her. "Not now, though. You will come to see me some evening, won't you? And then you will tell me." He spoke wistfully, like a little boy who had been waiting for his heart's desire for a long, long time.

Almost involuntarily Nancy assented.

"When?" she asked.

"At your convenience, of course."

"Tomorrow evening?"

"Yes. At seven. I live at the back of the shop here. You will enter from the alley in the rear. Thank you." He paused. "You see—I—I *loved* her."

In astonishment Nancy contemplated him. This was a totally unexpected development. It had never occurred to her that any but young people could experience love, and the idea of coupling Aunt Bea with a common cobbler was incongruous. Yet she caught his spirit of reverent awe and smiled back at him.

"Tomorrow evening at seven. I shall look forward to it. Good bye."

93

She was conscious of a sense of peace as she walked back to Cashes'. What had become of all the fretting little problems that had harried her when she left the office? Something of the same atmosphere—was it a fragrance?—that she had found in Aunt Bea's room seemed to envelop her, as if it had surrounded her in that little shop and still clung to her. There was nothing eerie or occult about it. It was simply as if she had met a Person who *was* Peace, and it—He—had remained with her.

That night as she lay in bed and thought over the strange encounter, she remembered Betty Martin's chatter that first day in the office. Of all the people that Betty had maligned or at least gossiped about, Lou Johns was the only one about whom she had had only good to say. He must be a remarkable person. She was actually looking forward eagerly to the next evening.

But the thought of what Betty had said brought back the jabs of insinuation that she had thrust at her that morning.

Well, if I do keep that church job, I certainly don't intend to give Betty Martin or anybody else a chance to make any cracks about me and that new minister. I want *no* parts of him. Me! A minister's wife! I hope his car breaks down and he *never* gets here.

But at that very moment Jack Warder's car was being efficiently overhauled for its trip to Pine City.

eleven

Nancy was glad when she reached home that there was nobody in evidence except little Ellenelle. The child sprang up and clattered over toward her lovingly with a book to be read to her. A warm comradeship had grown between them, perhaps because the little girl was necessarily shut out of much that concerned the rest of the family, both because of her age and also on account of her disability. More and more Nancy felt that she herself was not one of them, and that the feeling might be mutual. She could not bring herself to show any interest in their form of religious beliefs, and she soon became aware that anyone who did not was, in their minds, outside the pale.

Nancy accepted every invitation to dine out; she was never there for lunch; breakfasts she dreaded. Dunn Cash was sure to be out of sorts the first thing in the morning. Sometimes his ill temper was so blatantly obnoxious that the rest chose to omit breakfast and clear out, leaving him to his wife's placating ministry. As far as Nancy could determine, emotional disturbances stemmed always from essentially the same cause: anxiety over knotty business deals. She had often heard poor Mrs. Cash pleading with him in their room at night. She couldn't catch any words, only tones of voice. Apparently Alice never won her case. He would always make the plunge and then take out his worry upon her and all the rest of the family.

Sometimes Nancy reviewed the few weeks she had spent there and recalled her first impressions of the place and the people. What a blissful existence it had appeared to be then. Was every home rotten below the surface? She thought of her own. There was no open rift to deal with, such as Rose Trask, for instance, had had to put up with, but there was certainly much to be desired in the Lansing home life. The other people with whom she was fairly well acquainted all had their skeletons, too. There was Hank. What a life his had been. She was truly sorry for the boy, although she had never had any very high regard for him. He was fun to play with, that was all. The Martins? Nothing ideal there, certainly. Immermans?

She didn't know them very well. Nick was pleasant, but in her estimation rather lazy and easygoing. She guessed that Chuck might be the same.

As she read aloud to Ellenelle with her lips, her mind slipped secretly back to that little dark shop where she had just heard the strange, fascinating confession of the love of a mature man for a sweet middle-aged lady. How long had it existed? Surely it had not sprung up overnight, as it were, in the short years since Aunt Bea had been home from India. Nancy had heard of childhood romances and scoffed. Love never lasted that long. Bitterly she slammed the door on her own memories of last winter. Had some strange power possessed those two people? Nonsense! The man must be nuts!

Nancy finished reading and made haste to slip up to her own room. She was not anxious to be around when Dunn Cash came home. For there was another vague undercurrent besides his mere ill temper that kept gnawing at Nancy's subconscious thought about him. In view of the few meals she took at the Cash house, she knew that the food allowance on her salary was not an equitable arrangement. Yet she hesitated to go to him and say, "I eat only so much, therefore I want to be reimbursed." It was an embarrassing situation. After all, they had made her practically a member of the family. She had received so much more in their home than mere board and lodging, intangibles, that could never be paid for. So she had kept her own counsel. Still, she felt that Mr. Cash should be the one to come to her and make the adjustment. She would have looked for another boarding place, but after all, there was that invisible obligation to those who had taken her in so warmly. Perhaps they, too, wished to be relieved of the arrangement, yet disliked bringing up the subject. She was sure Meta would be glad if she were not there. But what about Ellenelle? And Elbert was certainly most friendly. There was nothing to do but watch and wait. But another four or five months of this? She could not take it.

96

Contrary to her fears, nothing at all was said at the dinner table about her having left the office early. No doubt Mr. Cash thought that Elbert or some other friend had picked her up. He might even have forgotten all about her.

The next morning Mr. Cash was unusually agreeable on the way to the church office. Nancy did not trust him, however. She had the feeling that he was working up to something.

"By the way, is the work here at the office taking all your time?"

"Why, no," she answered. "Frankly, I can't find enough to do." Perhaps he was going to suggest that she work part time and take less pay. She would resent that, but likely it couldn't be helped. "I suppose that when the new minister comes we'll soon make up for all this leisure."

"No doubt," he agreed. "But I was thinking that if you could manage it, perhaps you could help me out at my office a little. My secretary is taking her vacation starting today, and I haven't found anyone to fill in for her yet. If I try to handle everything it keeps me pretty well tied down, and I should be out a good deal on sales and closing contracts, you know."

"I'd be glad to do what I can," assented Nancy politely. "Would I be at your office or here?"

"Part of the time here and part time there, I guess. Or better still, I could have the operator transfer the church phone calls to my office for the time being. Miss Johnson will be gone only a week. I thought we might work it in, because I practically pay the salary of the church secretary anyway."

"All right, whatever you say." Nancy was often surprised to find herself agreeing with whatever Dunn Cash suggested, just as she had watched others do. Even the members of the church board seemed to follow his leading without question. It sounded to her as if he was planning to retrieve some of his church contributions. Well, that was his business. In this case, she actually would welcome more to do. The monotony of sitting hour after hour waiting for something to happen was boring to her. So it was arranged that he should take Nancy with him to his own office as soon as the telephone calls could be transferred.

That day, whenever Nancy had time to sit and think, her mind ran ahead to the strange conference she was to have that evening with Lou Johns. She was aware that if she went home to dinner beforehand, she would have quite a time persuading the Cashes not to take her to her appointment. She felt reticent about telling them where she was going. She had a strong feeling that there would be wisecracks. She had no intention of airing Aunt Bea's love affair, if such it was, before these people, who, kind as they had been to her, still did not seem to discern between hallowed and profane.

So she planned to take her evening meal at the Coffee Nook, window-shop a little while, and then make for Lou Johns' alley abode.

Promptly at seven she strolled down the back street. It was neat enough. It differed from the street in front of the shop only in its narrowness, and its trash cans, set out for the morrow's collection.

A store's rear entrance flanked the little home on the left, and a neighbor's pitiful back porch adjoined it on the right. Lou Johns' living space took up certainly not more than fifteen feet of the length of the block, and she recalled that the shop itself extended at least halfway through the depth of the building. Nancy had never met intimately such poverty before.

She knocked. A hearty welcoming voice called, "Come in," and she entered.

Instantly she felt at home.

The green-painted walls were chipped, the old rose carpet on the floor was threadbare; there was only a single easy chair, near a studio couch with a handsome India shawl neatly spread over it. But somehow she had the sense of being at a loving, warm, family hearthside. There was a green-painted wooden bookcase, a large one, filled with well-bound volumes that intrigued the imagination. It was a great contrast to the bare drop leaf table, whose drab paint was almost scrubbed away in places. Two straight-backed chairs were the only other furniture. A faded green curtain half hid the two burner hot plate and some cooking utensils in the corner. Yet the room held a cheerful welcome.

Her attention was drawn to the figure of the cripple wheeling himself laboriously toward her from behind the green curtain.

He smiled eagerly. There was a sort of quiet radiance about him.

"Am I too early?" asked Nancy shyly.

"Not at all. I was afraid you'd be late and then I would get to thinking that you had decided not to come. Will you sit down there, in the big chair? It's the most comfortable. I'll park right here; then, when we have to light the lamps, I'll be able to see you. You must forgive me, Nancy, if I keep looking at you. You are so like your aunt when she was young."

Nancy smiled, a smile that was rare with her in its gentleness. So often her smiles were hard and gay, for self-defense. " 'Except for one thing,' you said yesterday. I want to know what that is, of course."

He looked thoughtful. "Of course you do," he agreed. "Perhaps I will be able to tell you—sometime. Not just yet. Perhaps you will soon be able to guess it yourself, when I tell you more about your aunt."

He kept his hands at rest while he spoke. They were hard and calloused from his work, but clean.

"First," he began like a small boy on Christmas morning, "I would like to hear what you have to tell me. Then I will tell you my story."

Nancy raised her eyes in surprise. "Do I have anything to tell you?"

"Indeed, yes. You mentioned it yesterday. You said you saw —her—just before she left us. Tell me, please." He spoke in a low, earnest, breathless tone. "You see, I couldn't be there with her."

"Well, I—I don't know where to start. I came down here to Florida, expecting to spend—a while, six months, to be exact, with Aunt Bea."

He nodded, watching her closely.

"Yes, yes. Tell all about that. Why did you come?"

Nancy flushed. It seemed fairly sacrilegious to speak of money affairs here. Suddenly the twenty-five thousand dollars appeared almost unclean to her. She took a forced breath.

"Well, my uncle had died—that was her brother Harry. My father is her youngest brother, nearly fifteen years younger, I think. Uncle Harry made a will leaving me twenty-five thousand dollars if I would spend six months down here in Pine City. We assumed that he meant with Aunt Bea. But she was gone almost as soon as I got here. The lawyer insists that the money cannot be paid to me unless I fulfill the requirement regardless of her death. It's rather ridiculous, really, because I think Uncle Harry's idea was that Aunt Bea's goodness would sort of rub off on me—I'm not very religious myself. Now that she's gone, it's only a question of putting in the time. Silly, isn't it? I suppose some people would say it wasn't worth it, but I guess it's as easy a way to make twenty-five thousand as I know, short of a giveaway quiz program on TV." She laughed.

"I see," he said seriously, looking kindly at her. "I had an idea it was something like that. I used to know Harry well, but not in later years.

"Go on, please." His eagerness persisted. "Tell me, if you will, just how she looked, what she said. You don't know how I have longed to hear it from somebody. And to think it can be you! It's like having her tell me herself, you're so like her."

The pink came up prettily in Nancy's cheeks under his steady, earnest, admiring gaze. She decided he was almost handsome, in spite of his age and his handicap.

"Well, when I was met at the airport, I was told right away that she had had the accident and might not live. I was to go immediately to see her. Frankly, I was frightened. I had never before faced death like that. But when I went into her room—well, it was like"—she stopped a moment and searched for words, glancing round the room—"it was something like coming in here!" She spoke awesomely. "It was like a home-coming, if you can possibly understand what I mean." She had forgotten him now in her desperate attempt to find a way to explain to him, to satisfy his longing to have the scene reconstructed. "It was like this"—she waved her hand around—"only more so. I mean it was light, and fresh like sunshine on a field, or the taste of wild strawberries that I had once when I was little and I visited my grandfather's farm."

His eyes were upon her in delight, fairly snatching each word from her mouth.

When she paused, he murmured, "And you caught that! You recognized it! Glory be to the Lord!"

Her eyes were detached, distant. She went on as if she had not heard him.

"She smiled at me. The sweetest smile I ever saw, I think. She was such a dainty little thing, so gray, and yet so sunny. And she tried to speak to me. I had to lean down to hear her. Oh, I remember it all so plainly, for I had never experienced anything like it. She said—I could just make out the words—"

"Yes, yes, go on," he breathed.

101

"She said, 'I hope you enjoy it here, in Florida. I—can't stay. It's so beautiful over there.' "

The man's deep gray eyes shone.

"Then she said to me, 'But I love you. Do come—sometime. I'll tell Him about you.' I'm not just sure what she meant by that. Maybe you can tell me."

"Yes, I will tell you. Go on. Did she say more?"

"Just one word. We thought she was gone, but then she opened her eyes and smiled a sort of glorious smile and cried very clearly, 'Why—Harry!' Then she closed her eyes. And that was all."

As if the very intensity of telling had taken all her strength, Nancy leaned back in her chair, exhausted.

The man was gripping tightly the arms of his wheel chair. Nancy had a feeling that she ought to hold him fast lest he too float off to that far distant beautiful land where Aunt Bea had gone.

Then he turned and smiled again, with a long satisfied sigh.

"Thank you," he said simply. "I was sure it would be something like that. She is a wonderful person."

"She must have been," agreed Nancy.

"She *is*," he corrected gently.

"Do you really think she's existing somewhere?" she asked wistfully. "It would be sort of worth it all if we could be sure there was something better coming later on."

"I don't think so. I know so," he stated with unaffected sincerity.

"*How* do you know? How can anybody know?"

"Because of the integrity of the One who told us so. He's the only one who really knows. Don't you see that all truth hinges on that? The complete honesty of the person who tells you something is what convinces you it is true."

"I suppose if you *could* really trust somebody, it would

102

make a difference. So far, I've never found anybody like that."
A bitterness came into her face, but she said no more about
her own experiences.

"I have."

"Yes? You mean Aunt Bea?"

"No, Jesus Christ."

"Oh, religion. I don't go for that. Religionists are a bunch
of hypocrites. The more I see of them, the less I want to see."

The spell that had been over them both was suddenly
broken.

"I agree with you," he replied, and when she looked surprised, he added, "I hate religion. It is so futile. Every religion
in the world requires a man to *do* something to earn merit
with God."

"Yes," she agreed vaguely. Suddenly she glanced at her
watch. "Oh, I'm staying too late. I must get back. And you
haven't told me your story yet. May I come again?"

"You surely may, my dear. It would be my pleasure."

"How I wish I had a car. I would love to take you out for a
drive. It must become very tiresome for you to be cooped
up."

"In a sense, yes. But there's always a way up, you know."
He smiled. "Good night. I'll be looking for you."

Nancy said nothing at Cashes' about her visit. Somehow she
felt as if she wanted to keep that tiny room as a sort of sacred
refuge. It seemed like a place where ordinary things did not
intrude, a place of peace.

She was to start work at Mr. Cash's office the next morning. The discussion at breakfast turned on the expected arrival of Jack Warder. Nancy listened and kept her own counsel. Bit by bit she planned to build up an immunity to the
personality of the man for whom she would soon be working.
Let the rest of the unmarried girls run after him as they would.
Nancy Lansing was definitely not in the contest.

"He will probably be here the end of the week," said Cash. "I've arranged for him to occupy the Preston house until he finds something suitable. It's partly furnished and I believe he wrote that he was bringing a trailer with some of his things. He can make out there very comfortably. I wonder if he is bringing somebody to look after the children. He certainly can't have them hanging around the church office. Alice, can't you find a colored woman or somebody who could go over there part time at least, and help him? Maybe Meta could—"

"Not me," snapped Meta. "I'm not spending my life looking after brats in an orphanage."

In spite of Nancy's resolve to keep out of the discussions, before she thought what she was doing, she put in, "JoAnne Donaldson said the other night that her father was dismissing their housekeeper. JoAnne is going to take over." Then she could have bitten her tongue off. How much better if she had kept out of it.

But Dunn Cash caught up her suggestion.

"Donaldson's housekeeper? Fine. She's a daisy. I'll call him before somebody else snaps her up. If she's available she'd be perfect. It was last night you heard it?"

"The night before." Nancy nodded. Meta shot her a suspicious glance.

"I didn't know that you knew JoAnne Donaldson. You do get about, don't you?" There was an edge to her tone.

Nancy simply looked at her without expression and went on eating toast. Inside she was fuming.

"She's a little young for you to be running with, isn't she?" persisted Meta.

"She's a cute kid," responded Nancy noncommittally.

Meta's lip curled. Her father didn't see it. Her mother pretended not to. Elbert gave a scoffing sound and shoved back his chair.

"Fine housekeeper JoAnne will make," he growled.

"I saw her kissing Ted Martin in the church corridor once," spoke up Ellenelle. They all laughed.

For once Mr. Cash left the house in good humor.

"I'll call about Emma today, and see when she'll be available. Surely we can find someone to look after the brats until then," Cash said gaily on the way to the office.

"You have all sorts of responsibilities to take care of, don't you?" remarked Nancy conversationally.

He chuckled importantly. "What's nobody's business seems to be mine. It's always been so."

Nancy wished that she didn't have to despise him for that.

Nancy was quick at taking directions, and soon caught on to the routine of Mr. Cash's business. He himself was owner and manager, and Chuck Immerman was one of his assistants. She soon discovered that appliances were only a small fraction of his interests. He had a finger in many other pies, some to a large extent. He was on the board of one of the town banks; he was active in a scheme to buy and fill some of the shallow submerged land on the edge of town, and he owned considerable real estate. Nancy's desk was in an alcove open on one side to the showroom and on another side, to Cash's own office. It was a pleasant air-conditioned room, much more comfortable than the stuffy little coop at the church. It seemed like a fortunate break for her, and she began to have a more kindly feeling toward Dunn Cash than she had had the past few days since his outbreak at the breakfast table.

Elbert stopped in and took her out to lunch again. She had not seen as much of him since Hank Valentine had been dating her.

"How come you don't work for your father, Bert?" she asked innocently while they sipped iced coffee and waited for their dessert.

"Me work for Dad? No sir. He's too hard to get along with

at home. Besides, I don't believe in working for relatives. Makes trouble too often."

Nancy nodded. "I suppose it could. I've seen it happen."

"Yes. You both carry business home and talk it all the time. I'd be getting blamed every night at the dinner table for every wrong move I made. Besides—" He halted suddenly. "Well, I just don't like the idea of working for Dad."

She dropped the subject, but she couldn't help wondering what he had started to say.

The next day she was working at the books, trying to make sense of some entries that didn't seem to come out right. Mr. Cash was not around, so she decided to wait and ask him. Then she thought it would be smart to look back and see how the same situation had been handled before. If Cash had only given her a chance to have a morning with Miss Johnson before she left!

The discrepancy was in connection with a deluxe refrigerator that Cash had supplied to the church. It was entered in one place as a contribution, and in another place she found a receipt for payment to the company, signed by Charles Immerman, the church treasurer.

She sat a long time puzzling over the two entries. Nobody was about except one of the junior salesmen. She could not very well ask him. He wouldn't be likely to know anything about it if she did. She hated to admit what she was compelled to think. There must be some mistake. Surely Mr. Cash would make it plain when he came. But she didn't feel she could pass it by, since it involved several hundred dollars.

At last Cash returned, but he had a customer with him. They went into his office and closed the door. She could hear them arguing. The other man did not leave until almost closing time. So Nancy decided to wait until the next day to bring up the matter. Elbert was taking her home since Mr. Cash had errands before dinner.

Two or three days passed. Every time she tried to get Mr.

Cash's attention for any length of time, he seemed to have other pressing matters to attend to. Finally she did point out the discrepancy to him.

"Oh, that!" He laughed. "Don't let that worry you. Miss Johnson will straighten all that out when she comes back. Any business, you know, has to do a little finagling occasionally, to make the account balance at the time. It will be adjusted and will all come out right in the end." He laughed again, nervously, and went on to speak of something else. Nancy felt relieved that she had done her part in calling it to his attention. It was his business, not hers.

However, it came back to her later in the week when she happened to overhear a conversation between Mr. Cash and Mr. Manton, who was buying a large consignment of washing machines to be installed in his chain of laundromats in surrounding cities.

"But I thought I understood you to say in the beginning of our discussions that you would not be able to supply this number of machines by the first of August."

"I may have said so then, Bob. But"—Mr. Cash slid into what Nancy had dubbed to herself as his synthetic tone of voice—"there are ways if you just know how to use them. If you try hard enough and keep at it, I've discovered that you can find merchandise where there seemed to be none. The big dealers don't always tell the truth, you know. They hold out on us little fellows for various reasons. Don't you worry, Bob. Just sign your John Hancock right here and I'll see that the machines are in for you on time—uh—excuse me, Bob. I'll be back in a moment. You just go ahead and sign your name."

Cash tore out of his office, through Nancy's alcove and into the wash room at the back of the store. His eyes were staring and his face was a pale green color. He was gone several minutes.

Nancy sent one of the junior salesmen to see if he was all

right. The young man came back with the report, "He says he'll be all right shortly. He's being pretty sick right now." Then in a lower aside, "He has ulcers, you know."

There was nobody else with authority in the office, so Nancy decided that it was up to her to take care of the customer. She walked briskly into Cash's office where Mr. Manton still sat, with his pen in hand looking very sober.

"I'm sorry, sir," she explained. "Perhaps you are aware that Mr. Cash has a physical difficulty that seizes him at times. I will be glad to take the contract if you don't care to wait."

He bowed courteously. "Thank you, but on thinking it over, I have decided *not* to confirm the order at this time." He arose and stalked out of the building.

With a puzzled frown, Nancy glanced down at the paper that still lay on Cash's desk. It called for delivery of two hundred new washing machines by the first of August. Nancy was aware of the frantic letters, telegrams, and telephone calls that Mr. Cash had been scattering here and there trying to locate the appliances, for the past three or four days. She knew that he had so far been able to get only one hundred and fifty, but he had agreed to take over another fifty repossessed, guaranteed machines. Could it be that he was planning to slip them in on the order along with the new ones? Did Manton suspect that something was wrong? It looked strange to her.

She wondered what Mr. Cash would say when he returned and found that his bird had flown.

Five minutes elapsed before he came back. He went straight for the contract and seized it. Then he flung it down in a rage.

"Where is Manton?" he roared at Nancy.

"He went out," she replied calmly.

"What did he say?"

"When you left, I went in to see if he needed anything, and

he was simply sitting there, thinking. Then he got up and said he was not going to sign the contract, and he walked out."

Cash made an indescribable noise rather like a wounded bull and seized the telephone. He dialed and dialed, but he got no satisfaction.

Finally he slammed out of the office, threw himself into his car and went home.

"Spoiled brat!" muttered Nancy to the empty office as she prepared to lock up and take the bus home.

twelve

"Well, Em, how'm I doin'?"

JoAnne's round vivid face beamed at the old colored woman inversely from the mirror in the guest room which Henry Valentine still occupied whenever he was not out amusing himself. She was polishing the glass vigorously.

"It ain't how you're doin', but whut you're doin', Miss Jo." Emma filled the doorway disapprovingly. "There's all that wash has to be ironed yet before Monday's load will have to be put out. You spen' all yer time a-polishin' mirrors an' you'll soon git swamped with the real work. Now git! Switch on the iron to medium high or you'll scotch all yer daddy's shirts. Don' fergit to push out the ironin' board hard all the way er it'll give way with you."

JoAnne turned and stood with her own hands on her hips in imitation of the other woman, and the pretense of a sour look on her face. "Okay, okay, Emma. You think I'll impress my new boy friend by freshly ironed shirts rather than by a polished mirror, do you?"

"I don't think nuthin' 'bout it. Your daddy done hired me for a week to teach you how to housekeep, but it shore has been the hardest work of all my seven years here. An' lemme tell you somep'n you don' know, Miss Jo, 'bout that young man that's a-parkin' hisse'f here. Ef'n you don't lay off'n this chasin' him like youse doin', you is gwine git youse'f talked about but good."

"Oh, now Emma. You don't really mean that! Wouldn't that be terrible! Young girl makes headlines—the talk of the town. But I thought you used to tell me that words couldn't hurt me. Don't you remember?" JoAnne placed herself directly in front of the stout serving woman and shook her finger in her face.

" 'Sticks and stones can break my bones but words will never hurt me.' Wasn't it you who taught me that?" She danced around the room gaily. "Never fear, Emma dear. I've already learned about the birds and the bees and the butterflies, and I'm a bi-i-ig girl now." With a merry laugh she dashed underneath Emma's avenging arm and skipped down the corridor to her ironing. Emma stood still, provoked to despair, and shook a threatening fist at the man's sport shirt hanging across the back of a chair. Then she stamped away to see whether the invalid needed anything. She brought him a drink of water and then returned to the kitchen.

"Jes' two more days," she muttered. "Law' he'p me. I'll never live through it."

As she passed the front door she caught a glimpse of Valentine's long yellow car. With a scrape and a scratch of gravel he zoomed away, JoAnne snuggled down in the seat close beside him.

Emma took two frantic steps toward the door to call her. Then frustrated and infuriated, she turned back, shaking her head.

"They ain't no use. No use'tall. Time when Miss Jo shoulda learned was 'fore she could walk. She got to learn now the hard way—ef'n she ever does."

The telephone rang and Emma lumbered to the living room to answer it.

"Yes, Mr. Cash," she responded after a moment. "Yes, sah, I'll be glad to give it a try. But I ain't makin' no promises. Ef'n the chilluns is brats, I quits . . . Yes, sah. Tomorrow's my last day here." She tried to suppress the distress she felt.

She returned to the kitchen and stood gazing at the basket of ironing to be done. It would be a simple matter for her to do it herself. But she was a conscientious person and having promised that she would attempt to train JoAnne, she felt that it was up to her to carry the discipline through. So, although it was against her tidy routine, she left it untouched, and went about preparing an attractive dish for Dr. Donaldson.

JoAnne did not return until late afternoon. She was hot and sunburned from riding in the convertible with the top down. She rushed up to her bathroom before Emma knew that she was in. Between splashes in the tub she retorted through the door, "If you're so anxious to have those clothes ironed, do them yourself. I'm going out for dinner. I won't have time."

But Emma gave the clothes another look and left them. They were still waiting when JoAnne and Hank came in at half past two the next morning.

Emma had slept very little. She was trying to make up her mind just how to talk to the girl's father before her term of service ended. Evidently he did not realize how the girl was carrying on. It must be up to her to tell him.

She prepared a good breakfast for him, not without a nostalgic feeling that this was her last, after seven years, and carried it to him. Then she decided that she ought not to disturb him before he ate; she would talk to him when she came to get the tray.

It was a good two hours before he buzzed for her. JoAnne was not yet up. There were no sounds from Hank Valentine's room.

Breathing hard with righteous indignation, Emma entered the sick man's room.

She did one or two little pleasant errands for his comfort, straightened his bed, and puffed up his pillows. Then she picked up the tray and took a deep breath.

"Dr. Donal'son," she began, "I'se got to talk with you before I leaves. I has done my best with Miss Jo this week, but I has failed, entirely. Whut that girl will do after I'm gone, I jes' don' know. She has no more responsibility in her than a dragonfly. And I feel it's only right I should let you know that she is out with that young fellow whut's stayin' here, till all hours of the night." Her voice rose with anxiety and vexation. "Ef'n you know, that's up to you; but in case you didn't, I had to tell you, sah. There's no good goin' to come of it."

A worn troubled look came and sat on Dr. Donaldson's pale face.

"I appreciate your bringing the matter up, Emma. You have been very faithful and loyal. Yes, I have been aware that JoAnne has been inclined to be a little too gay and carefree. I'm hoping though, that it is just her age. Teenagers today tend to be more independent than in our day. I try to remember that and not to be too hard on her. I'll speak to her about it, though. And I'll have to suggest to the young man that he find other accommodations. It will not be good for the two of them to be here with so much time on their hands. Thank you, Emma. And don't worry about the work here. I believe JoAnne is a good girl at heart and when she is faced with real responsibility she will take hold and meet it. Perhaps as long as you are here she will always shift it to you as she has done for so many years."

He seemed to wave her away as if the conference was ended, so, with a heavy sense of defeat, Emma went back to the kitchen.

She remained at her work throughout the day, saying no more to JoAnne about the clothes. She prepared Dr. Donaldson's meals and took them up. JoAnne went out again with Hank as soon as she was up, and did not return all day. Soberly Dr. Donaldson gave Emma her check and she departed, still shaking her head.

Whut that pore man thinks he's goin' to do with no help but that scatter-brained gal is mo' than I know. I hates to go off an' leave him so. I reckon he figures to git married soon to that Mis' Constant. Well, I am shore glad to be out of that mess! I only hopes and prays that I'se not gittin' into another one.

Evelyn Constant had been in and out frequently during the week or so since her son had been staying at Donaldson's. They rarely met, however, since he was so often running around with the younger crowd. She had seen to it that most of his meals were available at her own apartment, whether she was there or not. Often she would come home and find that he had brought somebody or other there and practically everything in the refrigerator had been devoured. She usually laughed and teased him the next time he turned up. She and JoAnne were quite good friends, for he often brought her up to his mother's tiny place for a snack between pleasure jaunts or parties. Not infrequently Nancy was in the group.

"You'll stay down here, won't you, Henry, until you get me well married off?" his mother pleaded jokingly. "I ought to have somebody of my family here to give me away." She leaned over the back of the couch in her apartment and ran her fingers through his velvet-cut black hair, so like her own in texture.

"Ha! I don't think you really want me to 'give you away,' do you?" He spoke bitterly, fiercely. JoAnne was there and Ted Martin, with Nancy. JoAnne glanced up quickly at her future stepmother but she was laughing guilelessly and the girl thought no more of Hank's outburst.

"Are you visiting a justice of the peace or will you go in for a veil and bridesmaids?" he quipped to his mother.

"Don't make light of this marriage, Henry," she rebuked seriously. "I'm determined—we both are—that we are going to let God have his rights in us from now on. You don't think I mean it, but I do. I have found that Jesus Christ can save me, and He has. We'll have a minister marry us, even though we may not try to go to church much. Harvey is a lot better, but he still has to be careful. The new minister will be here by the first, and we are going to have him perform the ceremony. This marriage is going to *take*."

Her son looked at her skeptically. Then he shrugged and growled, "Okay. More power to you; I'm from Missouri."

"Oh, Henry!" she scolded. "You are so discouraging. You just don't believe what God can do. Can't you see what a difference it's made for me?"

He stared at her incredulously. "I'm still from Missouri. Come on, JoAnne. Let's go swimming."

After they left, Evelyn called Harvey.

"Honey," she piped in a wheedling tone, "I'm going to ask you a favor again. Do you mind?"

"You know anything you want is all right with me, Eva."

"Well, I would like it so much if you'd let Henry stay until the wedding. You see, he doesn't seem to take it very seriously that I'm a Christian now, and I'd like him to be in on a real Christian wedding. I'm afraid he hasn't had much chance to see that kind of life. I'd like him to meet that fine new young minister, too."

"Why, of course, if you think it's all right, Eva. I've let Emma go, and being shut off the way I am most of the time, I'm not a very good chaperone for JoAnne. But it'll only be a few days. Whatever you think."

"I certainly don't think people will talk as long as you're there," she argued hesitantly. "JoAnne seems like such an independent little girl, capable in so many ways. And of course Henry is so much older. They play around together just like brother and sister. I had so hoped it might turn out like that, and I'm so grateful to see them. It's the first really wholesome companionship Henry has had, I'm afraid, since he was a little boy. Well, if you think it won't make too much work for JoAnne, let's leave it that way. Good night, honey. You're all right?"

Harvey put down the phone with a sober frown. He was not so sure that JoAnne would be able to come up to the character of capable housekeeper, but of course she was basically a good girl and the responsibility was sure to develop her. The two young people did seem to be enjoying each other.

He soon forgot the problem and immersed himself once more in the notes he was sorting in preparation for writing a book on paraplegics.

thirteen

Dunn Cash was ill over the week end. Flemming Elder took his place as preacher and harped on juvenile delinquency.

He gave reams of statistics, interspersed with scripture quotations. He admitted that he had a whole scrapbook full of news items on vandalism and immorality, but he had to stop a dozen times to adjust his glasses so that he could read his clippings, and his remarks were made in such a preachy, monotonous tone of voice that half his teen-age-less congregation were dozing in the summer heat before he was finished.

Nancy did not attempt to listen. She would have stayed at home except that she did not care to share the solitude with Mr. Cash. The whole family had had to be hushed early the evening before, and also throughout the morning preparations. Poor Alice Cash looked white and fagged out. She had been kept awake many hours listening to her husband review the injustices of mankind toward him.

All through the day there was a funereal pall over the household.

"I imagine Dad's had some run-in with a customer who won't do what he wants him to," observed Elbert bitterly. He was lolling after dinner in the patio glider while Nancy was doing a picture puzzle with Ellenelle nearby. "He always takes it out on the rest of us when something like that happens."

Nancy said nothing. The incident in the office the day before came to her mind, but she did not feel that it was her business to discuss it. More and more, however, she was losing confidence in her employer. There was little in this Florida life now that resembled the glamor that had attracted her during the first few days. Scarcely more than six weeks had gone by. Six months seemed like an interminable sentence. But the twenty-five thousand still gleamed brightly at times.

Sunday passed at last, and the next morning the master of the house reappeared. But he was glum, and looked as if his very soul had been twisted and wrung out. The family scarcely spoke, and each one seemed impatient to get the routine business of breakfast over with and get away.

Mr. Cash's secretary was back on her job, so Nancy was to return to the church office. On the silent ride, she kept thinking of poor Alice Cash. How constantly she tried to cover up for her husband. Marriage! Was that what it entailed, if two were to remain together? It seemed as if one of a couple was always having to be a front for the other. While one would make things hot, the other would have to try to keep cool. Yikes! Marriage was a gamble with the odds against everybody!

Mr. Cash dropped her off sullenly without a word of thanks for her help at his own office. He was completely preoccupied.

Nancy tried to settle to her work. She scarcely knew what to do to keep busy. She half wished the new minister would come to get things going, and yet she was determined that she would not like him, that she would keep her distance and forestall the slightest intimacy.

It was late Tuesday morning when Winifred Windom made her first visit to the church since Nancy had been there. She walked past the secretary's office first, as far as the window of the minister's adjoining study. Then she returned and gave a fragile knock on the screen door.

"Good morning, Mrs. Windom," greeted Nancy in what she hoped was the tone of a perfect church secretary. "Come in. What can I do for you?"

"Oh!" exclaimed the lady in dainty dismay. "I had forgotten that Miss Forrest was gone. Do you know how her father is? I haven't called there once, I've been so busy. Isn't that terrible?" She laughed, a precious little laugh, over her shortcomings.

"She called here yesterday, and said that he was still about the same." Nancy had learned to offer no more information than was necessary.

"Oh. Isn't that too bad. I don't suppose Edna will be back soon." Winifred's voice trailed off. She always gave the impression that her mind was already on a new subject before she finished her sentence.

"I believe not." Nancy studied this woman whom she had heard mentioned so often.

Winifred was looking at her now, as if she had just noticed her. "Why!" she exclaimed. "I've just realized—how did you know my name? I'm flattered." She fingered a dangling turquoise pendant that hung nearly to her waist. Her hands were long and slim, but not well manicured.

She was wearing a pale blue blouse that dipped low in front and displayed her really beautiful white neck. Her eyes were blue to match her blouse. Nancy had the fancy that perhaps she changed her eyes to go with her costume. They were fringed by long curling lashes of golden beige. Some short locks, straying from her upswept coiffure snuggled into attractive little curls in the nape of her neck. There was an appealing tilt to her head as she turned it from side to side. Yes, Nancy thought, I can see why they go for her; but nobody would risk marriage. The gossips were right this time.

"I saw you in church," explained Nancy, not too coolly. "I'm getting to know quite a few people here."

"Oh," fluttered Winifred. "I think it is a friendly church, don't you? But not like our folks back home. My! I can remember the good times we used to have. All the young people went in crowds then. No going steady with just one. Why, the girls used to vie with each other to see who could collect the greatest number of boys' rings at one time." She indulged in a gloating little sound. "I think I had fourteen one year. I tried wearing them all at once, but the boys who had to double up on my middle fingers didn't like it. They each wanted their own finger. Isn't that perfectly ridiculous? Teenagers are so silly," she gurgled. "You'd never know it now, of course, but that was the year I won the state beauty contest. How time does fly!"

Yes, the gossips were entirely right, Nancy agreed with herself. But she only smiled distantly at Winifred.

"By the way," went on the visitor, in the tone of voice that told Nancy here was the real reason for her coming, "I hear that the new minister is coming soon. Isn't that wonderful. I hope he will be the kind who can interest the *young* people, don't you? I think it's so important to catch the youth for the Lord—while they are young, you know. Don't you?"

Nancy wondered how youth could be anything but young, but she didn't answer.

Winifred rattled on. "Did you hear him the Sunday he was here? I thought he was simply marvelous. So spir'tual, you know. And deep. If there's anything I like it's good sound *deep* teaching. I hear he simply *made* the church up north where he has been. It's a wonder he will come down here for the salary we can pay. He must have money." She lowered her voice. "I guess there's quite a bit in the Cash family, isn't there?"

"I really don't know," replied Nancy, going on with the work she had devised, of reorganizing some files.

"Well, I thought you would probably have some inkling, you living there right in the family, you know, and hearing a lot of intimate talk. You haven't heard them say anything about how the new man is fixed?"

"No, I haven't." Nancy was nearing the point of exasperation. If the woman wanted to marry for money why didn't she put a sign on her back?

"When is he due to arrive?" Winifred was a little breathless as she reached the real point at last.

"I haven't a notion," Nancy answered truthfully.

"Oh!" squealed Winifred prettily. "I do believe he's driving in *now!*" She had been standing close to the door where she could command a good view of the driveway. Now she pushed open the screen door and stood in an attitude of enthusiastic welcome.

Nancy went on with her work.

"Oh!" Winifred whispered back without turning her head, "he's just as gorgeous as I remembered him. Just look, Miss Lansing. Isn't he the best-looking man you ever saw?" Nancy was still occupied and paid no attention to her.

"And those must be his two children. Aren't they just *precious!* There they come. Mr. Cash is bringing him in. I hear he is his nephew. He doesn't look a bit like him. But if he's as smart as his uncle, he'll do. Mr. Cash is simply fabulous as a business man."

Nancy raised her brows slightly but she did not look up.

"Welcome to Florida!" cried Winifred prettily, holding out both her graceful hands. "You don't know how thrilled I am, to be the first to greet you. I just happened to be in the office talking to the new secretary. Oh, it is just too good to be true that you have really come, Mr. Warder." She was oblivious to the fact that nobody had taken the proffered hands. She chattered on, in the face of dignified bows from the two men and the briefest of introductions all around. "And these are your two little darlings. Come, little girl, give Winnie a kiss. What's your name?"

Cindy stopped stock still and scrutinized the gushing woman.

Then she looked at her father questioningly.

"Tell her your name, hon," instructed her father.

"Daddy!" reprimanded Cindy with precise dignity. "You have always told me not to talk to strange people or let them know my name."

Jack Warder and Mr. Cash roared with laughter. Nancy could not help joining in.

The child looked bewildered until Jack stooped down and explained to her that this was a woman in the new church and she would probably soon know her well. "It's all right, you know, when I'm around, Cindy."

"Oh," replied the little girl. "Well, I don't know why she is so interested. I'm not very important."

That remark passed unnoticed, since Mr. Cash already was busy explaining some matters of business to Jack. Nancy noticed that Cash looked as debonaire as ever. Evidently he was cured, or else his mind had been happily diverted from his week-end illness.

"You'll be able to get a lot of details from Miss Nancy here," said Cash to the newcomer. "She has taken over like a veteran, and there isn't anything she can't do, and do well." He smiled blandly.

"Oh, yes, Miss Lansing," put in Winifred. "We all appreciate you already. How fortunate you are going to be, working right here in the same office, practically, with Mr. Warder!"

Nancy froze. The men moved on into the corridor, with the children trailing their father.

In a moment Cash put his head in the office door again and asked tensely, "Can't one of you two ladies entertain these youngsters a few minutes while Jack and I go over a few matters to start with?"

"Oh, I'll be delighted to," offered Winifred. Cash ushered the two tots back into the office.

But after one or two futile attempts to get them to say their names and tell how old they were, Winifred kept glancing at the corridor door. "I wonder how long they are going to be," she fretted to Nancy. "I just have to get back to my housework. I left my clothes out on the line and I'm so afraid it's going to rain before I get them down. That happened last week and set me back for hours. With my two children home all summer there is almost more than I can do in trying to keep them clean and get three meals a day." She waved her ringed fingers ineffectively. "If I leave these children here in the office, *do* you suppose you could look after them for me, the few minutes until their father comes back?" She spoke as if they were her own responsibility of long standing.

Nancy nodded, and Winifred, collecting her purse, a parcel, and her handkerchief which she had dropped, along with a gold pencil that had slid out of her bag when she pawed for her handkerchief, finally took her departure.

The two children stood hand in hand solemnly and watched her go. It amused Nancy to guess their thoughts. Little Teddy was unmoved, but Cindy's big dark eyes showed her dislike. She turned to Nancy.

"Don't women like that just *bug* you?" she spat out.

"What is it about her that bothers you?" Nancy asked, suppressing her amusement.

"Well, she's just plain silly, *I* think. I hate silly women." Then as if the matter had been settled, she asked, "What do you do here? Are you the church secretary?"

When Nancy assented, she went on, "My daddy had a secretary at his other church, too, but she was an *old* lady, very ugly. She was not pretty like you. I think he will like you better. Do you like to cut paper dolls?"

Nancy quickly disconnected the train of thought in the last two remarks. "Why, yes. I haven't done it for some time, but I used to love it."

"That's good. My daddy doesn't care for it. But he does it anyway, sometimes," added Cindy in all fairness, "when he has time."

"He plays horsey, too," put in Teddy. "Can you play horsey?"

"Why, I guess I could, if I tried. Would you two like to take a little walk around?"

They agreed with alacrity.

Nancy took them by a hand each and started up the narrow, dim corridor toward the church auditorium.

"This is just great, isn't it?" Cindy giggled in an eerie little voice, snuggling a bit closer to Nancy.

"Oh, yes, isn't it!" Nancy whispered back giving a mysterious little shudder. "All sorts of exciting things could happen here, couldn't they!"

Cindy grinned and shivered in appreciative response.

"I don't like it here. It's dark!" stated Teddy bluntly.

Just then they entered the big airy audience hall. The long straight aisles invited running. Cindy started up one side, and Teddy the other. Their voices sounded happily, calling back and forth to each other. They hid behind the pews, and called to Nancy to find them. She entered into their game and enjoyed it as much as they did, realizing that they had been pent up in the car on the long trip south. Once Cindy reprimanded Teddy for putting his hands on the fresh blond wood of the seats.

"You know Daddy said your hands were dirty, Teddy. He won't like it if you get his new church soiled."

Teddy took his rebuke in good part, and they romped for several minutes.

Then all at once the outside door opened and a man entered from the street. He halted in horror.

"Here, here, *here!* Children! You must stop playing in here. Don't you know that this is God's house?" He spoke the last two words in a tone that intimated that the place he referred to was possibly a morgue, and the person who owned it was an ogre.

Nancy turned in dismay. The intruder was Flemming Elder. He was sputtering and fluttering. "My dear young lady," he addressed her. "I'm surprised at you. Don't you realize that you are actually teaching these little ones disrespect of God? The very idea! *Running* in the *sanctuary!*"

His fury had halted the game and all three gazed at him in amazement. Upon their apparent acquiescence his manner abated, and he trundled slowly down the desecrated aisle to the pastor's study.

Nancy's face flushed in anger. Cindy regarded her with aplomb.

"He really told you off, didn't he?" she observed. "Well, I wouldn't mind, if I were you. Daddy always tells us when grownups blow their tops over nothing, just to quit doing what annoys them and forget it. Let's go outdoors."

Pondering the precocious advice, Nancy agreed. She was surprised at the pleasant sensation it gave her to have a sticky. plump little hand nestle confidingly into each of hers on the way out.

When the men finally came out, Nancy and the children were bent over, engrossed in watching the efficient business of a colony of ants near the driveway.

"Look, Daddy. Come here! Look!" squealed both children. They scarcely wanted to turn their heads from the fascinating sight that must be shared with their father.

Jack smiled his satisfaction, and cast a glance of gratitude tinged with admiration at Nancy.

"What did I tell you, Jack? This gal can do anything, from typing to baby-sitting."

Jack nodded appreciatively. Nancy leaned down to fasten a buckle on Teddy's shoe, to hide her irritation at Mr. Cash's flattery.

The Warders piled into the car and Nancy returned to the office. But Dunn Cash took time to lean on the car window next to Jack and say under his breath.

"Let me as your uncle give you a hint. If you're looking for a—uh—replacement—" he jerked his thumb in the direction of the office, "you won't go wrong."

Jack gave him a steady look for a long moment.

"Thanks, but I'm *not!*" he responded, and drove away.

Cash stood gazing after him, a knowing smile curling his harelip.

fourteen

"Do you know you haven't given me a date for a week?" Hank strolled in, and sprawled his tall form across Nancy's desk.

"When have you asked me?" retorted Nancy.

"You turned me down so flat the last time that I haven't had the courage to try."

"I had another engagement that night," replied Nancy truthfully, remembering the evening she had visited Lou Johns.

"Who is cutting me out, I'd like to know?" Hank fretted.

Nancy laughed. "Wouldn't you like to know."

"Well?" Hank persisted. "His Majesty Elbert?"

"I don't think you're being very pleasant, Hank." Nancy frowned at him. "Since when have I been your property?"

"That's the trouble. Why aren't you? You know I've wanted you for over a year."

"Wanting is not a very good basis for marriage, my dear young friend. Not in my book it isn't."

"Well, what more do you wish? I'll put it any way you like. Look here, Nan, I'm twenty-two. I'm tired running around alone. I don't belong anywhere. I'd like a wife and a home. And you've known for a long time that there never was anybody but you on my list."

"Perhaps you'd better add some, then. Your choice is too limited in that case."

"Stop tormenting me, Nancy. Can't you see I mean business?"

"I'm not trying to torment you, Hank. I'm just not planning to marry you."

"Why not? You seemed to like me pretty well when you were up north. Don't tell me that you've been bitten with the deadly religious bug that has hit so many people around here."

"Yikes, no!"

"Well, how about a date tonight?"

"Can't, Hank. I have other plans."

"Cripes! When, then?"

"I can't be sure. Maybe Friday."

"Friday, then."

"I didn't say it was definite."

"I did. Let me take you home and you will."

"But I told you I have an engagement and I'm not going home for dinner tonight."

"I'll take you wherever you're going."

"Not tonight, Hank. Thank you just the same."

Nancy stood up and reached for her purse.

But Hank stood also and reached out his long arms, pulled her to him and held her close. She started to struggle, but her pride would not let her. She simply froze immobile.

Then a footstep sounded in the corridor. Mr. Cash put his head in. Hank released her suddenly, looking sheepish.

Nancy's face was aflame. She was too furious to speak.

A slow sneer spread over Mr. Cash's countenance.

"Caught in the act, eh? Sorry I interrupted—just stopped in to see if you needed a lift home, Nancy. But it looks as if somebody else got in ahead of me. Well, good night." He went out the same way he came in.

Until his footsteps had died away and the sound of the big door of the main auditorium slammed shut, their eyes locked. Nancy's were hard and steely; Hank's cool, swaggering, laughing.

At last Nancy spoke with frigid dignity. "I'm leaving, Hank. I'll have to lock up here."

"Okay, okay. Have it your way. I'm going to count on Friday."

He went out. Nancy closed the office and locked it, as slowly as she could, to give him time to be out of her way.

As a matter of fact, she had planned no special date that night, but she had quickly decided that this would be a good time to make her second call on Lou Johns. For she was not at all inclined to go out with Hank. Hank seemed trivial and immature to her lately. She recalled how delighted she had been to see him when he first turned up, a taste of her old life. But now he seemed aimless; perhaps her viewpoint had shifted. Was that a good thing or not? She didn't know. At any rate, she actually found herself looking forward more eagerly to a visit with the mender of shoes than to a gay evening with Hank and the others.

It was late afternoon, but there was a pleasant little breeze ruffling the air. She walked with unhurried steps toward the coffee shop where she had dined before. Her mind was still in upheaval over the unpleasantness of being found by Mr. Cash, of all people, in the arms of Hank Valentine.

There was another strong reason why Nancy had preferred not to go home for dinner: the Warders were coming. She chose to avoid Jack Warder. Besides, it made her hot all over again to think how Mr. Cash might depict the amorous scene in the office for them and they would laugh at her expense. Meta would enjoy it; Elbert would be angry. What would

Mr. Warder say? She set her lips and tossed her head. She was determined not to care what he would say or think.

She tapped gently at the screen door of Lou Johns' home. There was no light, although it was growing dusk.

"Come in!" He sounded refreshingly cordial. His voice had the ring of a younger man than his gray hair and worn face implied.

A soft shaded lamp flicked on. With a glad welcome, he greeted her.

"I was only just now thinking of you, Nancy. I wondered whether you would ever come back."

"I've really been eager to come, Mr. Johns," she said. "To tell you the truth, I find very few people to talk to; I mean people with whom I feel at home. Why is it that everything seems different to me these days? I don't know whether it's since I came to Florida, or since I met Aunt Bea, or—or since I met you. But all the old things are beginning to seem so childish. Maybe it's since I've seen and heard a little of other people's troubles, down there at the church."

"Yes? Tell me about it."

It was easy to talk to this man. He was like a big brother. He seemed to draw her thoughts out.

"Well, there was college. That was a full life, and I enjoyed it. I learned a lot. But now I see that what I had was mostly theories. I had lots of those, but I had never lived enough to put them into practice. I am finding now that many of my pet ones don't work."

"We all discover that sooner or later." He laughed gently.

"But living was different there, too. If you didn't like what somebody did, you simply cut them, and that was that; and then you went on your own merry way. There were always others to go with. But down here, I seem to be thrust into situations where—well, I don't know how to say it. There are many things the people do here that I don't go for, yet I can't seem to just drop people and get away. I seem to be stuck into a certain little niche and there I am, whether I like it or not."

"Isn't that all right, if you fit?"

"But I don't fit. Almost everything, it seems, goes against the grain. What do you do in a case like that? You know," she broke off haltingly, "it's strange, but I have the feeling that you are really my uncle—perhaps because you—might have been. Tell me about it, will you?"

He drew a long slow breath as if he were about to face something that he had long dreaded, that yet fascinated him.

"Yes, I will tell you. I have never told another human being. Even Beatrice knew only part of it. But my time is so nearly over now, it won't matter."

She settled to listen.

"It is a long story. I shall have to begin away back in the beginning."

"Good. I like stories like that."

"You have wondered why I am like this," he motioned to his legs, "and why I am doing work like mending shoes, when I can speak good English and I'm not exactly a moron." He spoke haltingly as if it were an effort to bring up the subject.

"Yes," she said. "I wondered the other day. You are a gentleman. You have read good books."

"I love to read," he agreed. "I was in my second year in college when I met your Aunt Beatrice. We both knew right away that there was nobody else for either of us. We made wonderful plans. We both wanted to teach, and so we were in many of the same courses together. We were very happy. We had both learned to know and love the Lord, and we decided right off that He must come first. So we never had any quarrels as so many lovers do. If we differed, as we sometimes did, we would pray together and try to find out how the Lord looked at the problem. It worked wonderfully.

"Then came the war. I went at the end of my junior year. We were sent to Burma. I was with the Marauders. It was dangerous work."

He spoke in short jerky sentences as if the very memory was still painful.

"Over there, we were pretty much on our own. Sometimes when one man of a group on a reconnaissance mission was wounded, there was nothing to do but give him his forty-five and his ammunition and leave him to make out the best he could." His voice had sunk low. He was living again some of those terrible days. Nancy listened intently, scarcely breathing.

"We had an officer, a second louie—never mind his name; the boys hated him. He was younger than most of them. He was pleasant enough but he had no guts—he was yellow. Excuse me, Nancy; I forget myself going back to those days." She nodded. She was not noticing his language. She was living with him through those days of horror.

"One day he and I were in the brush together. The rest of our men were scattered about, and I guess the Japs had got most all of them. I never did hear what became of them. Then they got me—both legs—shot away. I knew it was all up. And my officer did too. I begged him to finish me. He put tourniquets on—said he would stay and help me. The sun was intolerable, and I was losing blood fast. I passed out. When I came to, he was gone. He had taken all the water and all the ammunition except—one—bullet!" The words seemed torn out of him.

Nancy held her breath in a long gasp.

"I prayed that one of our safety patrols would turn up, but night came and there I was alone. I tried to crawl but I was too weak. Finally the sounds of fighting died away. By that time I didn't care. I must have fainted dead away again, or slept, for when I woke up I was in a filthy little native hut. An old

Burmese woman with a wrinkled face and dirty hands was trying to feed me goat's milk. She had bandaged my legs with dirty cloths; infection set in. I couldn't understand a word she said. All I knew was that I was still alive, and that somewhere, Beatrice was praying for me. She was all I had on earth, for my parents were dead.

"How long I was in that hut I never knew. It must have been months. I was delirious most of the time. And after the fever finally left me I was so weak that all I could do was crawl out to the sunshine and lie still. The goat's milk kept me going, physically, but all that time I was aware that the Lord's hand was on me. When I came to myself enough to pray, I knew He was right there beside my mat, that He had sat there night and day all those months, and He cared."

Nancy's eyes smoldered hotly.

"Did you ever see that lieutenant again?" she asked.

The man glanced up at her swiftly. Then he dropped his eyes. At last he lifted his head and looked straight at her.

"Yes," he said slowly, with strange emphasis, "I have."

"And you didn't—kill him? What did he say to you? How could he face you?"

There was a still longer pause.

"He—offered me—money, a loan! A thousand dollars. He said it was all he had at the time. I guess perhaps it was, *then.*" His voice trailed off, as if he were re-entering the shadow of the disappointment that God must feel when His creatures come short of the glory He intended for them. There was no sign of resentment or self-pity, only sorrow.

Nancy was silently scalding the unnamed officer with her hate.

"You see," went on the shoemaker at length, "it was five years later when I met him, in this country. I had spent those years in a prison camp."

Nancy caught her breath in a sob. "Besides all the rest?"

"Yes." There was more in that one word than if he had talked for an hour about his sufferings.

"It's a wonder you didn't lose your mind."

"Yes. But you see, God was keeping it." He smiled. "A man can't lose what God keeps."

"I never heard anybody talk like that before. I suppose it must make sense, for it's plain that you have something. But I don't understand it."

"You will some day, when you know Him. But really, Nancy, believe me when I tell you that all the physical suffering was nothing compared to the struggle I had with myself. When my wits and my strength came back in that Burmese hut, the first thing I wanted was to write to Beatrice."

"Of course," agreed Nancy.

"But, you can see that that was impossible. Not only months, but years went by before I reached any place of civilization where I could send a letter. She had been informed, of course, that I was dead. I knew she must have become resigned to the fact. In time I found that she had taken nurse's training and gone to India after the war was over, as a missionary. Very slowly, I began to realize that that was what the Lord had planned for her. If I had been in the picture something He wanted might never have been accomplished. So I knew that I must stay out of the picture. I came down here, as far from where we had lived as I could get, so that nobody would find out that I was alive and write to her in India."

"Oh, but she would have wanted so to hear from you, and know that you were alive!" cried Nancy.

"Yes, but you see, I couldn't offer to her the thing I had become." He glanced down at himself. "She would have been torn between keeping at her work, and coming home to nurse a useless cripple. No," he shook his head, "if I had to choose, I'd have to do the same thing over again."

"Maybe that's the way you see it, but if I had been Aunt

Bea, I would have *loved* to come back and take care of you."

His eyes shone. "I'm glad you feel that way. It's right that you should. But what I did was right, too. Those children in India needed what she had to give.

"Well, I landed here broke, with no college degree and no way to get one. I couldn't teach. All I could do was the trade I had learned of necessity in the prison camp. So—here I am."

"How did you get started if you were broke?" she asked.

"I told you." His hands clenched once and then were still again.

"You mean you had to take the money that yellow dog offered you?"

Lou Johns sighed. "I suppose I wouldn't have *had* to. I might have been able to get a loan somewhere else. But he was pitiful. He wanted to make amends somehow. He never got up the courage to mention what he did, but I knew he wanted me to know that he was ashamed. I took it to try to help him get his balance again. He had had a complete breakdown after he came back home, had to give up his own work for a long time."

"You speak as if he were still alive. Is he just the same?"

Lou nodded. "He would have been better if he had confessed it all. I guess he could not bring himself to do it. Well, that was years ago. I have paid him back every cent. I'm clear, now."

"You mean he *took* it?" groaned Nancy, shocked. "From *you?*" Her hands were clenching and unclenching.

Lou nodded. "Don't blame him too much! You see, money has a strangle hold on him. He serves it as his god. But let's forget all that. Let me tell you the rest of the story. Just like all of God's stories, it has a happy ending."

Nancy gazed at him in fierce incredulity.

"After I had been here a number of years, somebody wrote

to Beatrice that I was here, alive. I can never describe the day her letter came."

His face shone as if a bright light had been turned on. "I had always prayed for her and kept in touch with her work. Every cent I could spare I sent to the mission, without my name, of course. I prayed that God would accept it as unto Him, and not simply for her sake. I hope He did," he said humbly. The man's soul was laid bare; Nancy felt as if she were on holy ground.

"We wrote back and forth after that, for a while. They were happy years. We both agreed that we should remain where God had put us. Then she got the fever and the mission board sent her home. She came down here, and although we never broadcast the story, or made any attempt to be seen together, we saw something of each other. The last year has been the happiest of my life."

There was a long silence when he finished. Then he looked up with his sweet patient smile and said, "Now do you see why I wanted you to come and tell me the end of the story?"

"I never heard anything like it," breathed Nancy in awed tones. "I think—I can never be just the same again. I don't think I have ever *lived*." Then she paused, and added with a puzzled look, "But there is one thing that seems as if it ought to have been just a little different, to end the story right."

"What is that?" he asked.

"I—you'll think me foolish, but—why didn't she say—just before she left—why didn't she say *your* name instead of Uncle Harry's?"

An inner laugh gushed up in him because he understood. "Oh, but you have missed the point. I *know* she thought of *me*. I would never doubt that. But God let her have a glimpse of someone over there, just to confirm to me the fact that she is really in glory. And He sent you to tell me about it. Don't you see?"

Nancy shook her head. "I see what you mean, but I don't get it. I wish I knew things—knew God—like you do. There must be something, some Power, to keep you so sweet through all this. You're so different from the rest. I told you that you seem like my own uncle. I'm going to call you Uncle Lou. I wish you were." She came over to him and laid her lips on his brow. "I'm going now. It has been wonderful. May I come back sometime?" She paused again, her hand on the doorknob. Her tone suddenly shifted to harsh once more. "Don't get the idea that I'm about to get religion! But—I'll say this—if I ever do," she spoke fiercely, "it'll be all or nothing. None of that halfway business for me." She flung open the door and went out into the night.

Lou Johns sat looking after her, tears filling his eyes. "All or nothing!" he echoed. "All or nothing. Let it be all, Lord."

fifteen

The house was quiet when Nancy reached home. She went straight to bed and to sleep. The next morning she was to begin the new regime under her new employer. In imagination she had dreaded that first day.

Jack was already at the church when she arrived with Mr. Cash. He greeted her pleasantly, had a word with Cash, who left immediately, and then came into her office.

"Well," he said, "I guess you are going to have to be the boss for a while and tell me what the score is. I hear you have been holding down the fort here gallantly."

Nancy nodded with cool reserve.

"But first, before you give me the lowdown, let's have a little time of worship together. I always start the day that way, and I've found it gives the Lord a good chance at us before we get our minds full of all sorts of other things. What do you say?"

If Nancy had dreaded this time beforehand, she was near panic now. She darted a steely glance at him. "I'm not a religious person, Mr. Warder," she blurted out abruptly. "I may as well tell you now, I don't go for that sort of thing. I don't know anything about it."

Jack gave no sign that he was surprised or that he wondered why she had taken the position of church secretary if she felt that way. He smiled genially.

"No? Well, there's always a first time." He produced a pocket Bible, worn from use. "Let's start reading in the gospel of John. 'In the beginning was the Word, and the Word was with God, and the Word was God. The same was in the beginning with God. All things were made by him; and without him was not any thing made that was made.'" He paused just a moment, then read on with emphasis: "'In him was life.'" He noticed that Nancy's attention was caught. He made the most of it. "It's terrific, isn't it? To think all life is wrapped up in one Person! Einstein said that electricity holds everything together. The Bible says it's Jesus Christ."

Without further comment he went on reading: "'And the life was the light of men.'"

Suddenly Nancy spoke up, meditatively. "That must be what makes Lou Johns so sort of—*bright*." Then she realized that she had forgotten herself and her resolution to remain completely impersonal. She flushed and withdrew into herself again.

He smiled. "I wouldn't be surprised. You'll have to tell me who Lou Johns is sometime." Then he read on. "'And the light shineth in darkness; and the darkness comprehended it not.' "

"That's it!" she cried again. "That describes him. There he sits all day in his wheel chair, a marvelous person. Simply radiant. And nobody, but *nobody* recognizes how wonderful he is. Oh, I'm sorry. I didn't mean to interrupt again." She glanced at Jack and saw him observing her intently, with friendly interest.

He laughed. "That's quite all right. I think we have had enough to chew over, for this morning. Let's talk to the Lord now. Father, we just want to offer our thanks this morning for the chance to serve You for another day. Direct us in all that we do and may the very thoughts of our hearts be completely pleasing in Your sight. We ask this for the honor and glory of the Lord Jesus Christ." Then he added reverently, after a moment, "Amen."

"Now let's get to work," he said.

In less than ten minutes Nancy realized that he knew his job. He went at the work systematically. He soon had what information he needed for a start, and attacking the mail that had piled up awaiting him, he dictated half a dozen letters, then retired into his own study.

They worked, each in his own cubicle, for an hour. Then the telephone began to ring.

The first call was from Harvey Donaldson. He and Evelyn were to be married sooner than they had originally planned. Could Mr. Warder come to the house and talk over a few matters with them?

Nancy thought of Elbert's remark about JoAnne's housekeeping. She smiled all to herself. Living conditions at the Donaldsons' could be the reason for the change in date. JoAnne was fun to play with, but Nancy could not imagine the child shouldering all the monotonous routine of an invalid's household. She thought of the approaching wedding. What was it that would attract a vivacious woman like Evelyn Constant to a semi-invalid, older than herself? What a match!

Then Winifred Windom called. She had a very important "personal matter" on which she said she needed the minister's counsel. She wished to come over right away; she implied that she was desperate over it.

Jack frowned but reluctantly agreed to the appointment.

She arrived in less than five minutes, fetchingly attired. She marched into the pastor's study and closed the door behind her.

But almost immediately it opened again, and Nancy caught a significant look from Jack as he said, "Mrs. Windom, I always make it a practice to put confidence in my secretary. I think you may rely on Miss Lansing's discretion."

Chagrined, the widow replied, "Oh! Mr. Warder, I should feel so embarrassed to speak of my personal affairs to anyone but my pastor." She spoke the last two words unctuously.

"I think that anything you have to say will not be more embarrassing because of the presence of another lady, Mrs. Windom."

"Well, of course, if that's the way you insist on having it." Then she lowered her voice to an intimate tone. Nancy made no attempt to listen, but could not help catching a word or two that showed that the poor woman was only troubled about the behavior of her young son, and wished to know of a good school for him. Mr. Warder gave her one or two addresses, promised to make the boy's acquaintance at the earliest possible time, and stood up.

There was nothing for Mrs. Windom to do but take her departure.

A wicked little appreciative grin was playing around the

corners of Nancy's mouth as she watched her shadow pass the window. But the young pastor made no reference to the interview.

Calls poured in about the reception to be given for the new minister on the following Tuesday night. Nancy felt at home with those. She could phone committee members, arrange for flowers and ice cream, and attend to a score of other details that belonged to such an affair. That was easy. It was the sort of thing she had been used to doing in a smaller degree in her old life in New York. How far away that seemed now. Would she have taken the trip down here if she had known that she would land in the office of a young minister, and a widower at that?

Betty Martin called several times about the reception. She seemed extremely excited over every detail.

"My little sister is coming," she explained, "and I want her to get a good impression of our church and our wonderful minister."

Nancy wondered how old the little sister was, and why Betty cared so much.

The next caller was a thin, worn, anxious-looking woman, a Mrs. Jones, with a small baby. They were clean, but extremely shabby.

Jack greeted her in a kindly manner and seated her beside his desk. She was evidently loath to begin her story. It was a pitiful tale of a husband who drank and couldn't keep a job. He had threatened last night to kill her. She wanted to do the right thing. She thought a minister might advise her. Should she leave or try to stick it out? How could she work and support three little children? If she did work, who would take care of them? Would Mr. Warder come and talk to her husband?

"Does he know the Lord?" asked Jack.

The woman shook her head. "He won't listen to me."

"I'm going to be very personal now," said Jack gently. "How about you? What is your relation to the Lord?"

"Oh, I've prayed and prayed," she answered wearily. "It don't do no good."

"Do you know the conditions for getting answers to your prayers?" he asked her.

"I don't know what you mean," she said. "I try to live right. I haven't gone to church much lately. We don't have the clothes." Even her drab garments drooped in a discouraged attitude. "It still don't seem like it's me. We always lived right, in our home. We weren't rich, but we had things nice. We never had to ask nobody for help. But after I married my husband, everything changed."

"Did it ever occur to you, Mrs. Jones, that a situation like this was lovingly planned by God, just for you?"

"Planned by God?" she ejaculated in astonishment. "No. I can't see that. There ain't no love in it, that's for sure."

"You said just now that you never used to have to ask help from anybody. Did you know that God goes to great pains to bring each one of us into a place of desperation so that we will *have* to go to Him for help? He gets us to the end of our rope, where nobody but He can help. It's the only way most of us will pay any attention to Him. And some people won't, even then."

"Well, I told you I prayed. Why didn't He answer and do something about Joe? He could *make* him be different, couldn't He?"

"Yes, but He'd have nothing but an unwilling slave, that way. He wants people who come to Him voluntarily. And it takes a lot to change some people. What would it take to change *you*?"

"What should I be changed fer? I ain't making the trouble."

"Avoiding trouble is not what God is after. He wants to

140

make you, and Joe, and all of us, like His Son. Jesus died, you know, in our place, to get rid of our old sinful selves. He wants to give us life, His life. That's more important than having a peaceful home. If Joe had God's own life in him, he'd live differently, wouldn't he?"

The woman nodded hopelessly.

"If you had God's life in you, you could go to Him as His child, and put the whole problem in His hands. You would trust Him just as your little boy here trusts you to take care of him."

"It sounds good, Reverend, but I guess it ain't fer me. Well, I better be goin'. I jest thought you might talk to Joe and maybe make him see."

"I'll be glad to talk to Joe. But I didn't make you see, did I? Why do you think Joe will? Don't you understand, Mrs. Jones, that the whole problem of sin is a question of being out of God's will, outside of Christ? Sin is trying to make it on our own, without Him. He says, 'He that hath the Son hath life; and he that hath not the Son of God hath not life.'"

Nancy had stopped her typing and was straining to catch every word. What she had not been able to see for herself she was seeing in this other woman's life. If she hadn't determined not to have any more dealings with Jack Warder than necessary, she would ask him more about it.

She glanced through the door a moment, just in time to see Jack slip a bill into the woman's hand. Then he wasn't just a man of words! A gladness sprang up in her heart. But she sighed as she watched the woman go out. Jack had taken her address, and prayed with her, a loving, tender prayer, and Nancy was stirred with a strange yearning to be able to talk to God like that. How many people there must be in the world who were in deep distress. In New York she had never thought of such people. No doubt they were all about her in the city, in slums and tenements, or even hidden in the mansions on Park Avenue, but their lives had never touched hers. For the first time since she took her new job she admitted to herself that there was something fascinating about it, a sense of being in on the doings of the universe. Perhaps it was true that she had never really lived before.

Jack's first meeting with his church board was scheduled for Thursday evening. It was evidently very much on Mr. Cash's mind, for he referred to it several times at the dinner table.

Nancy noticed that it was never Alice who brought up controversial subjects; her role was invariably the appeaser. But Elbert had no such inhibitions. He seemed to take delight in throwing a barbed bait to his father, just to watch him snap at it.

"Well, is my dear cousin Jack going to make the grade with the powers that be?" he asked when his father made some remark about having to leave early to get to the meeting.

"He'd better!" responded his father threateningly. "Yes, I think we can handle him all right. He seems to be overboard on one or two ideas, but he'll go along with us when he finds that the consensus is opposed to them."

"What ideas?" questioned Meta. Nancy glanced at her in surprise. She rarely made any contribution to the conversation unless it directly concerned herself.

"Oh, he doesn't go for the every-member canvas, or any pledging, for that matter. I think he'd even do away with passing the collection plate if he had his way. When he veered that way I really put the brakes on him."

Alice spoke up. "Don't you think he ought to run the church pretty much as he likes, if he's the minister?" she asked timidly.

"My word! We can't let him do that. It would be crazy to let one man hold the reins. Besides, he's young. He doesn't realize that the church would be broke in six months if we followed his ideas."

"I thought it was God who sent the money to keep churches going," put in little Ellenelle with a troubled look. "That's what the teacher said the verse meant that we learned last week in Sunday school."

Dunn Cash looked condescendingly at her. "Of course, He does, Nellie, but He does it through people who give."

"Oh. They couldn't give if there wasn't a collection plate to put it in, could they?" she agreed innocently.

"Haw! You hit it, kid. They have to have it stuck under their noses so that they're ashamed not to put something in it. Somebody might be looking." This from Elbert.

Nancy held her peace. She had found it wise to let the tide of conversation flow past her. She learned more that way, and it kept her out of trouble. But the current subject bothered her. Somehow it seemed unfair and disloyal to be talking about the new young pastor behind his back this way. Of course, everybody in the church must be discussing him at their own dinner tables and he was probably used to it. But it rather nauseated her. Was everybody in the world false? Did they talk about her like this behind her back? Did they pick out her faults, and discuss them—at least what they considered faults because her standards differed from their own narrow ones? Her lips set and her jaws locked. She felt as if she couldn't swallow another bite. This *couldn't* go on. Twenty-five thousand or not, she had better get out of here. Tomorrow she'd look for another place to live. But how about her job? If she antagonized Mr. Cash he would not hesitate to fire her. And her father had no way to help her now. She'd have to stay. She tried to quiet her turmoil. Maybe it was much ado about nothing. She was tired. It might look better tomorrow.

She excused herself early and went to her room.

The night was hot. She slid out of her clothes and showered. How glad she was for her own bathroom. There, that was certainly something to be thankful for. Where else could she get such a nice room, good food, no housework, her own bath, and freedom to go and come? She gave herself a mental shaking. But the unrest persisted.

She lay down near the window. She felt more lonely than she ever had been in all her life. She realized for the first time that she must have had a comparatively easy, carefree existence. Since watching all the varied problems come and go in the church office she had had a revelation of the weariness and sorrow that continually go on in the world. She lay still for an hour, thinking soberly, reviewing the events of the last few weeks. Gradually, into her consciousness swam a refrain; words that must have been going over and over beneath the surface of her thoughts for a long time. At last they demanded attention. "In Him is life. He that hath the Son hath life; and he that hath not the Son hath not life." What did it mean? Nothing, probably. Just some words from an ancient manuscript. Who knew what they meant, if anything? But they persisted until finally she fell asleep.

She was awakened later by the sound of voices on the patio below her window. The silence of midnight, or else the direction of the light breeze, carried the words directly to her ear.

Dunn Cash was saying, "Yes, he's utterly impractical. We can't let him take too much authority. That nonsense about starting a school! It would never pay. And no every-member canvas! It's visionary. But I still think we needn't worry too much. Between us we can keep him in hand."

Another man's voice murmured a response. Nancy heard only a few words: ". . . if Betty's sister Marge can catch him we'll have him in the family for sure." They both laughed.

144

The murmurs went on but the voices were lower. Nancy gradually realized the implications of what she had heard. Instantly she found herself sympathizing with the cause of the absent young man who was being analyzed.

Why can't people be straightforward? "O what a goodly outside falsehood hath!" And what sort of person is Betty's sister Marge?

sixteen

JoAnne called Nancy at the church office next day.

"Hi, Nan. How about a little help? I'm swamped."

"What's the deal, Jo?"

"Well, you know my old man is getting hitched tomorrow and I'm supposed to hand out the feed bags. You're acquainted with the whole gang—Evelyn, and Hank, and you've met Dad, haven't you? At least you know me. Wanta do me a favor and manage things while I stand up with 'em and look pretty? I'd a lot rather have you than some old hag that Dad might pick out. I told him if I was going to do the work I want to choose my own staff. It won't be much work, really. Only a dozen or so people in all. Evelyn's going to fix the food and have it ready. Yes?"

"Sure, I'd be glad to. I may have to clear it with my boss."

"Oh, he'll be there too. He's going to tie the knot. That's why we can't ask for Emma. He'll need her to stay home for baby-sitting. Anyway, it's after hours, you know, five o'clock."

"Okay. I'll be on deck."

Nancy put back the receiver with a hesitating little scowl. Was she constantly going to be cast in a role with Jack

Warder? Well, after what she heard last night on the patio she was far more ready to go to bat for him. But only if she could keep well out of the picture herself. Let the unknown Marge have her inning, if she turned up. The kitchen would be Nancy's precinct. Probably Hank would hover around and pester her about that dinner date Friday. But she could handle him. Why not go? Maybe it would help to get her balance better. She had been so confused lately, it would be good to get back to her old way of looking at life.

JoAnne picked her up that afternoon and they went over the arrangements together at Donaldson's house.

"I believe you are glad about this wedding, aren't you, Jo?" Nancy remarked in the midst of her friend's eager chatter.

JoAnne shrugged. "Sort of," she responded. "It takes the load off of me. I don't know how to take care of an old man, and a sick man at that. It's been a raw deal. Let Evelyn worry now."

"But you do like her, don't you? As a mother, I mean?"

"I wouldn't know. She doesn't seem like my idea of a mother, but how would I know? I've never had one. I was three when my mother died. I don't remember her at all. Only Emma. She was a good egg, but it's not the same." JoAnne spoke more seriously and wistfully than Nancy had ever heard her. Most of the time she gave the impression that she never had a sensible thought.

The wedding was a pleasant enough affair. The easygoing Dr. Donaldson smiled upon one and all urbanely, while his new wife, vivacious and breezy as ever, flitted about in high spirits, telling a great many jokes on herself and laughing loudly.

Hank was not his usual self, flirtatious and carefree. He was more sullen than gay, and seemed inclined to stay in the kitchen and mope. Nancy chided him on it but he remained

146

heavily aloof from most of the festivities. He did not even mention the Friday night date.

The half dozen friends and neighbors were introduced to Jack and were obviously well impressed by him. Nancy found a glad little thrill of pride in him as her boss. But she quickly squelched it, in view of her predetermined resolution.

The couple were not planning to take any trip, so the company dispersed soon after the refreshments and congratulations were over. Nancy offered to stay a little while to help clean up, but JoAnne soon eliminated any thought of being saddled with that responsibility.

"Not a chance! I've slaved up to this point. I have a date with Hank tonight. They've made the mess, let them clean it up."

Nancy and Jack happened to be standing opposite each other at the moment. Their eyes met. Each recognized a wordless awareness of what the other was thinking.

Nancy slipped back to the kitchen under cover of good byes, and started on the dishes. Jack took a step as if to follow, but thought better of it; instead he made his adieus, and left. JoAnne was already up in her room preparing to go out with Hank.

Evelyn, hearing the slight clatter, came out and found her. "Oh, my dear! How sweet of you! But really that's not at all necessary. JoAnne can do it, or I will."

Nancy shook her head and smilingly shoved her out of the room. "Not on your wedding day, you won't. I'll have them done in a jiffy. Run along back to your bridegroom."

After she was gone Nancy paused a moment looking out the window. Hank was already in his long yellow convertible, obviously impatient for JoAnne to come. Jack noticed him and sauntered over to admire the car. He leaned on the low door, talking, for some minutes. Nancy worked as she watched, glancing from time to time at the two men. Somehow she knew, little as she had seen of Jack, that he had already progressed from the subject of cars to eternal things.

"You're wasting your time with that boy, Mr. Warder," she muttered over the dishes. "Save your breath."

They were still deep in conversation when Nancy wiped the last crumb from the sink and hung up the dish towels. She took her purse from the kitchen table and went out, just as JoAnne came down and climbed into Hank's car.

Jack smiled. "Let me take you home, Nancy. It's right on my way." She could scarcely refuse.

JoAnne glanced back. "Wait a minute, Hank. Come on, you two," she called. "Let's make it a foursome. At the Suncoast Inn. Yes?"

Nancy shook her head with instant decision. "No thanks, not tonight."

Jack smiled and waved them away, too. Hank had said nothing, only sat gloomily with his foot on the accelerator ready to roar away.

"Well, that was a strange interlude, that wedding, wasn't it?" said Jack conversationally as they started home. It seemed to Nancy as if he always knew what she was thinking and expressed it better than she could.

"Sort of ill-matched, you mean?" she replied.

"In a way. Although sometimes those odd marriages do seem to work out. I have an uneasy uncertain feeling about this one, though. What a cute little scatterbrain the daughter is."

Nancy glanced up at him archly. "How do you know, Mr. Warder, that I won't go straight to the Donaldsons and report what you called her!"

"I know you won't. Didn't I tell that neurotic Mrs. Whatsher-name that I put full confidence in my secretary? But actually, it wouldn't matter to me if you did. I meant it not unkindly. It's true."

"And I thoroughly agree with you. I feel sort of sorry for her, though, much as I'd like to shake the daylights out of her sometimes."

Meta was seated in the living room when Nancy came in. She looked up from her book and then gave a meaningful glance out the window at Jack's car pulling away. She looked back at Nancy again and curled her lip. Nancy caught the whole little scene, but she wouldn't for the world let on that she had noticed. Let Meta be as hostile as she pleased. Maybe in the eyes of the God she was supposed to worship, her regular church-going and her refraining from cigarettes would make up for ugliness of spirit. But Nancy's resentment smoldered hotly.

"I have a notion not to go to that infernal reception next week," she whispered to herself, up in her own room. "What do I care whether Jack Warder is 'received' by this hypocritical outfit or not? I'd think more of him if he weren't! Will this six months never end?"

But she did go, looking altogether enchanting, in a fluffy yellow formal with dainty butterfly earrings that gave the impression that she had just alighted and might take off into the upper air at any moment. Once or twice she caught a glimpse of Meta off in a corner with a blonde who made much use of a bewitching dimple near her blue eyes. The new girl turned out to be Betty's sister Marge. Meta kept looking her way and whispering, with an accompanying toss of the head toward Jack Warder. But Nancy was determined to ignore their cattiness and took pains to see that Meta was well served with ice cream and dainties. One thing Nancy made sure of, however; she kept a maximum distance throughout the evening between herself and Jack Warder. Let the Winnie Windoms and the Marges and other unattached females pursue as they would. That was not for her.

If the warmth of the welcome for the new minister could

be measured by the compliments that pervaded the conversation like cloying odors, then Jack was due to be a great success. Everybody gushed.

The Warder children were there for the first part of the evening, dressed in their fastidious best by Emma who had already taken them unto her ample breast and was endeavoring to mother them to the ultimate of her loyal capabilities.

Teddy submitted to flattery and caresses with pleasing aplomb. But Cindy warded off any undue familiarities with her usual acid frankness. The reactions of the congregation to them reflected the children's personalities respectively.

"The boy is a darling, but that sharp-tongued girl! My word!" exclaimed Sue Immerman after Cindy had announced with a significant gaze that she was not poor, if she was motherless, and her father was not looking for a new mother for her.

The consensus in the majority of homes after the affair that evening was that Jack Warder was the man for the hour. His looks, his clothes, his manner, his courtesy, his jokes, his fascinating smile, his sermons of the Sunday before, his tone of voice, the very grip of his handshake, all came in for notice and all passed the carping examination of board and church members alike. Westside Community Church heaved a sigh of relief, joyful and self-centered, and went to bed. The southern zephyrs caressed Westside consciences, already indolent, without hint of hurricanes that might be brewing.

But in the Cash residence and in the home of the new bride and groom sleep was not untroubled.

Not every member of the congregation had attended the reception. When her new stepmother had mentioned the party to JoAnne, her response was, "Not interested."

"Oh, but you'll like Mr. Warder," urged her father. "He's

young and full of fun. You know how you enjoyed him at the wedding."

"Oh, sure, he's all right," quoth the girl carelessly. "But I have something else I'd rather do. Hank and I have a very important date. I wouldn't miss it." Her tone of voice defied her parents to ask her what it was. She flounced out of the room and was not seen the rest of the day. She departed before dinner and did not return before they left for the church.

"I wish now that that boy of mine would go back to New York or somewhere," complained Evelyn on the way to the reception. "I have a feeling he is not good for JoAnne."

"Oh, they are young," soothed her husband. "Let them have their good times. I don't blame them for not wanting to go to church affairs. They will see things differently when they grow older. You have, you know."

"Yes," Evelyn sighed heavily. "But I have had to learn the hard way." A sad, bitter look tinged her usually gay features. "If anything should happen to JoAnne I should feel it was my fault. I think I should have sent Henry away when he first came down here, instead of asking you to take him in. But poor Henry has never had a real home and I did so wish that they could be like a brother and sister to each other."

"They are, Eva. Don't fret about it. Nothing is going to happen to JoAnne. She is careless and flippant sometimes, but that's all."

"But I'm afraid Henry may get to drinking and have an accident or something. You know, Harvey, I told you that he grew up accustomed to liquor in our home. I'm ashamed now that I didn't give him better standards."

Harvey patted her hand on the steering wheel. "That's all past now. We'll just go on from here with the Lord's help. Only trust, dear. Everything will turn out all right."

151

"That sounds well enough, Harvey, and I do trust the Lord. But don't we have to meet the results of our past failures? I know the one Bible verse my father used to repeat was 'Whatsoever a man soweth that shall he also reap.' Isn't that true?" Her question was packed with anxiety.

"Yes," agreed Harvey soberly. "I know that Dr. Glasser used to teach that even though God has pardoned us as far as eternal judgment is concerned, there is a certain consequence of our misdeeds that has to be suffered here on earth, for our learning. But really, dear, let's not bring up trouble until it comes."

"All right, honey, I won't. We'll have a good time tonight."

But when they returned from the church neither JoAnne nor Henry were home. The hours dragged on. Evelyn, at least, did not sleep. Three, four, five o'clock. What could have happened to them? She grew angry at her son, and then at JoAnne. Finally she became really frightened and woke her husband.

Meanwhile, Dunn Cash was having his own difficulty getting to sleep.

"Alice, I don't like the way the wind is blowing. I told you about Jack's suggestion of starting a school, didn't I? Well, I stayed pretty close to him tonight to get the drift of the general conversation. About one parent out of two, it seemed, was possessed with the idea that he must do something about the children. Drat it, why don't they know it's their own fault if their children don't turn out right? Why do they expect the minister to take all the responsibility? Besides, after they're in their teens there isn't very much anybody can do. What's the matter with people, anyway? We have never had any trouble with our children. They all go to church and live like decent citizens. They're not perfect, but they have never been any problem. Now these parents are getting Jack all stirred up and there's no telling where the thing will end. Jack ought to have sense enough not to initiate any innovations his first week here, but drat it, they're all ripe to go along with him in anything he may suggest. That crazy idea of having a school in the church buildings! If he'd as much as mention it there would be twenty families who would get on the bandstand for it right away. We've got to squash that right now or it will get out of hand. We just can't afford to go into something as big as that."

"Wouldn't it be a good thing to have a nursery school or even a kindergarten?" asked Alice meekly. "I think it would help many a young mother and make money for the church besides. Lots of churches do it."

Cash flew up in bed like a raging Jack-in-the-box. "And have to put out more on repairs than we'd take in? Not on your life. I've heard ministers tell how the kids wrecked their buildings. I want none of it." His voice rose to a shrill hiss. "Besides, Jack wants more than that. He even suggested working up through high school grades. He's crazy. We'd go broke in a year."

"Well," soothed Alice, "he can't start it if you all don't agree."

"But he has a lot of influence already. The people would eat it up."

On and on he ranted, with Alice agreeing and soothing her husband sleepily.

It was early morning before Dunn Cash joined his snores with the rest of the town.

seventeen

"Isn't this just heavenly, Hank?" JoAnne snuggled closer.

The convertible, quiescent after a wild orgy of speed through the county, faced the edge of a murky bayou where a weak moon was struggling to penetrate the vacillating, swaying palm branches that drooped almost into the water.

"It's not my idea of heaven," growled Hank, but he slid his arm around her.

"Oh, well, I mean, just being here alone, you and me, without a lot of pestering grownups throwing chores at us all the time."

"You couldn't by any chance be lazy, could you?" he teased.

"No, I'm not," she defended. "Basically, I'm not, Hank. It's just that I hate to have people *tell* me what to do. If I had my own home, I think I'd work real hard. I often wish I could go off and have a home of my own, don't you?"

"Oh, yes, sometimes. I never had a real home. My parents were always quarreling and then they got the divorce when I was ten. It was a *mess* after that."

JoAnne stroked his arm sympathetically. "Was it really? I always sort of thought you must have had a tough time. I've often wished—" Her words trailed off into the moonlight provocatively.

"Well? Go on, baby. What did you wish? By the way, do you know that you're as cute as a Georgia peach when you lie there and look up at me. I love to watch your eyes twinkle."

She cast her eyes at him, sparkling their very best twinkle.

"Do you—really?" she whispered softly, turning her full red lips up toward his.

He kissed them greedily.

"Oh-h! That was a *won*-derful kiss, darling! Did you know that I really never felt kissed until I felt your lips on mine? All the other kisses I ever had were just for fun, childish little pecks. Darling, you're wonderful!"

"Am I?" he breathed. "I think you're pretty nice, too. But you haven't told me what you wished."

He held her close and she stroked him lightly, hesitating prettily as she spoke.

"Oh, I know it couldn't ever be." She sighed.

"Why not? What is it, baby?" He kissed her again.

"Well, I've often wished, when I'd see you looking so sort of forlorn, and your mother not understanding and all, I've wished—you'll think I'm crazy," she purred, turning her face up to his once more.

"No, baby, I don't think you're crazy. I knew as soon as I saw you that you had a lot of sense for a kid, a lot more than many girls older than you are. Tell me. I'll understand." His lips were close to her ear.

"Well, I've thought how marvelous it would be to be able to make a real home for you. Honest, darling, I'd work my fingers to the bone to make it nice. I'm really not lazy."

He gazed down at her thoughtfully, longingly.

"You know, baby," he said soberly, "I really believe you would. You're the only one who never made fun of me or held me off. You always have seemed to understand."

"Maybe," she whispered against his cheek, "it's because I've always been unhappy myself. I know how it feels. Oh darling!"

They clasped each other in an embrace that seemed to shut out all the rest of the world, bayou, moonlight, palms, and all.

"JoAnne!" whispered Hank hoarsely, "You're not a kid any more! You're grown up! You do understand. Why don't we go ahead and *have* a home of our own?"

The girl drew back to stare incredulously into his face. "Do you really mean that, darling? Do you? Do you?" She gave him a little loving shake.

"Of course I do. I'm sick of lying around. Let's go get married. I know a place where we can get a license right away almost. It's pretty far, but we can make it if we drive all night."

"Oh, Hank!" She buried her head on his shoulder with a joyous sob. "But," she hesitated, "I don't have any clothes."

"We'll stop back at the house and pack a couple of bags. The folks won't be home from that shindig yet. Come on. Then we'll take off, and start living!" He started the car and with a scratch and a scrape they zoomed off down the road.

About five o'clock the next morning Evelyn gave up her vigil at the various windows of the house and shook Harvey awake.

"Darling! Harvey! Please wake up and tell me what to do about the children."

"Children? Whose children?" His eyes were still shut and his words came thickly.

"*Our* children, darling. They haven't come home yet. They haven't been home all night, Harvey." She was wringing her hands now and her voice was shrill with anxiety.

Gradually Harvey worked his way back into sensibility. His primary concern was to quiet his wife, before he made any attempt to grasp the seriousness of what she was saying to him.

When at last she made him understand, he found many excuses for the young people.

"Don't be so upset, Eva. Things aren't ever as bad as they seem at first. Lots of perfectly harmless things could have happened. They could be out in the Florida sticks somewhere with car trouble. Let's not worry until we know what's happened."

"But I feel so responsible about it because Henry is my son. He shouldn't have taken JoAnne out without proper precautions. Oh, it's my fault. I've known for a long time that I didn't bring him up right. I *am* worried, Harvey. I *should* be worried. I'm going to call the police!"

"Oh, no!" exclaimed Harvey. "We don't want officers swarming all over the place. I hate publicity like that. Let's wait. JoAnne has gone off on her own before. She'll turn up."

"Well, let's hire a private detective, then," insisted his wife.

"Evelyn!" he cried, shocked. "Calm yourself. Do you know how much a private detective would charge? Hundreds of dollars for a case like this."

"Well! Do you love your money more than your daughter?" she parried hotly.

"My money? Evelyn, I simply don't have it, honey."

"What do you mean, you don't have it?" she thrust back at him. "You told me long ago that your father left a hundred thousand dollars when he died."

"Oh, did I tell you that? Yes, he did," replied Harvey. "But it was left in trust for JoAnne. I have only a bare living."

"Then you lied to me!" Evelyn's black wiry hair seemed to stand up stiffer in rage. "Are we going to have to be strapped all our lives so that we can't even spend a little to take care of our own children, when they may be hurt, or killed, or in trouble? I never knew you were like this before I married you, Harvey Donaldson."

Harvey's breath began to come short and fast. Two pink spots appeared in his cheeks. "Now, honey!" he rebuked.

"You needn't honey me. You deceived me. I'd have been

better off to have stayed in Ohio and tried to salvage my own business there. I used to have plenty; I didn't have to pinch like this." She raised her voice to a choking wail.

Harvey simply stared at her. His startled hurt eyes finally caught her attention. She melted somewhat and knelt beside him. "Oh, darling, I didn't mean half of that. I'm sorry. I'm just worried. Forgive me. Now you try to get a little more sleep."

"All right, Eva," sighed Harvey. "I know you are worried. But let's wait and see if they don't come in later. They will likely call as soon as they think we are up. They may have stayed late at somebody's house and just decided to make a night of it. It's not a good thing to do, of course, but it may just be a youthful prank. Let's not get panicky about it. Why don't you go to the kitchen and get a cup of coffee? Bring me one, too," he suggested calmly.

So by easy stages Harvey put off her fears until nine o'clock. Still there was no sign of the young people.

Cagily, so that no one would suspect that anything was wrong, Evelyn called various people, including Nancy, but nobody seemed to have any clues. Frantic, she returned to Harvey's room. He was dozing. She stood watching for several seconds. Then an odd, sly look came into her black eyes. Scribbling a note to leave beside his bed, she stole out.

Harvey slept until nearly noon.

When he called for his wife, there was no answer. Then he saw the note. "I have a headache. Have gone to get some aspirin. Back soon." How long ago was that?

He turned to his books and tried to read. But as time went on he could not cast off his anxiety. Two-thirty. He reached for the phone and called the church office. Nancy answered.

In his usual placid tones he asked, "Miss Lansing, does

my daughter JoAnne happen to be there? I know she visits with you occasionally and I'd like to speak to her, or to my wife."

"No, Dr. Donaldson. I have not seen either of them all day. Is anything wrong?"

"Oh, no—that is, I trust not. JoAnne will turn up, I'm sure. You know these teenagers. Thank you very much. Good bye."

Harvey racked his brain to try to think where his wife might have gone. For years he had been used to having Jo-Anne disappear for a time and then turn up blithely, whole and unscathed; he was not nearly as concerned about her. But it was strange for Evelyn to vanish and leave no preparation for meals. He struggled to the kitchen and found some cold scraps. Then he turned on his television. The afternoon drama depicted the story of a teenager who ran away from her home with a scoundrel. Thankful that Evelyn was not there to see it, Harvey watched it through, not without misgivings.

He looked at the clock again. Where was Evelyn? Perhaps she had found some trace of JoAnne and was trying to follow it up herself.

Four o'clock. He turned the dial to Florida news. There was a strike at Cape Canaveral . . . A cruiser in the gulf had been boarded and robbed . . . The governor was planning a new budget request . . . Then, "A freak accident occurred early this morning just over the Florida border in a small Georgia town. A convertible car overturned flinging both occupants into a water-filled ditch. The driver, who gave his name as Henry Ballentine, of New York, said that he must have fallen asleep at the wheel. As there were no casualties, except wet clothing, there were no charges. The car was righted and the couple drove on . . . In Key West today—"

Harvey clicked it off. Could that have been Henry? It would have been easy for a reporter to confuse Ballentine with Valentine. He picked up the phone once more. Most definitely, he needed advice.

Meanwhile, the two young people had been having their own problems.

"Get your head outa my lap, will ya?" Hank ordered gruffly.

"Oh, darling, I'm so tired, I just feel as if I must lie down."

"Well, I can't drive this way. I'm tired too. I've been driving all night, remember. You wanted to come, and here we are. Now *take* it. Don't chicken out on me."

It was just then that the road turned sharply. Hank jerked the wheel to avoid hitting the curb, but JoAnne's head interfered with his elbow and the car ran hard against the curb. He yanked the wheel to get back on the road but at that instant JoAnne decided to obey him and sit up, and again she hit his arm. The car careened to the far side of the road and, leaping the curb, turned completely over. Hank and JoAnne were flung free, for the convertible top was down. They landed in a deep ditch at the side of the road. Sputtering muddy water and weeds, JoAnne found her voice first.

"You crazy fool!" she blasted him, struggling to lift her feet from the sucking slime.

Hank was having his own troubles in the slippery ooze. When he managed to climb out he turned on her with curses that could be heard far through the quiet of the early morning darkness.

"I told you to get out of my way, you little brat! It was *your* fault."

"It was not!" JoAnne wiped a glob of mud from her left eye. "I was doing what you told me to. I was trying to get out of your way."

"Cripes! How will I ever get this car back on its wheels." He cursed again. "I might have known better than to start on a jaunt like this with a *child!*"

Lights showed down the road.

"I'm *not* a child!" hissed JoAnne. "You said yourself I was grown up."

"Grown up, my foot! You're an infant. Can't even stay awake long enough to get anywhere. Get outa my way. I gotta flag down this car."

The approaching motorist slowed slightly. When he saw the accident, he slowed down still more, but warily. Without stopping to ask questions, he shouted, "I'll call a cop!" and tore down the road.

Hank roared all his worst thoughts after him but the balmy predawn zephyrs wafted them in the other direction.

The police soon arrived; a crowd collected; but it was three quarters of an hour before a wrecking car finally got the convertible back on its feet again. Its engine, at least, seemed to be none the worse for its acrobatics, so the young couple climbed in again in sullen mood and left the scene of their humiliation.

But the eager fervor of the night before had been dissipated, either by the shock or by the mud. They sat far apart in sullen silence, only occasionally throwing a barbed remark back and forth.

Finally, after a long interval, JoAnne burst out, "If you're going to be like this, Henry Valentine, I don't think I want to marry you. If you have to blame me with every little thing, when you were just as much at fault, you can go on being lonesome all your life. See if I care!"

She was very near to tears, but Hank's ill temper flared again.

"It's mutual, *infant!* I have no desire to marry a featherbrain. You don't know your head from a hole in the ground.

161

I gave up the marrying idea some time back, in case you want to know. What a sharp wife you'd have made."

"I guess I'd be as good a wife as you would a husband, wise guy."

"I'm wise enough to ditch you."

"Okay. If you feel that way about me," she flared back, "you can let me out right here."

"You wouldn't know what to do next."

"Oh, wouldn't I? You just try me and see." JoAnne was so angry by now that her words came in a hot hiss from her set lips.

"Okay with me. It'll save me some gas."

Hank stepped suddenly on the brakes, then gave a whoop of hateful laughter when she bumped her face on the dashboard. Furious, she reached out her dirty little hand and slapped him smartly across the cheek. Then in a flash she had the car door open and she was out. She grabbed her bag from the rear seat and started off down the road on what she thought was the way back to Florida.

A roar of mocking laughter followed her.

"Where're you going? New York?" yelled Hank. "You didn't even know we were headed back to Florida, did you, smarty! Haw! Haw! Haw! Good bye, Missus Valentine!"

Furious, JoAnne about-faced with a toss of her still dripping head and marched on her way. Hank watched a few moments and then he backed and turned his car toward New York. Only an instant he paused, then with a sudden scratch of tires he roared north.

Incredulous, JoAnne stole a glance back. She had had no idea that he would really leave her like this. Turmoil raged in her as she stamped on. Dawn was coming now, and the countryside looked harmless and peaceful. Why was her own life in such a mess? At last the tears came. She had to sit down on a stump at the side of the road and there she sobbed out her chagrin and discouragement to the empty landscape.

eighteen

Harvey paused, the receiver in his hand, mentally scanning the list of his friends. He shrank from calling on any of them, for it would mean airing publicly the fact of his family's triple disappearance. A minister was the only person to whom one could confide a thing like this. He called the church office again.

"Mr. Warder is just leaving, Dr. Donaldson," said Nancy. "I'll call him back."

She went to the door, and hallooed to Jack. He was just stepping into his car. While they waited for him, Nancy asked with friendly interest, "Did you finally locate your missing daughter, Dr. Donaldson?"

"No, I haven't. I thought possibly Mr. Warder might help me, or you, perhaps. My wife has disappeared also. Her son Henry, too, hasn't been seen since yesterday. It's very puzzling."

Nancy recognized the note of real perturbation in the man's voice. Just then Jack took the phone. Listening, he raised his brows and glanced at Nancy.

"Suppose Miss Lansing and I drop around there now," he said, looking for confirmation from Nancy. She nodded. "We were just leaving here anyway."

"I'll drop you at home after we call there," he said. "It's tough for the poor man alone. I guess he's pretty helpless. They all went off and left him no food. There's something wrong there."

Nancy covered her typewriter and took her purse, running a swift comb through her hair before her tiny mirror. Why was it that she was continually being thrust into Jack Warder's company? But she couldn't refuse a call like this.

"I don't know what I can do for him," she said. "I haven't a notion where JoAnne would be."

"I thought maybe you could get him a lunch, or something, while I find out what the score is. He impresses me as being very dependent."

Just as they turned the corner Dunn Cash pulled up to the church driveway to pick up Nancy. He caught sight of them, and went on, but not without a significant grimace. "I *thought* it wouldn't take her very long," he muttered. "I think my lady Marge had better get busy."

They had passed through the center of town and out to where the shops were thinly scattered, when suddenly Nancy exclaimed, "There is Evelyn's car. She must be somewhere nearby. Why don't I stop and wait till she comes out? Then she and I can go home together."

"That's a good idea. I'll go on and tell Dr. Donaldson that his wife, at least, has been located."

Nancy jumped out and ran across the street. The car was parked in front of a drug store. She peered through the glass doors of the store, and then poked her head in and looked around. Evelyn was not there. Doubtless she was on some other errand nearby and would be back soon. Nancy got into the car and prepared to wait for her. This was the only way to be sure not to miss her. Surely it wouldn't be long.

But a half hour went by. People came and went. The evening rush was over. Pedestrians thinned out. Traffic was less now at the dinner hour. Nancy was getting hungry. She thought of slipping in to the drugstore for a snack, but she was afraid she might miss Evelyn. Maybe she ought to phone Donaldsons'. Jack would be wondering what had become of them. But she kept putting off making a move, thinking that Evelyn must turn up soon. There was practically no store open now, except the drug store. Where *could* the woman be?

Nancy began to scrutinize every spot in the area where she thought Mrs. Donaldson might have an errand. The grocery store was closed. There was a dry cleaning establishment next to that. It was still open, but no possible cleaning errand could last this long. Beyond was a florist's; it was closed and the night lights already showed the store to be empty.

In the uptown direction two vacant lots stretched. Beyond them a little hamburger drive-in was serving two or three cars. Perhaps Evelyn was in one of them. She might have met a friend. Nancy decided to stroll down and have a look. She could still keep an eye on Evelyn's car.

She felt like a sleuth, walking closely past the three cars, scanning the figures in each. One held an elderly couple; the other two were filled with chattering teenagers.

Discouraged, Nancy glanced around the area. There was only one other small building left, before two more empty lots intervened, and then the residential section began.

She took a few steps farther. The little shop displayed a neon sign: Three-D Bar. Surely Mrs. Donaldson would not be in there, but Nancy was determined now to leave no stone unturned. She could not imagine anyone connected with the Donaldson family drinking in a place like that. Nancy was not averse to a cocktail herself, occasionally, at parties; but she had been brought up to think that no lady would be seen in a common bar.

Feeling very self-conscious about it, she walked slowly past the place, glancing cautiously in through the open door.

She could see a U-shaped plastic counter, clean and neat, with several high stools about it, and two or three men seated at one side drinking and talking in low tones. There were alcoves against the wall, like breakfast nooks. A few other men and a young couple occupied these.

Nancy could not get a good view of the other side of the

counter until she walked past and returned. Scarcely expecting to find the woman she sought, she gave only a cursory glance on that side. There at the counter, sagging over a half-filled glass was Mrs. Donaldson!

Nancy was thoroughly shocked, but at least her search was over. In she walked, and straight up to Evelyn, who looked sheepish. Her eyes were heavy and her whole face looked as if it were pushed out of shape.

The men stopped drinking, as if they were aware that an alien element had entered. Even the young couple in the booth glanced up in surprise. For Nancy had a patrician air about the way she wore her clothes, and the very manner in which she bore herself, that was not in keeping with the general character of the place.

"Hello, Evelyn," she greeted tentatively. The woman showed that she had been drinking for some time. Nobody could appear so bloated unless she had been at it for hours. Nancy was not sure how to deal with her. Would she be drunk enough to be rough?

Mrs. Donaldson stared at her defensively, uncertainly.

"'Lo," she responded thickly. "Have a dring wizh me?" She started to signal for the bartender.

Nancy shook her head. "Not now, Evelyn. I came to get you. Your husband is waiting for you to come back, you know." She spoke in a placating tone, as one would address a little child.

"Heh, heh!" quoth Evelyn. "Yesh, I tol' him I'd be right back. But wha's the rush? He can't eshpect hish wife to sit all day an' hol' 'ish hand. If you don' wanta dring, you go tell 'im I'll be right home."

Nancy saw that it was not going to be an easy matter to get this woman out of here, into her car and home. She decided to try to make Evelyn think she was asking her a favor.

"Well, I don't have a car, you see. I saw yours parked down

the street and I thought maybe you would take me. I'm so tired. I've walked a long way."

"You walked? Then have a dring. Tha'll make you feel be'er. Here Joe, get thish la'y a dring, an' fill mine, too. I'll be shochiable."

"No, I don't care for any, really." Nancy threw the bartender a decidedly negative glance. Then she tried appealing to him. "I've come to take my friend home, sir. Please don't give her any more. Her husband is ill and needs her."

"Ill? Harvey? Oh, no, don't believe it, Joe. He'sh alwaysh pretending to be ill. But he really ishn't sho bad. He can manage when he wantsh to. Besides," she leaned close to Nancy confidentially, "Harvey lied to me. I wouldn't ever lie to any pershon. He lied. He told me he had money. He lied. I gave up a lot for 'im. Tied to a wheel shair, I am. Now J'Anne'sh gone. Sherv' 'im right. He 'sh too eashy on her. J'Anne'sh gone. My shon's gone too. But my shon'sh a goo' boy. Never gave trouble. Only he lied too. Hish ozher mozher taught him to lie. He doeshn't trush' me any more. Now he'sh gone. I'm goin' to *get* her. Some day she'sh gotta be killed for that. He'sh a goo' boy." Then she finished in a thick stage whisper in Nancy's ear, "Tomorrow I'sh goin' to drive to Teckshas an' kill 'er."

Nancy seized Evelyn's glass and tried to persuade the bartender to take it. But he refused. "I can't, madam. She paid for it. It's hers."

"But she must come home right now. Her daughter is in trouble. She is needed!" Nancy insisted. The man was rotund, with only a ring of thin gray hair around a spotty bald dome. His too-small baggy eyes looked distressed. He gazed first at Nancy, then at his customer. Finally he took sides.

"Look, lady," he said dully to Evelyn, "you got a nice friend here. You oughta be glad somebody cares about you. An' you got a daughter that needs you. Now go on."

Evelyn merely stared at him and laughed in a silly way.

Nancy took her arm gently. She looked at her in befuddlement, rose and started to take a step with her, then turned back and sat down on the high stool again heavily, solidly. Nancy could not budge her.

The radio was blaring rhythmic hillbilly tunes. She began to grin and shake her shoulders in time to the music. But she was too sodden to keep it up.

Nancy grew desperate. She *must* get word to Jack. Perhaps he would be able to manage her charge. She dreaded calling the police.

She glanced around the place to see if there was a phone booth. Then she asked the bartender in a low tone.

"Naw," he responded sullenly. "We ain't got a phone here. Nearest one's down the street in the drug store."

Nancy reverted to her attempts to coax Evelyn to go with her. The whole barroom was watching with interest. The bartender began to urge her again to go with her "nice lady friend." But she sluggishly held her ground. Nancy wondered what Jack would say in a situation like this. No doubt he would advise prayer. She actually wished she knew how. Certainly she felt the need of a power greater than her own. It never occurred to Nancy, as it might to some girls, to retreat and leave the woman. She had been given a job to do and do it she would.

Suddenly the radio program changed. Children's voices came on the air, singing together.

The bartender was pleading now with Evelyn to go. He was evidently afraid that his business might suffer. "Go on, lady, go with your friend. You know you've had enough to drink."

The children began to sing lustily. It was not possible to ignore the words of their song:

> "What can wash away my sin?
> Nothing but the blood of Jesus.

What can make me pure within?
Nothing but the blood of Jesus."

Incongruously the words rang through the little shop.

The big bartender, startled, caught the unintentional cue and cried, "There, lady, that oughta show you. You ain't got no business in here. Now get."

Evelyn looked at him, shocked for the moment into something like soberness. Then she stared at Nancy, who was smiling and drawing her gently. Slowly, with uncertain steps, she permitted the girl to lead her outside. But she was leaning almost completely on Nancy and she was heavy.

They managed a dozen steps. How will I ever get her two blocks to her car? thought Nancy, panting with the exertion of holding her up. Then they came to a rickety bench discarded in the weeds edging the sidewalk. "Here," cried Nancy, "you don't feel up to walking. Your car is way down the street. Give me your keys and I'll bring it up here. You just sit down and rest a minute."

"Okay, okay," agreed Evelyn, reaching in her purse and pawing about. She handed over the keys and Nancy, with relief, rushed off, feeling that she had won a great victory. Was it the bartender who had won? Or perhaps the Lord Himself? She hadn't time to decide now.

She flung herself into the car and drove as fast as she could back to the Three-D Bar. There was the bench. But Evelyn was nowhere in sight. Aghast over losing her prey, Nancy locked the car and jumped out. She ran into the bar. Was the whole scene to be enacted over again?

There were the same men; there was the young couple; and the bartender, looking at her peculiarly. But no Evelyn.

"Did she come back in here?" she cried.

The men stared stolidly. The young couple snickered. The bartender shook his head. "No, lady. I ain't seen her," he said glumly.

Utterly discouraged, Nancy returned to the car. She drove back and forth several times up and down the street and even over on the next block, thinking perhaps Evelyn had managed to make it through the weeds at the rear. There was not a sign of her anywhere. At last Nancy gave up and drove back to Donaldson's house.

Jack met her at the door. She told him the wretched tale. Instead of showing shock or disgust, he merely shook his head sorrowfully.

"Poor, poor woman. And poor Dr. Donaldson, too. Only the Lord can handle a situation like this and bring something good out of it."

Nancy stared at Jack in amazement. "How on earth could *anything* good come out of a mess like this?" she asked.

He smiled, that smile that she had learned to watch for. It seemed as if it was lit from another world. "It's the sort of mess God uses to show His grace. We forget that He's the God who brought light out of darkness; He can even bring life out of death. You watch and see. It may be a long time, but He will do it. These two people are His children."

Nancy didn't answer. There was nothing for her to say, but she was disappointed in Jack. He seemed so ridiculously visionary.

They went down the corridor. "Here, let's go in the kitchen and talk," he said.

"Yes," agreed Nancy, "I've got to scrounge a bite of something. I'm starved."

While she made a couple of sandwiches he told her about the newscast. "It seems there was an accident in Georgia—car overturned. Nobody hurt, but the driver was announced as Henry Ballentine of New York. He had a lady passenger. So we called, but that was all they could tell us. If Henry and JoAnne are driving to New York they would not arrive until tonight at the earliest. It may be that's where they are. The police are alerted all through that area to watch for his car. If they don't find him they're going to page him over the radio."

"You don't suppose they eloped, do you?"

"Could be," said Jack. "I have discussed that with Dr. Donaldson. He doesn't think so. He seems to have an idea that JoAnne has a great deal of common sense. Do you know her well?"

"Not too well, but well enough *not* to think so. She's like most kids—hare-brained; thinks she knows more than she does. I was like that at her age. I don't know why I didn't get into more scrapes than I did."

Jack laughed and stole a keen look at her while she finished her cold drink.

"I started out the same way," he confessed. "The Lord got hold of me just in time."

It was her turn to glance at him and wonder. There was something rather special, she felt, behind his admission.

"Well, what do we do next?" she asked. "I'd be glad to help, but how?"

"The first thing will be to tell Dr. Donaldson about his wife."

"Oh, no!" she gasped. "I can't do that."

"He'll have to know sometime. It never does any good to hide the truth. It's a rugged deal," he added gently. "I wish it could be avoided. But it's his problem and he must know it. She's an alcoholic, for sure. I wonder if he knew it before they were married."

"I don't think so, from what JoAnne told me. She said Evelyn had told him she used to drink more than she should but that that was all over now."

"It'll be a blow. We'll stick with him and try to help him face it. He dreads publicity. I think he's more frantic about how people will talk than he is frightened about what may have happened to JoAnne. Do you think you can tell him yourself?"

"Yikes! What a task!" Nancy shuddered. "It's bad enough to have your daughter gone, but this! I don't know how to start."

Jack smiled soberly. "It's rough. Suppose we go in together. I'll prepare him and then you tell the whole tale. He's got to know sooner or later. Can you do it?"

Nancy put both hands over her eyes as if to shut out the look that she knew would come on the poor man's face.

Jack watched her a moment. "Let's ask the Lord to give us the right words to say," he suggested. Then in the same tone of voice, as if God were there in the kitchen with them, he said, "Lord, our hearts go out to this poor family. We believe they are dear to You. Show us how we should act, what to say, how to share with them this new sorrow. Guard the woman and bring her back safely, and JoAnne and Henry too. We commit the whole matter to Thy care. Bring glory to Thy Son through it all, and use us in any way You can. Amen."

While he spoke, Nancy peered through her fingers at his bowed head. What was there that seemed so different about him from the way—well, Mr. Cash, for instance, would have attacked this problem? Was it that Jack was so ready and available to share in the family's problem and bear it with them? She could picture Cash standing critically aloof, frenzied but helpless, or too busy to bother.

She trembled as they took their way to the invalid's bedroom. She had to admit to herself that it was comforting to have a strong person like Jack around.

Dr. Donaldson was seated in his wheel chair, staring at the black square of the front window.

"Miss Lansing has returned, Dr. Donaldson," began Jack, "and she has news of your wife. But I'm sorry to say that it's not very encouraging news. I'm going to ask her to tell you herself." He nodded to Nancy.

She told her tale as simply as she could, leaving out the more sordid details. "I looked everywhere for her. How she could have escaped in those short minutes is more than I know."

Dr. Donaldson turned his face away and groaned. Nancy and Jack glanced at each other with compassion for him. It was hard not to be able to do something. Nancy waited for Jack to speak.

Just then the telephone rang.

nineteen

Several times during the long hot ride through Georgia, South Carolina, North Carolina, and points north, Hank Valentine was bothered by the vision of a plump, wet young girl trudging down a path of dust in the burning Florida sun. But the farther he went the more futile it seemed to turn and go back after her. Again and again he argued with himself that surely by now she had come upon a place where she could get a bus or a train. He knew she had twenty dollars with her, for they had discussed finances the night before.

Hank was bitter against the whole world, his own lot in particular. He tried to think where to go next, what to do. His life so far had been unsatisfactory. He had left high school just before graduation, all because he got angry at the baseball coach over what he considered unfair treatment. He had no desire to go to college or to any training school. He had always hated the discipline of school, although he liked books and was generally a good student. He tried to imagine himself getting a job. What kind of work could he do that would seem worthwhile? He was smart enough to realize that he lacked sufficient training for any job that would challenge his intellect. Anything less would bore him. Well, why bother? He had money, enough to live on comfortably all his life if he was careful. So far he had not been very careful, but he always intended to be the next year.

He had gone to Florida with a faint idea of trying once more to live with his mother. He was fond of her in a way. But her habit of being brought home drunk so often had disgusted and embarrassed him. He had paid her bills many a time when she drank up everything at hand. Why start that all over again? Yet he felt rather righteous to think that he had made the effort. It had failed. So what? He was more bitter than ever. Other people seemed to be able to live happily. Why was life so unfair to him?

It was by grapevine that he had heard that Nancy Lansing, whom he had dated often in New York, was in Florida. That also had influenced his trip there. But she had not fallen into his arms with eagerness. The only person who went for him was that kid JoAnne. The thought of her infuriated him again. He was well rid of her. He'd be back in New York tomorrow. Maybe he'd find some new friends, or something that seemed worth living for.

He stopped at a wayside motel the second night and was just getting into bed when a knock came at his door. There was a police officer.

The officer's questioning angered him. "It's her own fault!" he kept muttering bitterly, until the officer reprimanded him not too gently. He was shaken but still more angry after the police left with a suggestion that he call Pine City, and a warning that he could be charged with contributing to the delinquency of a minor. That JoAnne was still missing did not disturb him greatly. She might have taken it into her scatterbrained little head to stop off somewhere and visit a friend. He knew she had school friends here and there through the south. He had made up his mind that it was she who was to blame. He resented the public's intrusion into his affairs. Hereafter he would keep out of touch entirely with his family.

Nancy and Dr. Donaldson were breathless as Jack picked up the phone. The call was from the police, a report of their talk with Hank. It left them all worse off, if possible, than before. All three of them voiced righteous indignation at Hank's irresponsibility but that did not help to find JoAnne. Dr. Donaldson and Nancy looked to Jack to know how to proceed. He had discussed the case with both Florida and Georgia police, since he found she had school friends in Georgia. The highway patrol were doing everything possible to locate her. They wanted to hold Hank for further questioning but his stepfather said "Wait!"

The night wore on. Finally, after midnight, Jack suggested that Nancy should take Evelyn's car and go home to get some rest.

"I'll stay here with Dr. Donaldson," he decided. "I called Emma long ago and told her I might be very late. The children were both asleep. Everything is all right there. I won't dare to work you hard tomorrow if you have been up all night." He smiled at Nancy as they walked toward the front door.

But they had no sooner turned the corner of the corridor than they heard the sound of the door gong, accompanied by a heavy knocking on the door.

They glanced at each other in startled alarm.

"There's one of them, at least," whispered Nancy.

Jack opened the door.

A taxi driver stood there, impatiently.

"I've got a woman out here. Her driver's license has the name of Evelyn Constant. A paper in her purse has this address. That right?"

Jack nodded.

"I'll bring her in."

"Okay, I'll be right with you," said Jack. "Get her a bed ready, Nancy, in the guest room."

The men went out.

In a few moments they were back, carrying the drunken woman like a bag of cement. Her head lolled to one side and she was breathing huskily, her mouth sagging open. Her dress was torn badly so that she was crudely exposed.

Nancy had never seen such a repulsive sight. It was hard to believe that this was the stylish Mrs. Donaldson. She looked anything but smart at the moment.

Nancy turned away in disgust only to see Dr. Donaldson wheeling into the corridor. His patrician face twisted in horror, and then suddenly froze into gray lifelessness. His whole frame slumped and he would have fallen out of his chair but that Nancy rushed to him in time to catch him and balance his dead weight in the chair.

Frightened lest he actually was dead, she managed to hold him until Jack and the taxi driver got Evelyn onto the bed.

"I—I think he's gone!" she breathed with white lips.

The man gave a startled exclamation, and bent to examine him.

"He ain't dead, miss, but you better get a doctor right quick. Looks like a stroke to me."

He helped Jack lift the man into his own bed, and called the hospital himself.

"They say they're full," he reported. "Better get his own doc; maybe he can get him in."

After he had gone and the call had been put in to Donaldson's physician, Nancy and Jack simply stood and looked at each other in dismay.

"I never heard of so much happening to one family at once!" exclaimed Nancy. "It's fantastic."

Jack shook his head sympathetically. "It's rugged," he agreed. "I guess it's going to be up to us now to keep on the track of JoAnne. Have they any family around these parts?"

"None that I know of," said Nancy. She spoke in a hushed voice. "He seemed to be a rather reserved old gentleman. I don't know what special friends he had. He'd want to keep this quiet, I'm sure. Few people came here. That was always JoAnne's pet gripe. I guess she must have come along rather late in life and her parents were too old to understand. I always felt sorry for the kid. She tried so hard to live life to the utmost and couldn't seem to make it go her way."

"She's not the only one," Jack reminded her. "There are millions like her."

"I suppose so," agreed Nancy. "I never thought of it that way. I never saw much of real trouble, I guess. I only heard of it indirectly through kids that were sort of unhappy, like I was sometimes. I can see now that I have a lot to be thankful for. Since I've been here in the church office I feel as if I'd been plunged into all the misery of the world. I don't know how you ministers keep from losing your minds over it all. What do you do, sort of unhitch your thoughts when you go home at night? How do you stand it?"

Jack smiled again. "I don't. I have to roll it all off on the only One who knows how it's all going to end. Hark! There's the doctor."

Jack went in with him while Nancy took a look at the other patient. She seemed to be snoring soundly. Now and then she would give a groan and babble some gibberish, turn over, and snore again. It was revolting.

At last the doctor and Jack came out to report.

"He will do as well here as in the hospital," said the doctor, "if he can have some care. All he needs is someone to watch him and call me if anything goes wrong. He may come out of it and he may not. It will take time. He is not a young man. If his daughter returns it may do wonders for him."

Out of consideration for Donaldson, Jack said nothing about the wife's condition. That might solve itself with nobody the wiser. JoAnne's disappearance had already been noised abroad on the radio, and the police were considering showing her photograph on television if she could not be found soon.

Meanwhile, JoAnne herself was meeting some experiences that hitherto in her mind had belonged only in moving picture dramas.

She had dried her tears finally, and trudged on several miles before traffic became fairly frequent. Her youthful spirits began to rise as she reviewed her present status. She was still so angry at Hank that she found herself gleefully relieved to think that she had escaped being married to him. Right now she might have been in his power, bearing his name, condemned to suit his whims. But she was still free. The experience of being practically thrust out and deserted in the lonely countryside still rankled, but she comforted herself by thinking that surely she would soon come to a town where she could get a bus for home. The reception she would get from her father when she arrived there did not loom brightly, but she shrugged it off. That she was assuredly able to manage; she had done it often before. She was glad she had some money with her. Money had pulled her out of many a jam.

As the day grew hotter, her clothing dried, and her hair, though muddy in places, was none the worse for her dousing. Her overnight bag was still damp around the edges, but most of it was plastic and she trusted that her nicest clothes, which she had chosen to bring along, were not too badly damaged.

Finally, however, her feet, unused to long hot walks, began to blister and burn. It was nearly noon. She sighed bravely. In the distance she could see smoke stacks and soon the tops of tall buildings showed between the pine trees. A city of some kind was ahead, at last. It might still be miles, but there was hope that she would sometime reach civilization. Each mile, however, seemed longer than it had in the early morning. The few cars that turned up whizzed past her, even though she put out a plump thumb waving in a southerly direction.

She went on and on. She was so exhausted that it seemed as if the city must be receding. Another car sounded far behind her. She stopped this time and deliberately stood almost in its path. It was a recent model, fast, and sleek. A man and a tall angular woman were in the front seat. To her dismay, they flew past her, but suddenly they slowed down. They seemed to be arguing. She drove her tired feet to catch up to them. The car began to back slowly.

With vast relief she saw that they were actually going to pick her up. When they came alongside the woman looked at her sharply, eying her bag and her generally bedraggled appearance.

The man spoke first.

"Where you goin', girlie?" he asked in a friendly manner.

"I am on my way to Pine City," she answered. "Ever heard of it? It's about the center of the state." She tried to speak brightly.

"You're a long way from there," he replied gruffly. "You weren't planning to walk all the way?"

"Well, no," said JoAnne gaily, "not if I can help it." She suddenly realized that she didn't care to tell all of her story. "I—I missed my bus."

"Oh." The man and the woman looked significantly at each other and then down at her mud-stained garments.

"You're just a kid. How old are you?" the man asked.

"I—I'm—going on eighteen," lied JoAnne, assuring herself that eventually she would be eighteen if she ever lived through this.

"Do you drive?" He questioned her again. "Got a license?"

"Oh, yes," she assented quickly.

"Well, get in. We might want you to take the wheel awhile. The wife here doesn't like to drive and I'm pretty beat out. We've come a long way ourselves. We're going down your way, so we might as well give you a lift."

With a feeling that she had been put through a cross-examination and passed, JoAnne heaved another sigh of relief.

"Here, you sit in between us. You're shorter than her. She don't like to straddle the transmission."

Obediently JoAnne climbed in across the woman's angular knees. She slipped her little bag onto the back seat and off they went.

"What is the town we are coming to?" she asked. "It seemed ever so far." She forgot that she was giving away the fact that she did not know where she was.

The man looked at her closely. "I dunno its name," he replied cagily. "Tain't far now."

JoAnne subconsciously wondered at the rough illiterate speech of the man; it didn't fit the slim luxurious lines of the car. But of course a man didn't have to be cultured or well educated to own a nice car.

The woman did not seem inclined to talk. They flew along and JoAnne was happy just to be able to rest her legs and wiggle her toes a little, although she would have given a great deal for a glass of something cold to drink.

It occurred to her that maybe these people would expect

some remuneration for taking her. At least she could offer to share expenses.

"I will be glad to pay my part of the trip," she offered cheerfully, "if you will tell me about how much it will be."

The man turned and gave her another scrutinizing look. But he only growled something about their going south anyway, and showed no further interest in talking.

"Where are you from?" JoAnne asked to make conversation.

The woman started to answer but the man cut her short.

"From up north a ways," he evaded.

"Oh," said JoAnne. "I thought maybe you were from one of the northern states. So many people come down from Pennsylvania or even Maine in the summer time. I should think they would find it too hot, being used to the cooler summers up there."

"Humph!" was all the response she got.

Deciding finally that these were rather grumpy uncommunicative people, JoAnne relapsed into silence herself. She had tried to be friendly. Well, she couldn't fuss about them, for they certainly had been friends in need. Once or twice she tried again to thank them for their kindness, but she received little answer.

At last they came into the outskirts of a city. JoAnne tried in vain to catch a glimpse of some name that would tell her where they were.

They drove on down through the center of town. It was about the noon hour. Heat shimmered up from the pavements. The traffic was light, though pedestrians were many, probably on their way to lunch. The weary girl glanced wistfully at several drug stores but her chauffeur seemed not inclined to stop.

They crossed railroad tracks. Then the man spoke again. "Now miss, if you want to drive a bit, we'll be very grateful. I have to leave you here, but my wife is going on to Pine City. She'll be glad to take you all the way down, if you'll do most of the driving. Funny thing, she doesn't like to drive, but she sure does like to ride fast. So don't poke. I'm goin' to park right here an' leave the engine goin'. Be sure not to shut it off, because it's right hard to start." At that point the woman got out and hastened into the bank. "When she comes out, you git goin'. Follow 301. I'm goin' to shove off now. Be sure to give her a good *fast* ride, hear?" He gave a nervous ugly grin and walked away.

In less than two minutes the woman came out and literally flung herself into the car.

"Get goin'!" she commanded roughly. "Faster!" she whispered hoarsely, as JoAnne hesitated a little, to maneuver a bend in the road.

JoAnne felt jittery driving a strange car and being hounded by the owner, but she was determined to do her part agreeably. She had no time to give attention to what the woman was doing, though she noticed that she drew a pair of dark glasses out of her enormous bag, and that she tucked something into it.

They were soon at the edge of town and the woman kept hissing under her breath, "Faster! Faster!" JoAnne glanced at the speedometer. It registered over ninety. To the teenager that was not an excessive speed, but she did wonder at the older woman.

"You really like to go, don't you?" she exulted, secretly delighting in the roadability of the superb machine. Her eyes danced as she neared the hundred mark, passing the few cars there were, easily and deftly. JoAnne knew that she was a competent driver, if not always a cautious one. She had had a fierce argument with Hank the night before because he would not let her drive his convertible.

"I like to go where I want to," retorted the woman in a deep gruff voice and so sharply that JoAnne shot her a quick astonished glance. Dumbfounded, she took her foot off the gas and her mouth fell open from amazement. The woman was not a woman any more. She had a ring of thin sandy hair around a bald head, and the dark blouse she had worn was gone. In its place was a light blue T shirt.

"Turn down that road to your right!" ordered her companion with a fierce oath. As JoAnne still hesitated he whipped a tiny automatic from his right pocket and poked it at her.

Terrified, JoAnne swung jerkily into the side road.

"Keep goin'!" ordered the man, still holding the gun near her ribs. They tore down the dirt road about two hundred feet, then he ordered her again, "Turn right." She turned and at that moment she could hear sirens screaming down the highway they had just left. Sweat poured out on her hands till she could scarcely hold the wheel steady. For the first time in her life, JoAnne Donaldson had met a situation which she could not conquer.

twenty

Dunn Cash spun his car off the street and into his own driveway with a vicious lurch, shut off the motor and stormed into the house.

"Alice!" he yelled. "Alice!" No answer. "Meta, where's your mother?" he demanded.

"How should I know?" retorted Meta. She made a hateful grimace at his back.

Ellenelle came clattering in just then from the patio.

"I know. She's out in the back yard, Daddy. Shall I get her?" she offered meekly.

"Tell her I want her. Right now."

It was two weeks since the day that Mr. Cash had had the unfortunate seizure in the office. Whatever had caused it, his family had decided privately that he had grown more impossible to live with each day. He was home hours before his usual time this afternoon.

His wife appeared, flustered and breathless, clothespins still clutched in her hand.

He hauled her into their bedroom and closed the door. Meta narrowed her eyes. She resented being shut out of important conferences.

"Alice, I'm in real trouble." Alice waited sympathetically. "I've got to have some money."

Alice still made no response; she had no money to produce.

"I tell you, this time I've got to. I'll *have* to get it somewhere."

Alice tried to be patient. She had heard this so many times.

"Dunn, I think the people in *real* trouble are the Donaldsons. Did you hear that JoAnne has disappeared?"

"That might be anything but trouble," he retorted harshly. "That girl is more trouble when she's around. She'll turn up."

"But Dr. Donaldson has had a stroke."

He glared at her. "That's tough. But listen! You think this is just a tempest in a teapot. I tell you, I'm serious. I mean, it's so serious that I'm completely sunk if I can't get that money. I'm done. Lost."

He stood over her trying to impress her with the importance of what he was saying. "This is no laughing matter, I tell you."

Once, long ago, Alice had dared to say facetiously, "Well, I'm not laughing." She never said it again. It wasn't worth the consequences.

"Aren't you going to say anything? Are you just going to sit there like a moron and watch me go down like a foundered ship?"

Alice had discovered that "What shall I say?" was also anathema. So she said something else.

Gently she suggested, "Dunn, why don't we get down on our knees together and ask the Lord to undertake in it?"

He tossed his head impatiently. "This is not the time for that. We can't expect a miracle."

"Why not?" reproached Alice lovingly. "I think God loves to have us come when we are helpless. Remember how Jack brought that out in his sermon Sunday? Please, Dunn."

"*Jack!* Don't bring Jack into this. He's nothing but an upstart. I wish sometimes I had never brought him here. He has the earmarks of a troublemaker."

"Dunn, *you* didn't bring him here. I believe God Himself sent him. Don't you? Isn't that what everybody prayed for when Dr. Glasser died—that God would send the man of His choice?"

"Piffle. Of course. But man can often go far astray from what God wants."

"I sometimes think that *you* do, Dunn, or you wouldn't get so panicky and upset when things seem to go against your plans."

"So you're going to preach to me, are you? Now, when I need you more than I ever needed you in my life."

"What can I do, Dunn? I am trying to help you, with the only help I know to give. I've depended on the Lord many a time when you—" She halted abruptly, then went on to finish vaguely—"when things seemed dark. He always answered. He has always brought us through, hasn't He?"

"That's all very well, but it's beside the point right now. Alice, I'm in over my head and ears. I'll lose everything—

everything, if I can't lay hands on at *least* twenty-five thousand dollars by next Monday."

"Perhaps it would be good for us to lose everything, Dunn."

"What?" he screamed. "You don't know what you're talking about."

"Yes, I do know. I mean just that. I know it would be hard for me to do without a lot of the luxuries that you have given me, but I never used to have them, and I could do without again. Sometimes, Dunn," her voice grew wistful, although she was surprised at herself for daring to speak as she did, "I think of the happy days of our early married life. We didn't have much money, but we were happy. You were so eager and earnest then. All you cared about was to win souls to Christ. You were a wonderful preacher then, Dunn." Her eyes tried to seek his in understanding. "I have wondered whether it hasn't grieved the Lord for us to turn to just making money. We'll have to leave it all soon."

By this time Dunn Cash was rigid. He stood by the window with his back to Alice, trembling, clenching his thin knuckly hands.

"This is just what I might have expected!" He was cold with rage. "This is just the right time for a preachment. And you are such a fine preacher. *You* had better turn preacher yourself. Maybe God would be more pleased with you." He spoke scathingly, and Alice cringed under it.

"If you want to go back to living in a hovel, like a *missionary,*" he sneered, "you can. I don't and I don't intend to. I'm sure the Lord never intended all Christians to go without everything that makes life pleasant. If you don't appreciate all I've tried to do for you and give you, it's too bad. But I'm going to enjoy it. And I'm *going* to get that money, somewhere."

He slammed out of the room, letting the door bang, and stamped through the house into the garage. Then, like a returning thunderstorm, he blew himself in again. Back to Alice he strode and shut the door behind him once more.

In a hoarse rumble he whispered, "Do you remember how long it is before that boarder of ours gets her money?"

Alice, shocked into speechlessness, shook her head dumbly. Cash detonated like an unseasonable firecracker and erupted once more into the garage. He started up his car furiously and backed out. But his family heard a long sickening screech of metal on metal and knew that he had scraped the paint from the side of his car for the third time that year.

Meta grinned contemptuously to her book. Ellenelle looked distressed. But Alice bowed her head in discouragement.

"Will he ever learn?" she murmured sinking into a chair and covering her face with her hands.

That was Friday afternoon. Just after Cash left, the phone rang. Meta answered it.

"That you, Meta? This is Betty Martin. I just wondered whether you had heard about the Donaldsons." Her tone was flavored with excitement as if she were about to indulge in a new and tempting dish.

"Which thing about them?" hedged Meta. She wasn't sure what the latest news was, but she didn't intend to let Betty know that.

"You mean Nancy Lansing didn't tell you? She has the tightest mouth! As if she can't trust anybody. Who is she to know all the dirt when she's just new here? It makes me boil! Well, you surely knew that JoAnne and Hank disappeared the night of the reception? Yes, and the new wife got absolutely pie-eyed drunk." Meta gasped. "Poor old Dr. Donaldson had a stroke," went on Betty glibly. "I don't blame him. I never cared for the guy; he's a stiff old duck, but I feel awfully sorry for him. He thought he was getting a nice new bride and she gets stewed the first thing. But *wait* till you hear! That's not all. Guess who came to the rescue and stayed *all Wednes-*

day night. Our new minister and his beloved secretary. *Both* of them! I can't imagine what they found to do all that time. Sat and held his hand, I guess, or each other's, more likely. That girl is the fastest worker! She takes advantage of situations like nothing I ever saw. I froth at the mouth when I think how hard my sister Marge has worked to get him, and what a time I had to get Tom hooked and tied." She giggled.

She then proceeded to discuss the reception, what everyone wore and who said what to whom.

Meta curled her lip in disdain when Betty finally hung up. Meta was a girl of few words. She listened much and committed herself little.

Nancy came home soon after that. Meta was very conscious of her presence going through the room but she did not look up. She wished she could bring herself to ask Nancy if there was any news of JoAnne, but the words would not come. Her pride kept her from disclosing the fact that she did not know as much about the affair as Nancy probably did. Many of Meta's caustic remarks were blurted out to hide her hurt pride. She always felt left out of everything, and therefore, she usually was.

As a matter of fact Nancy herself was bewildered and puzzled over several things. As she showered and rested a few minutes before dinner, she reviewed the events of the past few days.

After Evelyn had been brought in and dumped into the guest room bed, Wednesday night, Jack had sent Nancy to get some rest in JoAnne's room.

"You might look in on her now and then," he suggested. "She may get very sick, or she may just sleep it off. You should be able to get a good three or four hours of sleep. I'm going to stay with Dr. Donaldson. I'll lie down on the couch in his room. It may be that Emma will be willing to come over tomorrow part time at least, if I take the children with me to the church. It won't be the easiest arrangement, but until Mrs. Donaldson comes to herself, I don't know whether to try to get a nurse for him or not. They are pretty expensive articles. I'll have a talk with her in the morning. If she's really born again, I can show her how to get the mastery of this thing."

So Nancy went upstairs and the household relaxed for a few hours. She was so exhausted from the excitement that she did not stir until nearly five o'clock. Then she awoke with a start. It was not yet light. She remembered that Jack had told her to keep an eye on Mrs. Donaldson, so she stole softly down the half flight of stairs and peeked into the guest room.

There was nobody there. Alarmed, she poked her head into the living room. Maybe the woman had gone to the kitchen. That was it. She would be hungry. But the kitchen, too, was empty and silent. No one had been there to fix anything to eat, apparently.

Nancy tiptoed down the corridor and tapped lightly on Dr. Donaldson's door.

"Jack!" she called softly.

Instantly he was up and came out.

"She's gone! I'm so ashamed. I should have watched her more carefully." Nancy's distress made her look like a little girl.

Jack showed no surprise. "I was afraid of that. She's going to go after the stuff until she's had enough, whenever that is. It seems as if alcoholics have to go through a sort of cycle of thirst. Then it's over and they're all right for a while. I've seen this sort of thing before. It's ghastly. Well, at least Dr. Donaldson won't know it this time."

"Oughtn't we to go out and look for her?" asked Nancy anxiously.

Jack smiled down at her quizzically. "You're a bear for punishment, I'd say."

"Well, how about you? You didn't even know these people two weeks ago. Now you've married them, and you may bury them before long! How about your strength and your time?"

"That's what I'm for, I figure. A minister is just an errand boy for the Lord." She watched that special smile come again. It always fascinated her.

"Well, I can certainly do my share of something. If you're going to take responsibility that isn't yours, I guess I can, too."

"I don't know that there's any use in doing any more surveillance work until she's had her fill. I believe you would be more good at the office this morning. I ought to stay here in case any calls come in about JoAnne. Let's see, this is Thursday morning. Yes, you had better go. You can call me from church if anybody needs me."

Nancy agreed. "I'll have to call Mrs. Cash first. Maybe Elbert will pick me up. I hate to advertise all this mess."

"Why not just tell them that JoAnne has disappeared and Dr. Donaldson has had a stroke because of it? That ought to be enough for the town to gossip about without the rest! Tell them you spent the night here, to help out."

Mrs. Cash took Nancy's call with her usual equanimity. Nancy often wondered whether she ever did get excited about things, or whether she had learned long ago never to show it.

Elbert was pleased to go out of his way to get her. They stopped back at home for Nancy to freshen up and she was soon at work.

So it came about that Nancy held the fort for Jack for a day or two while he divided his time between Donaldson's and his own home; for Mrs. Donaldson was still out of the picture. Emma, in the goodness of her heart, consented to come back and take care of her old master whenever a change of guardians seemed expedient.

But the events of the last few days had made a deep impression on Nancy. There were certain questions she had to have answered. For one thing, if all these other Christians, or so-called Christians, regarded drinking and even smoking as beyond the pale of their religion, how was it that Jack Warder, who to her seemed the most sincere of them all, could acknowledge even the faint possibility that Evelyn Donaldson, in her condition, could be a Christian? It didn't make any sense at all to her. Except for Lou Johns, Jack was the only one who had aroused in Nancy the slightest desire to become a Christian herself.

Another concern was JoAnne. Nancy knew Hank Valentine better than most of the people down here, and she was well aware that he was completely heartless when it came to a question of his own interests. What would JoAnne's reaction be, if Hank took advantage of her? There was something frank and wholesome about the girl, in spite of her giddy-headed mannerisms. She was eager for excitement, and she didn't know how to go about really enjoying life. Nancy herself felt years older than JoAnne. In fact she felt as if she had lived a whole lifetime in just the short time she had been in Florida.

She thought of the months yet to go. If she had known all that the twenty-five thousand dollars would involve, would she have made the decision to come? She was not sure at this point.

The third question that bothered her, and which had been pestering her subconscious for a couple of days, was what people like Betty Martin were going to say about her staying all night at Donaldson's. They'd be sure to find out that Jack Warder had been there, too. In vain she had tried to persuade herself that there was little else she could do. But she knew that there were those who would choose to put the worst light on it. Betty's sister Marge was obviously setting her cap for Jack. It would be no wonder if idle chatter should join with jealousy and spawn a scandal. She made a fresh resolution to keep at the greatest possible distance from Mr. Warder from now on.

Then the telephone rang. Meta answered and called her. It was Jack.

twenty-one

"This is the bureau of missing persons," teased Jack.

Nancy giggled. "What's new?" she asked, her resolution thrown to the winds.

"One mother recovered. I finally called the police and they brought her in just now. I think she's had it this time. They picked her up yesterday and kept her in the city jail. She wouldn't give her name. All they knew was Evelyn Constant, from her driver's license. She was evidently trying to protect her husband. She is very repentant. I've had a good talk with her. Now, the deal is this. We still don't dare to trust her. I'm going to sleep outside her door tonight. She's willing for it. But we need somebody to watch Dr. Donaldson. His wife plans to help but she isn't fit to, yet, and there's no nurse available tonight. Are you busy? Could you sit beside him? You could rest a little on the couch in his room when he sleeps."

"I'll be there."

"Good. I was sure you would." There was a sort of deep, satisfied admiration in Jack's tone as he said that. Nancy wondered why it gave her such a pleasant feeling inside. She threw a few things into her big envelope purse and went out to the bus, with just a word to the cook to tell Mrs. Cash that she would not be back that night.

JoAnne drove on, breathlessly, scarcely daring to turn even her eyes toward the man beside her. All she could think of was that wicked-looking gun poking its nose under her right arm. She had always dreamed of exciting adventure; now she had it.

After about ten minutes of wild whirling down the uneven dirt road her captor said, "Okay, okay, you can take it easy now. Turn left at the next road. It's narrow. You'll have to go slow."

They wound between scrub pines and palmetto wasteland until they came to a small lake with an old frame house on its bank, so laden with alamanda vines in bloom that it looked like a huge basket of yellow wild flowers.

Scared as she was, JoAnne caught her breath at the loveliness of it bursting on them out there in the desolate wilderness.

But her companion was not interested in esthetic values. His glance darted here and there as they entered the clearing around the lake. There was no sign that anyone had been there; not even tire tracks showed in the sand.

"Get out," he commanded as soon as they stopped. He piloted JoAnne into the house. She had a horrible dread that she might feel a shot in her back at any moment.

Brother! If I ever come out of this alive, I will certainly have a lot to tell! she thought to herself. Her busy brain was trying to notice every detail as she passed it, just like the heroines on television. She would have to think up a scheme for getting out, and quickly. She still felt that she would be able to outwit this fellow, whoever he was. He didn't look very smart, to her.

The house was surprisingly luxurious inside. It had evidently been a gentleman's mansion years ago. JoAnne noticed a framed certificate of some kind on the wall, with government insignia decorating it, as if the former resident might have been in a branch of the coast guard or the navy. There were comfortable armchairs and a deep-cushioned davenport, all of a style of forty years ago. There were handsome rugs on the floor, and bric-a-brac here and there. Books, moldy and worm-eaten, lined a whole wall. Strange that none of these things had been stolen, for the house must have been empty a long time.

JoAnne was desperately hungry, and fiercely thirsty. She had had nothing at all since late last night when she and Hank had stopped at a late drive-in for a hamburger and a Coke. She turned cautiously to get a glimpse of her taskmaster, to see whether that gun was still in evidence, or whether he might let her stop for a drink. It was still there, ugly and menacing. He hounded her on, through the living room, and the old-fashioned butler's pantry, into the kitchen. Here there would surely be something she could scrounge! But no. He flung open a door revealing a short flight of stairs up to a shallow dark attic.

"Get up there!" he snarled.

Tears were threatening JoAnne's brave composure.

"Couldn't you let me have a drink, or just a little something to eat?" she begged.

"There ain't nothin' here," he said. "Maybe Jim'll bring some grub. I dunno. Git."

He practically shoved her through the door, so hard that she stumbled and skinned her shin on the steps. He slammed the door behind her and locked it, leaving her in what seemed like complete darkness.

Her inclination was to pound and push on the door. In the movies she had seen, heroines always did that first, but it never got them anywhere. She might as well save her strength.

Well, here she was, in the midst of an absolutely *corny* drama. If she had to be kidnapped, why couldn't it have been in some romantic unusual way? However, corny or not, she intended to get out of here. Gingerly she felt all around her. There were walls on both sides. She cautiously raised her foot until it touched the step above. Only five steps and she found herself at the top. The floor was partly boarded over, but the ceiling was so low she couldn't stand up straight.

By this time her eyes had become accustomed to the gloom somewhat, and she saw that it was not as dark as she had thought at first. At each end of the room there were little square openings for ventilation. They were screened and louvred with wooden slats, very dirty. She doubted whether she could possibly squeeze through even if she could get the slats open.

She decided to examine the place while there was still a little light, to see whether there was any other exit than the door at the foot of the stairs. But just then she heard the sound of a car driving up to the house. It stopped, and heavy steps scuffed across the porch. She heard voices in the living room below her. One sounded like the man who had been in the car when they first picked her up. They were arguing.

She crept cautiously over the loose boards to the corner where the voices sounded clearest. They seemed to be discussing where to hide something. Their loot, no doubt. If she could only hear, she would be able to tell the police when they finally caught the criminals. For every story she had ever read, or seen in the movies or on television, had ended happily for the "goodies" and the "baddies" had been caught. It surely would not be long before some fine strong character resembling a comic strip detective would come riding up and shoot the thieves out of their hiding place. JoAnne's romantic spirit was not dampened yet, in spite of the darkness and dirt, and her hunger and thirst.

She peered around through the dingy shadows. In one end of the attic there was a table, thick with dust, and littered with various discarded objects. At the other end were several old chairs, piled hit or miss as if they had been tossed up there to get them out of the way. An old trunk and a couple of broken table lamps blocked the way to the chairs, or she might have been able to sit down. It was uncomfortable to stoop all the time. She could not stand upright even under the ridgepole. Then she spied a couch, one leg of which was bent under as if it had sprained its ankle. Gratefully she worked her way over to it, but when she sat down there was a hideous rustle as of some little stealthy living thing bustling out of her way. She jumped with fright and smothered a scream. What a place! Florida was full of bugs and scorpions, horrid creatures that crawled and might bite. How long was she to have to stay in this loathsome place? Her hunger pangs were growing worse, too. At last, in anger at the two who were putting her through all this misery, she descended the steps and banged on the door, demanding food and drink.

She called a long time before they paid any attention. Finally one of the men came and swore at her through the door: "Shut up!"

"But I'm hungry," she wailed. "You have no right to starve me."

She could hear a whispered growl of consultation.

"Okay! Okay!" came the response. "We'll get ya somethin'. Keep your trap shut."

She heard noises in the kitchen. After what seemed a long time the door opened and one of the men handed in a cup of what he said was coffee. JoAnne was so famished that she didn't care what it was. She took a long swallow of it. It was wet, and that helped. It tasted musty, like no coffee she had ever had, but she decided they must have made it from some old stuff that had been left there years ago. At least it quieted the gnawing in her stomach. She crept to the couch and sat down while she drank.

She tried to turn her thoughts to planning her escape, but

all at once she was aware of being very sleepy. That was not strange for she had slept very little in the car the night before. The baking heat of the stuffy little attic seemed to overpower her. Bugs or not, she laid her weary head down on the couch and drowsed off.

Night came and she still slept. The little creeping inhabitants of the attic came out and inspected the new tenant who was disturbing their home for the first time in years, but Jo-Anne slept on. She might have been thrilled to know that her name was being broadcast over the state and beyond, but if she stirred it was only to groan and turn over on her narrow bed.

Sometime after midnight she began to be aware again of existing. She had a frightful headache, and she felt as if she had been fighting her way for weeks through thick jungles, where creatures of all sorts kept making passes at her. She struggled for light and freedom only to be thrust back time and again by some invisible power, into darkness, pain and near oblivion.

At last, after what seemed like hours of wrestling with such nightmares, she managed to get her eyes open. It was still so dark about her that she actually had to put her hands up to her face to make sure that her lids were not closed. For a horrible moment she thought that she must have been blinded, for there was not even a shadow visible. But at length, staring around, and forcing her eyes to focus, she could make out the outlines of the louvred spaces at the end of the attic room. Then she remembered where she was. A frenzy seized her. She began to shake all over with a fear that she had never before experienced. She had always been one to laugh off fears, to try to show herself bold and daring. But now there was no one to show. Only herself, and—perhaps, God.

As her senses slowly returned to normal, she was more and more conscious of God there in the cramped little attic. She had never been alone with Him before and she was frightened. Every other time in her life when she had been even slightly aware of His presence, demanding her attention, she had been able to run off to her friends, or a book, or the radio or television, to help her shake off the thought of Him. Now there was nothing and nobody. Even the two thieves, one each side of her in the car, with their sparse conversation, would have been like a refuge from the silent invisible insistence of His gaze upon her. She wanted to scream. But her voice stuck in her throat. She put out her hands as if to thrust Him away, but they fell in her lap, futilely. She bowed her head, turning it to ward off the unremitting inquisition of His righteous eyes.

But she could not escape Him. Before her shrinking soul He spread the pages of her life. One by one He turned them, giving her time to look and abhor her own self. When at last —she had no idea how long it took—she had read the whole book, even to the last hour before she stepped out of Hank's car, she seemed to see herself not a girl at all, but a worm, filthy, writhing and twisting, in frustration and impotence.

She cried out aloud in her agony, "Oh, Lord, I'm a sinner! I never knew it before. I never broke the laws of the land, but it's You I sinned against. Forgive me, Lord, I knew better!"

It was as if she had flung herself at the feet of the One who stood before her, sobbing and clinging to Him for mercy. She seemed to see in His feet scars, like nail holes. She knew that she had caused them and she wept afresh.

Then like a mother's arms around a grief-stricken child, came peace. Words she had learned from her father in her childhood sounded in her heart: "If we confess our sins, He is faithful and just to forgive us our sins, and to cleanse us from all iniquity . . . The blood of Jesus Christ His Son cleanseth us from all sin." Tears came again, cleansing, refreshing tears of relief and release. For a long time she wept quietly, surrounded as she was by those loving, comforting arms. At last her weary body, worn with hunger and turmoil, dropped again upon the old dirty couch, and she slept once more. This time her sleep was deep and sweet.

twenty-two

After Evelyn was brought home the second time, and Nancy was ensconced in the Doctor's room, the Donaldson household settled down. During the night, Jack awakened several times, and listened. When he heard Evelyn Donaldson's heavy, regular respiration, he breathed a prayer of thanksgiving and dozed off again.

Nancy ministered to her patient once or twice, but she, too, managed to get a good sound rest. Friday morning they were both ready to get back to work.

They planned for Emma to come over for the day, just to keep an eye on things, until Mrs. Donaldson was thoroughly back to normal. Jack stopped for her and picked up the children. Between them, he and Nancy could look after them at the church for one more day.

Dr. Donaldson was no better, and the anxiety over JoAnne had increased. As time went on and not a trace of her whereabouts was reported, Jack discussed with the police the necessity of apprehending Hank. He had already been questioned more than once, and apparently knew no more than he had told them at first. But it did not look good for him. They were keeping a close watch on him. Farmers living in the rather desolate area where he said JoAnne had started to walk had also been interrogated. One or two who were accustomed to

leave for market in the early morning said they distinctly recalled seeing a girl of JoAnne's description, with a small
suitcase, walking along the road Wednesday morning. That
was all. She had completely vanished.

At first no one thought of connecting her with the much
publicized bank robbery that had taken place at noon on
Wednesday. But Thursday afternoon a small boy turned up,
who told police that he had been standing outside the bank
just before the alarm was given, admiring a late model car
that was parked immediately in front of the door. He said its
engine was running, and a girl was at the wheel. He noticed
her, he said, because a tough-looking man who "didn't seem
to belong to her" was talking to her. After he walked away,
a "big ugly woman" came out of the bank and got into the car
"in a hurry." He was greatly impressed by the speed with
which the girl shot through the town. He had said to himself
at the time that she sure was going to get a ticket.

That was not much of a clue, but police were encouraged,
for the boy was able to give them the make and model of the
car. However, the scent did not lead them far, for the car was
found within three hours, parked innocently in front of a
store on the edge of town. Nobody seemed to know who had
left it. A check of the license number showed that it must
have been stolen from the garage of a family who were on a
trip to Bermuda for three weeks.

The more details Jack learned, the more he suspected that
there was more to JoAnne's disappearance than a childish
desire to get it back on Hank, or to earn publicity. If she
were simply visiting school friends, somebody would surely
have seen the notice in the paper, or heard the broadcast, and
notified the police or the family.

All through the morning's work, Jack was praying continually for the girl. He felt the responsibility heavily, since her

father was so ill, and her new stepmother had troubles of her own.

Nancy had no difficulty in keeping Jack's two children happily occupied. She had brought crayons and scissors and reams of colored construction paper. She didn't mind their cutting on the bare tiled floor. A few sweeps of a broom would clear away all their mess. Now and then she took them out for a run or a game under the trees on the church lawn. Cindy's acid observations about Jack's various callers amused her continually. Then came Betty Martin, with her sister Marge.

Betty opened the screen door and at first she just stood and stared at Nancy, snickering sardonically, while Marge moved on to Jack's outside office door. Nancy was puzzled and angry at Betty's insolent attitude. However, she tried to cover up her feelings. Forcing a smile, she asked, "What can I do for you, Mrs. Martin?"

Betty glanced at Jack's children, and then at the open door between the two offices. Jack had no callers except Marge just then.

Betty gave forth with, "Nice little family group, eh?" in a sneering tone inaudible in the next room. "Well, you sure do work fast. Some of us could probably win our bets easily, except that I'm sure Mr. Warder's principles would never permit him to be 'unequally yoked with an unbeliever.' It's too bad for you, isn't it?"

Nancy flushed crimson and turned away to her typewriter. She was afraid to speak. Did they consider her a heathen? She tried to control her rage.

"Did you want to see Mr. Warder?" she asked. Her voice was pressed and unnatural.

"Ha, ha! I did get your goat then, didn't I? Well, I'm just expressing admiration, really. We simply don't know how you do it. But I think it's only fair to warn you. You probably don't realize how people would feel about you being the minister's wife. You really had better lay off. Personally, I'm not the narrow-minded sort. So don't think *I'm* trying to throw in a wrench. Actually, I just stopped in to see if there's any news of JoAnne."

"Not that I know of," answered Nancy coolly.

"Okay, you don't need to be so snooty about it. We all know that you get the lowdown on everything, and we would just like it shared now and then. All was quiet at the Donaldsons' last night?"

"Yes," replied Nancy, burning with fury.

By this time Cindy had halted her cutting operations and was giving close attention to the visitor's remarks. With her usual arrow-like penetration, she put in, in a high pitched innocent tone, "I know your little boys, Mrs. Martin. I met them in Sunday school last week. Jimmy said he's awfully tired of baby-sitters. I told him he ought to be glad he had a mother."

She returned casually to her play. Jack appeared just then with Marge hovering near, looking up yearningly, waiting for an answer to some question she had just put, which Jack had ignored. Nancy's rage melted into a fiendish desire to laugh. But Betty simply glared at the little girl, slowly comprehending. She simply couldn't let on that she understood; it would be too embarrassing. So she chose to ignore her remark and make much of the child's interest in Jimmy.

"You must come over and play with Jimmy sometime, Cindy. He would be so glad to have you. And it would relieve Miss Lansing, too." She couldn't resist that last dig.

"Oh, *she likes* to take care of us, Mrs. Martin. It's not a chore to *her* at all." She spoke pleasantly but her implications bit.

Betty Martin froze. "Well, I guess we'll be getting on, if

you won't tell me any news about the Donaldsons. Good bye."

Nancy slid a sheet of paper into her typewriter and began to type, furiously, anything, just to keep busy.

In a few moments she became aware of someone standing in the doorway to her left. Startled, she turned to see who it was. Jack stood looking down at her with a combination of hilarious amusement and admiration. She wondered how much he had heard.

He made no reference to the incident except to say, "Well, there's never a dull moment, is there? Come on, kids, time to go home for lunch."

For some reason which she couldn't fathom, Nancy felt better.

Scarcely five minutes after he had gone, the police called for Jack.

Nancy thought quickly. If she relayed the message it might take longer than if they spoke to him directly.

"I'll give you his home number," she replied instantly.

They sounded excited, she thought to herself. I wonder what they have discovered?

twenty-three

When JoAnne began to stir on Thursday morning, even before she was wide awake, she was aware of a feeling of peace, like the easing of great pain. Then all the memories of the last two days came flooding back to her. Nothing peaceful in them, certainly; nothing but horror and dread. Then she remembered what had happened in the middle of the night, and she knew instantly that those arms were still there, strong and faithful. She drew a deep breath of relief and gratitude.

Then she opened her eyes. Even though it was broad day, the light in the attic was dim. The heat was stifling, too. Added to that, her tongue felt like dirty carpet, and her hunger pangs were almost unbearable. She had had nothing but that vile-tasting coffee since Tuesday night. She was not sure how long she had slept. What day was this? Even her watch had stopped. She tried to rise from the couch with some idea of rousing those two thieves downstairs, if they were still there. But she was dizzy and terribly weak. Were they going to leave her there in that attic room to starve? Panic began to seize her. She struggled up from the sofa and worked her way, cramped with stooping, to the stairs. She had to sit down and move from step to step in a sitting position, for her legs would scarcely hold her. She began to pound on the door and kick with her feet. Perhaps if she made enough noise and disturbed them they might be frightened lest someone would hear, and they would come to her just to get her to keep quiet. But each time she bastinadoed the door and yelled, she was met with utter silence. She might have been in the hall of the dead.

At last she concluded that there was no one in the house. She sank down on the steps and sobbed in a frenzy. But gradually, as she wore out her frustration, she began to be aware of those arms once more.

With a last helpless cry she let her head sink down onto her arms on the step.

"Oh, Lord," she wailed aloud, "You must know that I'm here, and that I can't do anything about it. It's my own fault, I know. I'm *sure* You're going to take care of me and get me out of here, because You're like that; but I'm so tired, and hungry, and thirsty, and so dirty!"

She thought afterward that she must have fainted then, or

at least slept again a long time there on the stairs, for when she roused next, the sun showed in thin slant rays at the opposite end of the room.

She tried to bestir her brains to think of some way to get out. She ought to work fast before she fainted again, or grew so weak that she couldn't run if she had to.

She made her way up the stairs again and began a systematic search of the attic to see what weapon or tool she could find. Perhaps if she could come upon a hammer or a hatchet she could chop the door down.

She examined every inch of the room. The trunk was empty except for a couple of old service uniforms.

There were no odds and ends about the floor. But the table invited exploration. There were some technical navigation books piled on one end, a box of electrical fittings, rusty and worthless; some nuts and bolts, and an odd-shaped object that did not seem to be worth bothering with. JoAnne decided at first glance that it might be an antique coffee grinder. But it had a wire connected to it. Had somebody tried to save grinding by hand? Because it was the last object in the room which had not been examined for possible use, she picked it up. It was rather heavy. She noticed some printed directions on it.

She turned it over and there on the other side were the letters SOS Coast Guard. She halted. What the thing could possibly be she hadn't a clue, but she knew what SOS meant. She took it to the last rays of afternoon sun struggling through the dirty louvres.

She had to rub several places clean enough to make out the words, but gradually she began to realize that this was actually some kind of signal. Feverishly she read through the directions again, almost memorizing them, for the light was growing dim and she might have to work in the dark. Finally she thought she knew how to operate it. Would it still work? No telling how long it had been up there in the old attic. There was a long fine wire extending from the signal box which, the directions said, should be attached to an aerial. She shook her head. No aerial here, certainly. There was not another bit of wire in the attic. Or wait! The screens across the ventilating louvres! At school the kids had often used wire screens for radio aerials in their rooms. Hope renewed her vigor. She hurried to the other end of the attic and came back with a chair. Gingerly, lest she break her new treasure, she climbed up with the end of the wire in her hand and tried to poke it through the screen. But the wire was just a little too thick to slide through the holes in the screen. She hopped down and felt around in the dust on the table until she found a big screw. This she worked into one of the interstices in the screen until she enlarged the hole enough to take in the signal wire. She slipped it through, but now there was no way to bring the end back and fasten it. She felt in her hair. No bobby pins. But there might be one in her purse. She pawed around. Yes, there it was. After much poking and twisting she managed to fasten the wire securely. She was exhausted after that, and had to sit down and rest for several minutes. Then horror possessed her lest she would not live till morning without food or drink, and she seized the handle of the signal box according to directions and began to turn it. It resisted at first, but with some effort, and working it gently back and forth, she finally got it to moving fairly freely.

Round and round she turned it. Squeak, squawk. Was she doing any good? Or was she going to spend the last few days of her life like a lunatic, winding a rusty crank around? She became almost hysterical at the thought. But she took a firm hold on her fears and began to pray as she turned. Her brain was so fatigued that she fancied herself a heathen priest turning a prayer wheel. Sometimes she would laugh wildly at herself and her fantastic situation; other times she would weep and sob, and cry out for those comforting arms about her. For hours she kept at her task, intermittently. Sometimes she dozed, sometimes she fell into a sort of coma. But every little while she would rouse and go at it again.

All night long she persisted. But the only sounds she heard were hoot owls and bats and none of them came to her rescue. Just before dawn her hold on the box loosened. It fell and she collapsed on the floor on top of it.

It was some time after midnight that a young recruit in the Coast Guard watchtower twenty miles or so from where Jo-Anne was imprisoned, suddenly became aware of an insistent call: SOS-SOS-SOS. It was faint, and sometimes it died out altogether. It was not like any modern signal he had learned in his recent training. This was the first time he had been left alone at the post and he was eager to prove himself. Should he give an alarm? Or was this merely a routine call that nobody had remembered to tell him about? Perhaps a child was playing a prank. What a fool he would feel if he roused the rest and there was nothing to it. They would never get over teasing him.

For some time he listened, trying to get used to the signal, persuading himself that it was nothing unusual. But he could not shake off the weird sensation it gave him that somebody, somewhere was in trouble. At last he called a buddy of his on the phone.

"Joe," he said, "I'm sorry to rout you out but I want to know what I should do." He told him what he had heard. "It's something new to me. I didn't want to make a big scene over nothing."

"For cryin' out loud!" ejaculated Joe. "That could be a ship at sea, or a small boat in trouble. You never ignore that. Sure, call in. We may be able to spot it."

Before long, messages were flying and boats and helicopters

began a search. They called another watching station and found that they also were getting the signal, but very, very faintly. Soon the location was plotted between the two stations. But by that time the signals had ceased.

After the police call came for Jack at noon on Friday, Nancy sat by the phone to eat her lunch. She hoped he would call her if there was any new development.

Sure enough, in a few minutes he reported the news that an SOS had been received in the area where JoAnne had last been seen.

"Of course it may not have anything to do with her," he said. "How she would ever get hold of one of those old wartime signals is more than we know. But it is something. The only trouble is, the calls stopped about dawn this morning. They were faint, at best. Let's hope it's not too late. They have plotted the exact section where the calls must have originated, and the highway patrol are searching with cars and helicopters. Keep praying. I'm going to stay here and work this afternoon, at least until the children wake up from their nap. I'll call if I hear any more."

Keep praying! It had never once occurred to Nancy to do any praying. She had never formed the habit of taking her problems to someone else. Everything in her resented the ridiculous idea that a God who *could* do anything about a situation like this, would have allowed it to take place in the beginning. Yet Jack was not a gullible man. Nor Lou Johns. They both believed in prayer. It was puzzling. She toyed with the idea of trying it. How would one go about it? She certainly did not intend to stand and close her eyes and reel off long involved sentences such as she had heard the deacons do in church. Neither did she have any inclination to kneel and clasp her hands. But she would truly like to have a part in helping JoAnne if she was in trouble. And if people like Jack and Uncle Lou felt that it would help, she was willing to try.

She raised her eyes as a start. The first thing she saw was Edna Forrest's motto: "Delight thyself also in the Lord; and he shall give thee the desires of thine heart."

There was a recipe, all right, but she had no idea how to meet the condition even if she wanted to. Delight thyself in the Lord! What did it mean? Was that hateful Betty Martin delighting herself in the Lord? Or a man like Mr. Cash? To her, it seemed more as if he were delighting only in money and all the luxuries and power it would bring.

She thought of the Christians in this church where she had landed so unexpectedly; just what were they all delighting in? She began to evaluate them in her own mind as she saw them. She forgot that she had started out to look to the Lord.

There was Mrs. Cash; she, apparently, delighted in keeping Mr. Cash happy.

Elbert; his delight was certainly to glorify Elbert and enjoy him forever. Nancy had heard the children reciting something like that and it seemed to fit Elbert.

Meta? Poor Meta seemed to think she had nothing to delight in, as far as anybody could tell. Maybe her delight was to be miserable.

There was no question about Betty Martin. Her delight was gossip, and Tom's was Betty.

Winnie Windom? Well, hers was not worth mentioning. It was no secret.

Hank had no delight, as far as she could tell. Maybe he and Meta were in the same class.

She began to bring before her mind's eye all the other people she had met since coming to Florida. There was that absurd author fellow, Arthur Pease. He delighted in his "masterpiece" of philosophy. She laughed again to herself as she remembered how funny he had looked when she rebuffed him.

Evelyn Donaldson, pitiful woman, rushed to her bottle for

delight. As for her husband, Nancy had always sized him up as one who had never got over wanting a mother's arms about him. JoAnne, obviously, wanted fun, excitement, adventure.

How about Chuck Immerman? Assign him to the band wagon. Flemming Elder? His delight was to think well of himself, Nancy decided acidly. If that were taken away, would he have anything left?

Nancy, by this time, was fairly sure that she had a pretty keen discernment of people. Perhaps she ought to have gone in for personnel work, or psychology.

Even little Ellenelle had her own goal; she was always wanting things and people to be right and true. Poor child! She was always being disillusioned.

The picture would not be complete, mused Nancy, if she did not include her own family. Well, no difficulty there; her mother never had cared for anything more than money. Dad? She thought a moment. Yes, Dad probably cared to be considered to have "made the grade," more than anything else. Not once did it occur to Nancy to analyze her own heart. But there were two others whom Nancy was subconsciously avoiding in her list of characterizations—Jack Warder and Lou Johns. She was honest enough to know that in both of them she would find a whole-hearted delight in the Lord. When she finally faced that fact, she suddenly halted in her complacent analysis. The corollary to it was startling, to say the least. For of all the people she had evaluated, she undoubtedly admired most those two whose lives she had just admitted to herself were wholly committed to the Lord. Then that meant that she, Nancy Lansing, the irreligious heathen, preferred out-and-out Christians above all others! She was dumbfounded. It didn't make sense, because ever since Betty had pointed the finger at her, she was more than ever determined to have nothing to do with religion.

Hastily she replaced her fingers on the typewriter and

went on with the letter she had started to write. The implications of her last deduction were far too cataclysmic to face at present. At some other more convenient time she would take them out and examine them.

There were a few other unsolved riddles, too, that she knew she had laid away to wait until she was ready to attack them. Aunt Bea's last words, for instance, and one or two remarks of Uncle Lou's. But not now. There was too much else to take her attention now. Wait until JoAnne was found.

But like the striking of a clock before one is ready, came the triumphant telephone call from Jack:

"They've found her! Praise the Lord! She's alive, but not much more. They have taken her to a hospital near Starke. She's weak and they want her to rest twenty-four hours. I told Evelyn we'd go up tomorrow afternoon to get her. It's not too long a ride from here. It may do her father a world of good to see her back."

Nancy laid the phone back on its rack slowly, awesomely. She felt as if she had been suddenly challenged by her own words. But there was a rush of glad eagerness, too. Was it only because JoAnne had been found?

twenty-four

The news of JoAnne's rescue soon spread. Saturday morning, just about noon, Betty Martin popped into the church office again. Nancy dreaded now to see her chic blond head appear at the door. It seemed as if Betty always had some poisoned barb ready to let fly at her.

"Hi!" she greeted Nancy gaily. "I hear that JoAnne's all

the rage for the latest TV heroine," she jibed. Another person could have said that, thought Nancy, and it would have been just a harmless figure of speech. How was it that Betty always spiced her thoughts so that they emerged as catty remarks? Nancy could not find any way to smile or take it lightly.

"Who's going to bring her home?" prodded Betty undaunted. Her eyes held Nancy's, daring her not to tell the truth, the whole truth and nothing but the truth. Nancy's fell before her and instantly Betty knew that she had something to hide.

"Mr. Warder is going up this afternoon," she answered coolly. How glad she was that Mr. Warder was not there. He had gone home to lunch.

Betty laughed, an ugly giggle with a sharp hook in the end of it.

"Mr. Warder *and* who?" she persisted.

Nancy changed color, much to her own chagrin. Why did she have to give away her thoughts by that mortifying red that always rolled up under her fair skin? What could she say? How had this woman discovered that she was to go? There was no reason why she should not take a drive of a few hours with Mr. Warder, to be company for JoAnne on the way home. Nobody else knew the whole story of trouble and shame that must be told to JoAnne. It would not be easy for her to hear. Oh, why in the world did this offensive person have to make an issue of it?

Nancy did not answer. She busied her fingers with some copies of the church bulletin which she was preparing for the next day.

Betty's eyes remained on her, waiting, until finally the woman burst out into mocking laughter.

"What sage was it who said that well-timed silence is more eloquent than speech? Well, apparently you don't care who is saying what about you and Mr. Warder. But remember I warned you! Have a good time while you can. Ta, ta."

The screen door clicked shut and Betty's high heels clicked down the walk, leaving Nancy in a furor of indignation and uncertainty.

Was it true that she was guilty of bringing shame to Jack? As the minister of the church it was probable that all these people looked to him to set standards. For the life of her she could not see that she had broken any rules of modesty or convention. But perhaps they had some far-fetched ideas of their own that conflicted with what she had been used to. Surely, however, Jack himself would have known if there was any basis for criticism. Impulsively she seized the phone to call and tell Jack that something had come up which made it impossible for her to take the trip with him. But before she could dial his number, Elbert appeared to take her home to lunch. She shrank from making the call in his presence, so she locked the office and went home with him. But she was silent and distraught. She would have liked to ask some stable sensible person whether she was wise in going with Jack, but whom would she ask? And it was rather late now, anyway. Jack was stopping for her at one.

She ate very little and excused herself as soon as she could. But even that caused comment. Meta remarked acidly to the rest before she was out of hearing, "I'd be ashamed to show my eagerness the way she does. She's so hipped over Jack that she can't even eat. As if he'd ever *consider* marrying *her!*"

Nancy, halfway across the living room, whirled right-about-face and stormed back to where the family were still seated around the lunch table. The fire in her eyes and two crimson spots on her cheeks turned her into a flashing beauty. Elbert gloated.

She looked straight at Meta.

"I'm sure you meant me to hear that, so I'd better let you know that you succeeded. I've heard a lot of other innuendoes, too, and I would like you to know that I am definitely *not* interested in your cousin Jack Warder. He is *years* older than I am, and besides, *I* wouldn't marry a minister if my life depended on it. I might become too much like the rest of the *hypocrites* I see all around here! I'll thank you to leave me and my affairs out of your conversation from now on!"

She turned on her heel and stamped out and up to her own room. They all stared at each other in amazement.

Mrs. Cash looked hurt, and sought to find words to soothe and at the same time reprimand her daughter, not too harshly, for calling forth such a tirade.

Meta herself wore a sneer on her lips and sat with her head held high in stunned haughty silence.

Mr. Cash hissed, "Spitfire! That's what she is! And after all we've done for her, too!" He flung his napkin down and shoved back his chair.

Elbert wore a broad grin. He had hugely enjoyed the little scene. For one thing, it put Nancy on record about not caring for Jack. He intended to bring that up and use it to his own advantage with her if possible.

But little Ellenelle gazed in sorrow from one of her family to another. Finally two big tears rolled slowly down her face.

Nancy, back in her own room, let silent, furious sobs have their way for several minutes.

She felt as confused and hurt as she had last winter when she had had to face the fact of her bridegroom deserting her. It seemed that you could never depend on *any*one to stand by you.

At last, still angry, she dried her tears, washed her face, and prepared hastily to go out. She had decided that it would be ridiculous to change her course because of the gossipy chatter of two women. Why should she care what they thought anyway? How did they find out that she was going?

She was determined to let them know that she was not accountable to them. She made herself immaculate in a dainty pink gown and matching sport cap. But she was ready ten minutes ahead of time, and she couldn't sit still. So she walked to the corner and mailed a letter in the corner box.

She felt like a common little teenager, sneaking away from the house. For the third time, she decided that this was *it*. She would start tomorrow to look for another boarding place. She was tempted to pass up the twenty-five thousand even at this late stage of the game, and just pack up and go home, even though her common sense reminded her that she had had just as hard a time at home last year; was there *no* refuge in the world where she could find peace?

As she paced up and down, waiting for Jack's car to come along, she thought of all the peaceful places and people she had ever known. Actually, the list was short: Aunt Bea's death bed—who would ever expect that, of all places, to be peaceful? Edna Forrest's office, the first day Nancy came. What had happened to it since? And Lou Johns' little abode. There was one more, only one; but that one, Nancy would not even permit to enter her thoughts. It had been desecrated by the unlovely words of the two women who had recently destroyed what peace of mind she did have.

Just at one, Jack turned up. He gave her a curious look while she climbed into the car, and then he glanced at her again. He opened his mouth to say something, but then he closed it and made no reference to the obvious redness around her eyes, or the fact that she had been waiting out on the street.

In companionable silence they rode several blocks. When they reached open country, Nancy heaved a deep, deep sigh and began to relax.

Jack stole another look at her, but waited for her to speak. Finally she said, "People are funny."

He grinned. "Where have I heard that remark before? I agree."

She laughed a little, then sobered. "I mean they *aren't* funny." She said it so fiercely that he refrained from any more quips. Her rage rose again and she spoke in a strained voice. "They're horrible!" She turned her head away so that he would not see that she was struggling with tears again.

He waited, understandingly. Then he said, "I still agree." Then after a moment, "My relatives especially?" He spoke almost sadly.

She was looking at the distant landscape when he said that, and for a moment it seemed as if she had not heard, or as if she took the remark dispassionately. Then all of a sudden she turned and looked at him.

"Why, no!" she said. "How stupid of me. Honestly, I scarcely ever think of them as your relatives. They're not a bit like you. No, it's not only they. It's—" her voice trailed off, "everybody. Just people."

Then, as if she were flinging off a hated disguise, she suddenly broke into laughter. He laughed, too, and the day seemed brighter.

"This is really a break, this holiday," she said. "I feel as if I had been shut up in Pine City for ages."

"How long have you been here?" he asked conversationally.

"Just a couple of months longer than you have," she replied. Then impulsively she told him how she came to be there. "Nobody knows how many times I've determined to throw up the deal and leave. I hate so much of it. I suppose I seem like a heathen to you. You never feel that way, I'm sure."

He grinned. "Don't I? I'm 'people,' too, you know."

"No! You're not!" She shook her head vehemently. "Not the kind I meant."

"You don't know me. I used to have an awful time keeping my temper when my mother-in-law wanted to spoil the children. I blew my top more than once at her." He cast her a glance like a sheepish little boy. Her eyes rested on his big capable hands on the wheel. It was hard to imagine him failing to cope with a mother-in-law.

"It's tough to learn to live with people," he went on. "I had a beautiful wife, and I loved her, but she was not easy to get along with. She was like her mother, always saying the wrong thing." He shook his head forgivingly. "Poor Lu, she made so many enemies! But I'm sure the Lord planned that I should have all those experiences, to learn a little more psychology, as it were, and know how other people feel. My little daughter, I'm afraid, is going to be just like her. I often wonder how I'm ever going to handle her. It seems to me the Lord surely chose a *dud* when it comes to my being a father to those two."

"Really, Mr. Warder? I never would have thought that *you* felt anything but competent."

"Oh, my aching back, no! I'm anything but! If I didn't have the Lord to go to, I'd be sunk." He shook his head. "But— right here let's cut out the 'Mr.' business."

Nancy caught her breath. "Oh, but that wouldn't seem right for me to talk to my boss, and a 'reverend' at that, in such disrespectful terms." She twinkled at him.

"Don't make me a boss. Not right now, anyway. I certainly haven't been talking to you like a boss, have I? I don't know why I told you all that about my family. I've never said it to anyone else. But I sized you up that first day as a person who didn't blab."

"Thank you," she said simply. "That's a compliment that I prize highly."

They chatted on, discussing what might be JoAnne's condition when they reached the hospital.

They were both shocked when they saw her. It was not that she was actually thin, but her fresh little-girl plumpness had disappeared and a maturity of spirit had taken possession of her. It gave an impression of quietness after storm.

She was pitifully glad to see them. She introduced them to the tall young Coast Guard officer who had come to say good bye to her.

"He is the one who first heard my SOS," she explained gratefully. "And guess what? I found he is a Christian. Isn't that wonderful? He knows the Lord a lot better than I do. He was praying for whoever it was all that night when he heard the signal," she added wonderingly. "Oh, I have so much to tell you!"

Jack and Nancy exchanged glances of amazement. This was not the old flippant JoAnne. Jack glowed.

"I'm glad to make your acquaintance, brother," he greeted the boy, shaking hands warmly. "You and I must have met before, at the Throne!" he chuckled with delight.

They put JoAnne between them lovingly and waved a farewell to the young man, who promised to make a visit to Pine City as soon as he had opportunity.

"Brother! Is this ever different from the last ride I had between a man and a woman!" exclaimed JoAnne. Then she began her story and told them every detail, not omitting the night of despair in the attic when she found that the Lord was with her.

Nancy listened open-mouthed. She had heard sermons and even testimonies since she had been in Pine City but this was different. This she was seeing with her own eyes. JoAnne was not the same girl who had left them that Tuesday night. She would never be the old JoAnne again.

"Oh, it's so good to be going home," cried the girl. "I never *wanted* to go home before."

Nancy threw a quick look at Jack. How were they ever going to tell her about all that had happened at home? It would be too cruel.

"I'm glad you said that, JoAnne," began Jack gently. She looked at him, startled. "Because it's going to take some loving on your part to meet what you will meet at home."

"You mean—" she halted. Then, sorrowfully she added, "People are down on me, of course, for running off the way I did."

"No, I don't think they have paid much attention to that," explained Jack. "But you must realize that your disappearance hit your father and your new mother very, very hard. I don't know whether you knew it or not, JoAnne, but your stepmother has had an almost unconquerable enemy to meet in her life, for some years. I say 'almost,' for the Lord can give victory and I believe she's on her way to it. She's what is sometimes called an alcoholic."

"Oh, *no!*" cried JoAnne. "I—I knew she drank some, before we knew her. But— Oh, poor Dad!"

"Yes, it was hard on him, coming at the same time as his worry over you. She resorted to her old false refuge, and he saw her brought in. I'm telling you frankly now, JoAnne. It's better that you know the whole story before you get home."

"Yes, I want to know," she answered tremblingly. "Is Dad—?"

"He's not in good shape. He had a stroke."

"Oh-h! *Poor* Daddy!" JoAnne was silent. For some minutes no one spoke. "You know," she went on at last, "I have always blamed him a lot for my life being so mixed up. But I know now it wasn't all his fault. He *was* too easy on me. I guess I needed a lot of spankings that I didn't get. I

219

got to thinking I could get away with most anything. I'm glad the Lord stopped me and gave me a real spanking, before it was too late. I *always* knew better. I think most kids do. At least those who have grown up in any sort of a Christian home. I hope I can make some of the kids I knew see it now. I'm going to tell them all exactly what happened to me. But how is Dad, really?"

"He is able to move one hand a little, to motion. That's all. The doctor thinks he may improve a great deal when you come home."

"Do you really think I meant that much to him?" JoAnne asked in wonder. "I always thought he sort of wished I wasn't there in the way to hinder him with his books and all."

"I'm sure you mean that much to him," replied Jack confidently.

Again she was silent. Nancy, too, had very little to say all the way home. She was doing a great deal of thinking. She was ready to believe that what she was seeing and hearing was real. But how in the world did it synchronize with the state of things as she left them that morning? If a girl as scatter-brained as JoAnne could be so different, why not Betty Martin? Or Meta Cash? Or Mr. Cash himself? It was a mystery.

Just before they reached Pine City, JoAnne spoke up again.

"There is somebody I'd like to see on the way home. Will you stop at your house for just a minute, Mr. Warder? I want to talk to Emma."

"Be glad to," said Jack.

"You know, she brought me up. I've treated her like dirt. She's a wonderful person."

"I've found that out," said Jack. "I don't know what I'd do without her. The children love her, too."

They drove into Jack's garage and let JoAnne slide out.

Through the glass door, they could see Emma getting dinner.

"Emma!" cried JoAnne, rushing in and throwing her arms around her old nurse. "Oh, Emma! Can you ever forgive me?"

"Well, if it ain't my honey chile!" Her big arms enfolded JoAnne in a warm motherly embrace. "Sure, I'll forgive ever' thing you ever done, honey chile! Bless de Lawd!"

They stayed only a few minutes. Emma watched them out yearningly, wiping the tears from her eyes with her big white apron, and exclaiming over and over, "Bless de Lawd! Halle —loo!"

twenty-five

The last whispering chord of the organ faded and the congregation settled itself to hear what their new preacher had to say to them. This was his fourth Sunday in Pine City. On the first three he had given stirring doctrinal sermons; by now there was nobody in the congregation who had any doubt about his orthodox views. He believed that the Bible was the word of God, from cover to cover. He held the same views on salvation by grace that the Westside Community Church had been faithfully taught for twenty years. The members settled down in their respective pews with a feeling that all was well; they could enjoy the fine delivery, the good looks, clear pleasing voice, and the earnestness of the young pastor of their choice. They were congratulating themselves, each in his own way, on their wise selection of a new minister. Some, it is true, gave credit to God for sending the right man, but many either praised Dunn Cash, or managed to squeeze some little glory for themselves out of making the successful choice.

This was also the Sunday after JoAnne Donaldson was

brought home. A hangover of excitement was in the atmosphere.

Winnie Windom was there, in soiled pale blue silk, sitting near the front, directly in the center, gazing up at the pulpit adoringly.

When Jack rose to his splendid height, Betty and Tom Martin glanced at each other and then at Marge. Betty could not resist a sidelong glance toward Nancy Lansing, too, even if she did have to screw her head around a bit to be able to catch a glimpse of her. For Nancy was seated far at the back of the church, off to one side, almost underneath the gallery.

Bob Manton wore his most prosperous manner, sitting ramrod straight and filling adequately his expensive new suit. He turned his head neither to right nor left, as if to establish the fact that nobody, not even Dunn Cash, had sufficient authority to direct the thinking and the activities of Robert P. Manton. One could imagine that even the Lord Himself was merely Manton's junior partner. Mrs. Manton, immaculate with white gloves, which she wore even on the hottest Sundays, roosted meekly on his left.

Flemming Elder, with his faded wife, was discreetly and modestly off to the side, near the aisle. His hand always shaded his eyes during the opening part of the service.

One whole row was taken up by Dick Blount and his family—an efficient, plump wife, and five little girls, all dressed alike by the skillful plodding hands of their mother.

Chuck Immerman sat near the front, directly behind the Cash pew. His wife and thin, frustrated young son were with him. His older brother and his family were somewhere at the back of the church.

Elbert Cash and young Nick Immerman sat in the gallery, at the rear, so that they could slip out early without being noticed if they got too bored.

The rest of the Cash family always took the second row

from the front, with Dunn Cash at the end, which put him directly under the nose of the pastor, so that he could assay by odor, as it were, every thought as it came from the lips of the shepherd, before it could reach the flock.

Dunn Cash was strangely uneasy. Apart from his own business affairs, he had told Alice that morning that he had a hunch Jack was going to get out of hand. He wore a frown and he chewed on his harelip during the opening hymns and throughout the offertory.

Jack paused a moment before he began his talk.

"Let us ask the Lord's special blessing for us all today," he suggested and bowed his head with reverence.

"Spirit of God, search each heart today. May we hear Thy word, and only Thine. Anoint my lips to speak Thy word and only Thine, to the glory of the Lord Jesus. Amen."

The words were spoken so earnestly, and with such measured emphasis that they seemed to bear special significance to this particular sermon on this particular day.

Dunn Cash's frown grew deeper. A general alertness was apparent throughout the room. Then Jack began.

"Last week the turn of events alerted us all to eternal issues. Because of that, I feel that we should take stock of our spiritual life, as Christians.

"I will read first a short passage from the book of the Revelation of Jesus Christ. He sent seven messages, you remember, to His church, through John. The last of those seven we might call His 'last words' to the church. There has been no further message to us, except His 'Surely I come quickly.'

"Because we believe that His coming is near, we must also believe that His last message has particular significance for these last days of the church age. Listen to it, in chapter three.

" 'I know thy works, that thou art neither cold nor hot; I would thou wert cold or hot.

So then because thou art lukewarm, and neither cold nor hot, I will spue thee out of my mouth.

Because thou sayest, I am rich, and increased with goods, and have need of nothing; and knowest not that thou art wretched, and miserable and poor, and blind, and naked:

I counsel thee to buy of me gold tried in the fire, that thou mayest be rich. . .'

"Let's stop right there and see what He is saying. Does this have anything to do with us? What would a 'hot' church member be like? What would a cold church member be like?

"Perhaps when you think of a hot one you think of the Apostle Paul, or Timothy; maybe David Livingstone or Hudson Taylor, or those consecrated young men recently martyred in Ecuador. They were all 'on fire,' as we say.

"If so, then who would be the cold ones?" He paused.

"It's a common thing for a wife to be cold to her husband, but it's an alarming thought that anyone who professes to have been saved by the blood of Jesus Christ could be cold to Him. Do you think it's possible? Well, I've known of people who said they joined some local church because they thought it would be good for their business. That seems like a fairly cold attitude; it's practically impossible for a child of God.

"Then what is it to be lukewarm? Can you think of anyone who is neither cold, like such a one as I just mentioned, nor on fire like Paul or David Livingstone?"

He waited several moments. Eyes dropped. Heads went down. Jack bowed his own head. "Lord, help us as we see ourselves. We are all guilty, every one of us." He remained quietly in prayer a minute or two. There was a deathly hush over the congregation. It was as if there was a cleansing power at work.

Then Jack took up his Bible again. "I guess we don't have to wonder who is lukewarm, do we?" he said humbly.

"Well, what does He tell us to do about it? 'I counsel thee to buy of me gold tried in the fire.'

"Now of course we don't *buy* salvation. It is the free gift of God's grace, free to us because Jesus Christ paid for it Himself, an infinite price. But this 'gold tried in the fire'—*that* is expensive. It is not a gift. What does it represent?

"The Apostle Peter mentions 'your faith, much more precious than gold, though it be tried with fire,' and all through the Bible, gold is a symbol of God's glory. Then what is He saying?

"Well, let's imagine a man who is saved from hell. He is like a man snatched from a burning house in the middle of the night; he salvages nothing, not even his clothes. Such a man would be naked and ashamed, wouldn't he? There would be no glory for him in such an event. But if a man, having escaped himself, should risk his very life to save others, he would, in a sense, *buy* glory for himself. True, he might actually die in so doing. In that case he would pay the price of his life; still there would be glory for his name. Do you see what our Lord is saying here? We've been saved from hell. Yet if that is *all*, we should be ashamed. Oh, He must be eager for us whom He has saved at such cost, to pay any price to have His glory shine in our lives, so that others, too, may be saved.

"Have you ever asked yourself questions like these? What price did I pay to serve Him this last week? Did I lose any sleep? Did I spend any energy in prayer? Did I do without some little extravagance that I might send more to missionaries and those who have real need? Did I leave bitter words unsaid—for His sake? That would be a real sacrifice to some people. Have I sacrificed the pleasure of repeating a juicy bit of gossip? Have I *ever* gone without a real need to supply a need for someone else—for His sake? How about money? What do I think of it? The press, the radio, our very conversation as human beings, is constantly harping on the subject.

Yet all this money talk seems to trend toward *getting* money for *ourselves*. None at all of *spending* it for *Him*, to 'buy' the heavenly gold He talks about. When He comes, where will your bank account be? On earth, or in heaven? He warned us: 'Lay *not* up for yourselves treasures on earth.' Oh, people make much of 'Thou shalt *not* kill,' 'Thou shalt *not* steal,' 'Thou shalt *not* commit adultery,' but most of us pay no attention to this other command, 'Thou shalt *not* lay up for yourself treasures on earth.' God forgive us all.

"Ye know the grace of our Lord Jesus Christ, that, though He was rich, yet for your sakes He became poor, that ye through His poverty might be rich. 'I counsel thee to buy of me gold tried in the fire that ye may be rich.' Fellowship with Him is costly. But that is the only real riches. What would it cost you? Are you ready to pay the price? You don't know what you're missing if you aren't. Let us pray."

But before Jack could bow his head, someone on the back row, next to Nancy Lansing, stood up and tremblingly made her way to the front where she turned and faced the audience.

"I'd like to say something!" It was Evelyn Donaldson. She was shaking from head to foot but she stood her ground.

The audience, already convicted, was electrified.

"Some months ago I took Christ as my Saviour. But I was not ready to pay the price for this gold Mr. Warder talks about. I was still bitter about the loss of the money I used to have. I was so bitter that I used to get in a frenzy about it, and—well, you all probably know of our trouble and how I dishonored the Lord last week. I did it publicly, and I want to say publicly that I am sorry and ashamed. I won't say that I won't do it again, for I'm no better than I was. But I will say that I have committed myself wholly to God. If He takes everything I have, it's all right. And I know that He *can* keep me if I let Him. I want Him to do it at *any* cost."

Her voice broke many times; tears were streaming down

her face and many other faces, too. With trembling lips she went on bravely.

"And now I want to thank Him before you all for saving our dear daughter JoAnne. She went through some very difficult times to find out that she too was a sinner. I want to thank you folks, too, all of you who were praying for her. I'm sure many of you were, and I love you for it. Won't you keep on praying for us all, for my husband and—my son, too?"

Jack had stepped quietly over to the organist during Evelyn's last few words and now the music of "For You I Am Praying" stole softly out into the hush that followed her confession.

Jack led in the chorus, and one after another joined with him.

Nancy was tremendously stirred. To hide her emotion she slipped out just before the benediction and went into her office as if she had an errand there. Not for anything would she let those people see that she was moved by a religious service.

She felt as if she must be alone. So, rather than go home to listen to a carping rehash of the morning's events, she wandered downtown.

Passing a drive-in, she saw a man hurrying away with a double order of hamburgers. How nice, she thought, if she had a family to take a lunch to. Suddenly she thought of Lou Johns. Hastening up to the window she gave her order. When it was ready she fairly flew down the two blocks to Lou's little sanctuary.

Thus it happened that Nancy was not at home when the call came for Dunn Cash to come immediately to Chuck Immerman's house.

As soon as she heard Lou's hearty, "Come in," Nancy felt better, as if she had been blessed by a holy hand on her head.

He was as pleased as a child over her visit, and they chatted happily. She told him about JoAnne, and her rescue; about Evelyn's lapse, and about her remarkable confession at the church service that morning.

"I can't understand any of it, Uncle Lou," Nancy burst out after a long silence.

He waited.

"It has been puzzling enough to see all those *hypocrites* behaving like beasts all along, ready to scratch each other's eyes out. But I can't help feeling that Evelyn Donaldson is sincere. Yet if she is, why did she go under like that? If God really is able to change people, why couldn't He keep her from getting drunk and making all that trouble for herself and everybody else?"

Lou Johns smiled. He wore a calm, patient attitude that Nancy always said made him look "like the eternal hills."

"There are three tenses to being saved," he replied.

"What on earth do you mean?" queried Nancy.

"Well, she *was* saved from the guilt of sin by trusting what Christ did on the cross for her. She *will be* saved from the presence of sin when He comes to take her to heaven; even her body will be changed and glorified. But there's a way of *being* saved every day from the power of sin. A lot of people don't realize that. Being saved now is taking His strength against temptations, and His courage in danger, and His patience in trials. Perhaps she doesn't know about that kind of salvation yet. Or maybe, as she said, she was hindered by still wanting her old wealth back. To be saved every day requires that we commit ourselves and all we have, to Him *at any cost.*"

Nancy stared at him. Her eyes began to take on a faraway look. A long time she was still. Then gradually a light of understanding grew in her face. She was not aware that Lou Johns was praying fervently for the light to dawn in her heart.

At last she turned to him. "I think I begin to see it now," she spoke very slowly. "It's like what Jack said this morning in his sermon. It *costs* to be real! And most people don't want to pay the price." Suddenly she stopped and gazed straight at him. "Uncle Lou," she said solemnly, "*that* kind of Life is what I want. I want *all there is* of it. How do I get it?"

A radiance not of this earth glowed in his worn face.

"Just take it," he said simply. "Here. Read this." He handed her his Bible and pointed to a line or two.

" 'For by grace are ye saved, through faith,' " she read wonderingly, " 'and that not of yourselves, it is the—gift—of God.' " She looked up at him. "I'll take it." She drew a deep breath.

"Tell Him so," he urged gently.

She gave a start. "You mean—*pray*? I don't know how."

He laughed a little. "You know how to thank a person for a gift. Well, He's a person. Your new life is a gift."

"Oh-h! You mean—just—thank Him?"

"Just that." He closed his eyes. "Father, here is Nancy, come just now into Your family. She wants to talk to You." He waited a moment. "Nancy, thank Him."

Hesitatingly at first, she spoke. "Thank You, *Father*—may I call You that?—for the life I believe You have given me. Thank You, too, Jesus, *Lord* Jesus, for making it possible. I want it to be—real. I don't want to stop halfway. Thank You."

She looked at Lou. His eyes were still closed. There was a smile on his face. She waited.

When he glanced up she said shyly, "That wasn't much of a prayer. I don't know how yet."

"Does a child have to be taught how to talk to his father? He just talks, doesn't he? And I think likely there's nothing sweeter to God the Father than His new child's baby-talk." He smiled again.

"Oh, I wish I could stay here with you, Uncle Lou. I dread going back to Cashes'. I blew my top at them yesterday. I'm ashamed of myself."

"Just tell them so and go on. If your Father doesn't want you there any more He'll move you."

She leaned over and kissed him. "There's a quietness inside me," she said. "There never was before. I hope it won't go away when I leave this room."

"It won't," he promised. "He has said, 'I will never leave thee nor forsake thee.' You may think He has sometimes, but He won't. The devil will try to make it seem false. You'll be sure to have a time of testing, maybe soon, but trust Him through it. He will not fail you!"

They talked a long time. It had grown quite dark when Nancy finally left, and black clouds were gathering for a storm. Lou made her promise to take a taxi home.

The house was dim and silent when she reached there. A gloomy palm bent its crooked hand ominously above the roof. It seemed to hover like fate clutching, clutching, to strangle any life that might be in its power.

Nancy shuddered as she stole up the stairs. She had told the taxi man to wait, for she had a new desire to go to the evening church service, and the house looked so deserted she thought that there was no one home to take her.

But she no sooner reached the upper hall than Dunn Cash appeared and blocked her way.

twenty-six

It was four o'clock when Chuck Immerman's call came. The family had just finished its Sunday dinner and nap. Cash tore down the stairs to answer the phone. He snapped at Chuck in monosyllables, his voice rising into a tight shrill scream.

Then he slammed the receiver down and rushed out to the garage. He raced the engine to warm it, roared out the driveway and up the street. After he was gone, the whole house seemed to heave a sigh of relief.

Chuck began without ceremony.

"I sent for you," he said, "for two reasons. First, about you know what. Also, because I wanted to talk to you privately about that church secretary you hired. Sue here knows the whole thing, so I'll not ask her to leave. In fact, it was she who first brought the subject to my attention."

Cash narrowed his eyes. Chuck was watching him closely.

"Sue was out shopping all day yesterday with Betty Martin and some things came out in their discussion that I think you should know. It'll be up to you if you want to do something about it."

Cash raised his eyebrows and produced a sound which gave Chuck to understand that he was in accord with what he might have to say. So Chuck continued.

"It's not that she has committed any great crime. I really don't believe that she has actually done some of the things that are being rumored about her. But there's talk. And it seemed to me that as a church, standing for the right things, we can't afford to have someone here working in the office about whom there is any breath of scandal." He paused, observing Cash's expression. "The way things are going, it looks as if Jack is going to fall for her, hard. Naturally, as worldly as she is, we can't have her for a minister's wife. I don't want to harp on my own family, but my sister-in-law Marge, even young as she is, would be better. At least she's a Christian! Well, I can see that all this is not entirely news to you."

Cash nodded.

"Well, it seems there's an accumulation of the little things that we have all been more or less aware of," went on Chuck. "The women sort of itemized them, I guess, in their talk, and it doesn't look good. You know what I mean—the constant running after men, the rumor that she smokes on the sly, maybe even drinks for all we know, on some of the wild parties I hear she goes to at the country club. She never even pretends to be interested in the spiritual life of the church. I don't know that she has ever made any profession of being a Christian, has she? She certainly has been very intimate with JoAnne Donaldson and that new stepmother of hers, and that's not a good sign. I hear that she was practically engaged to the son in New York before she came down here, and everybody knows that he is no good. Betty heard somewhere that she was so wild up north that her family had made some deal to get her away and down here with her aunt Miss Lansing to see if she couldn't get her straightened out. Then there are those nights she spent at Donaldsons' when Warder was there. She doesn't attempt to deny that. Do you know anything about it?"

Cash twisted his face in assent. He managed to imply without words that he knew a lot more about it than Chuck did.

"The thing that bothers me most is," Chuck sat forward on his chair, "if she is so unstable in her personal life, how can we afford to trust her with the confidential matters at the church? How do we know, for instance, that she is not going to juggle the books somehow? I've been watching lately. I haven't found anything wrong yet, but you never know when something like that will turn up. How did you think she was when she worked at the appliances office?"

Cash shrugged. "She's a good worker all right, but she is nosy. She thinks she knows too much. In fact she does." Cash flung a swift significant look at Chuck that vanished instantly lest his wife should notice it. "And after all we've done for her, she blew up at Meta yesterday inexcusably. She implied things about all of us that weren't very nice." He shook his head. "I hate to fire her, but I guess it's best. I've lost confidence in her altogether."

Both men wore expressions of sorrow, as if they were losing a dear friend. Sue's eyes gleamed, but she had been primed to be silent.

"I'll think it over. The trouble is, there's nobody available right now to take her place."

"Marge could do the work. She'd be glad to."

"Really? Well, that's fine. Because Jack can't hang around the office all the time waiting for the phone to ring. By the way, what did you think of the display this morning in church?"

Chuck shrugged again. "Sensational. Rehearsed, I'd say. But it'll haul in a lot of people. Folks like that sort of sob stuff. I don't go for it myself. There are lukewarm churches that need to be stirred up, but there's no need of that in *our* church."

"The trouble is," said Cash, "that Jack is going to antagonize the people who have money, and they are the ones we've got to hold, to keep the church going. He's so everlasting extreme about his position. If he'd just go a little easy, he'd draw the crowds all right, and things would be smoother. It's not wise, and I'm going to tell him so. He'll pipe down when I get done with him. Maybe Marge will be good for him, too. He probably figures that with me as his uncle he can get away with a lot. But he'll have to pull in his horns. He's been here how long? Scarcely a month, and he's trying to get people stirred up already. It's not healthy. Well, I'm glad you called me, Chuck. We'll hold the line. Just keep your shirt on, and we'll have a change of end men."

They laughed good-naturedly, but there was a tense undercurrent of anxiety in Cash's voice that Chuck did not miss. He strolled out onto the porch with Chuck to be beyond earshot of Sue. There Cash fairly pounced on his friend. "Well, what's the verdict? Did they go for the loan?"

Chuck shook his head. Cash's whole being tightened. He started chewing his nails viciously.

Finally he burst out, "I've only one more hope. If that doesn't work, I'm sunk!" He flung himself into his car and drove home through the gathering clouds at a furious speed. A few minutes later Nancy's taxi drew up.

Cash's intention had been to talk to his wife before making his last try for money downtown. But the house was empty; evidently the family had all gone out to supper or left early for church. He felt bitter, hurt, resentful, as if they should have known that he wanted help and sympathy.

In his frustration he came face to face with Nancy in the hall and blurted out, "Here you are! This is as good a time as any to talk to you. I've had a time of it this afternoon. It seems the church people are up in arms about you working at the church. We're going to have to make a change."

He said it gruffly, without softening the bluntness of it.

Nancy was speechless. The new-found peace in her heart was so rudely and so suddenly shattered that she felt actually dizzy.

"But—Mr. Cash!" she stammered. "I thought you said— my work—was—"

"Your work's all right." He shrugged her off roughly, bitterness twisting his features. "It's just public opinion. A church has to be particular, you know, especially a church like ours, with its extremely high standards, and more especially of course, with a young, handsome, *unmarried* pastor. I'm sure you understand."

Nancy stared at him, the ugly truth piercing her.

In a small, frigid voice, she answered, "I—understand." Then she turned away lest angry tears should disgrace her.

She walked into her own room and closed the door, very, very firmly. She would not lower her dignity so much as to slam it. That was the sort of thing a Mr. Cash did.

She heard him in his own room pacing the floor, stomping heavily, back and forth, back and forth.

Only a moment she stood in front of her closed door, then she flew to her closet, dragged out a dress or two, snatched her toilet articles from the bathroom, and threw them all into a week-end case. The family returned, but she was too distraught to notice. Tonight, now, this minute, she would leave this house and never come back. She could write Mrs. Cash to send the rest of her things. She began to pack them all, feverishly, into her two big suitcases. But before she could finish and slip out, there came a tap at her door. It was Mrs. Cash. She had been crying.

She cast a glance of dismay about the disheveled room. Then she came straight to Nancy and impulsively put her arms about her.

"Oh, my dear! Please don't do this!" she begged. "You must not mind my husband. He is sometimes very brusque. I should feel terrible if you thought you had to go off like this. Please do stay, for a while anyway. We—we—love you!" The poor woman, harried for so long by her husband's vagaries, quite lost control of herself and wept on Nancy's cold, rigid shoulder.

For a minute Nancy was nonplused. Was this, too, a front? Then she realized how much Mrs. Cash had had to put up with. Slowly her arms stole around her and she laid her own head against Alice's straggly hair and wept with her.

After a few moments Alice raised her eyes, damp and pink, and the two women searched each other with a long, long look. Then Nancy slowly smiled, pitifully, compassionately. Alice Cash clung fiercely to her again and sobbed with relief.

She could find no words. What could she say? She would not speak disloyally of her husband, wrong as he was. But Nancy understood and Alice was satisfied.

As silently and suddenly as she had come, she slipped out again.

But the terrible ache in Nancy's heart refused to go away. She was determined not to stay in this place another night.

She listened intently. Sure enough, in another few minutes, some of the family, at least, went out again to church.

Stealthily Nancy slid out and ran down to where her taxi still waited.

Trying hard to control the breathless trembling of her voice, she leaned toward the driver.

"Do you happen to know which leaves first for New York, train, plane, or bus?"

"Bus leaves at nine-ten, ma'am. It's seven-thirty now. Nothing else till midnight."

"Thank you. Then you may take me to Fourth and Central. Just drop me at the drug store near the bank. I can easily walk to the terminal in time for the bus."

Nancy was determined to have one more visit with her beloved friend Lou Johns before she left him forever.

Nancy paid the taxi fare and hurried away with a nervous gait.

Never had she felt so lonely or yearned so desperately to talk to somebody who would understand. She turned her steps to the weather-beaten little refuge, down on Fourth Street's alley. Faster and faster she went as she neared the haven. It was as if she were fleeing from an actual enemy. The darts and jibes, the insinuations, the sneering, prying eyes, and finally Cash's cold dismissal, all seemed pressing in on her to choke her to death.

twenty-seven

By the time she reached the battered screen door Nancy was out of breath. She knocked hurriedly, calling, "Uncle Lou! Uncle Lou!"

The same comforting calm voice sounded a welcome. "Come in, child. What is it? Tell me all about it."

She flung herself down in the big chair and hid her face in her hands with a sob.

"Oh, Uncle Lou! I can't take it any more. Not any more. You said there would be testing, but I never knew it would be like this." She poured out her story.

With infinite compassion he waited, smoothing her bowed head with his calloused hand, praying silently.

At last when she had utterly spent all words, he said softly, "Have they spit in your face yet, Nancy?"

Startled, she raised her head. Could he be joking?

When she saw his serious tender smile, she slowly shook her head. But she was puzzled.

"They did that to Him, you know. And they pulled out the hair of His beard. His face was so marred that He didn't even look like a man any more."

He was silent. Nancy said nothing. Lower and lower her eyes dropped.

After a long time she drew a tight choking breath. Her words came with effort. "I see what you mean. I *can't* chicken out, can I?"

He shook his head slowly. "There's a war on, you know, not between man and man, but between God and Satan. We have taken sides. We can't be turncoats."

He held her gaze a long moment and then deliberately carried it along with his own, to a motto on the green painted wall: "As He is, so are we in this world."

"It isn't time yet for the war to be over. Stand fast. Leave it *all* in your Father's hands. He will bring you through."

Nancy saw the lines of his face strengthen and tighten. It must have been so that he had appeared when he faced the desolation and danger in Burma, alone. As she studied him, her own lips slowly set in a firm line of courage that grew sweeter as it set. She took another breath, a deep, free breath this time, and smiled. Triumph sat in her eyes. She rose. "I'm going to wash my face and get us something cool to drink. May I?"

"Fine," agreed Lou. She slid behind the green curtain and reached for a glass.

Suddenly the brakes of a car, driven crazily, squealed outside. A car door slammed furiously. There came a pounding knock.

Before Lou could answer, a man hastily pulled open the screen and hurried in.

It was Dunn Cash.

Nancy shrank back behind the flimsy shield, glad that she had not flicked on the light switch over the stove. She felt in no condition to meet Mr. Cash just now. She would wait. He'd likely be gone in a minute.

He threw himself down in the chair Nancy had just vacated.

"Lou," he blurted out in a sort of smothered terror, "you've got to help me. I'm in an awful jam, the worst I was ever in."

Lou Johns gazed squarely at him. His hands lay quietly in his lap, as they always did when he was under extreme emotional strain.

Nancy could see Lou's eyes. They were narrowed, scrutinizing the man before him.

"I've got to have some money, Lou." Cash was chewing his

lip. "Tonight. Or at least the very first thing in the morning. Twenty-five thousand dollars." He talked rapidly, in spurts, his voice still suppressed. "I know you must have it. I may as well tell you, Lou, I used to watch your deposits in the bank all those years you were paying me back. I figure you must have saved over a thousand a year, for you have done well, and obviously you never spend any. I know Bea Lansing left you something, too. Lou, I've got to have it. If I don't, this is the end of me."

Lou Johns sat still, his lips compressed, his eyes still boring into his visitor.

Cash was biting his nails now, and breathing hard. Under Lou's steady gaze he faltered and grew still more jittery. Every nerve in his body seemed to be in motion.

"They've got me against the wall, Lou." His voice rose tensely. His words came faster. "You'll do something, won't you, Lou? Remember I lent you the money in the first place. If it hadn't been for me you never could have got started. You never could have made it."

Lou opened his mouth. Even then he did not make a sound immediately. At last he spoke, deliberately. "The *first* place? Where was the *first* place? Once, long ago, I could have used your help, Cash."

"Oh, come now, Lou. You're not going to bring all that up again, surely. That's all under the bridge years ago. You don't hold that against me, or you would have talked before this. I know you've forgiven and forgotten and I appreciate it. It's like you. That's why I feel free to come to you."

"When did you ever *ask* to be forgiven, Cash?"

"Well," sputtered the little man, "of course I—I—oh, come now. I tell you I haven't time to go into all that now. They're practically breathing down my neck. There's not another soul I can go to. A brother Christian, you know, means a lot at a time like this."

Lou continued to look at Cash, steadily, calmly.

Finally he spoke again.

"Cash, if I'm to be any help to you at all, you've got to come clean and tell me the whole story. There's something wrong that you, a bank director, can't go to your own bank and borrow money."

"But that's the trouble!" cried Cash in agony, twisting his hands, rising, sitting down, distorting his face. "I—I *have* borrowed from the bank. Not even Chuck Immerman knows it." He bit his lip till the blood came. He licked the place and smeared the blood on his chin, wiping it nervously with one hand and then the other.

Nancy's horrified eyes were riveted on Cash.

Without any sign of astonishment or shock, Lou Johns continued his cross-examination.

"You mean," he prodded, "that you misappropriated funds belonging to your own bank." He made a statement rather than asked a question.

Dunn Cash sprang up and then sat down again hopelessly. He spread his hands. "Oh, call it what you want to. It wasn't that. I have every intention of replacing the bonds. It was this way: first a big order fell through; then I gave a bank check from Cash Appliances; certain other things didn't materialize, so I had to put up something. Now tomorrow's the deadline. Lou, you've *got* to help me, don't you see?"

"And if I gave you twenty-five thousand dollars, how would you repay me?"

"Oh, you know my word is good, Lou, and I'll give you my personal note. The money will be back in your account in three days. I promise you." He breathed fast and eagerly.

"I'm to believe that?"

Cash gave an exclamation of exasperation. "Look here, Lou, this isn't like you. You've always been what I considered a real Christian. Doesn't the Word say that if one of you see a brother have need, that you should help him?"

"Hm-m. Yes. That has *always* been in the Book, hasn't it, Cash?"

Dunn Cash fidgeted like a frightened horse.

"I don't know what you mean."

"No?" Lou waited. "If 'you see a brother have need,'" he quoted again with measured emphasis. Then he suddenly spoke with swift penetration. "I can see that you have a need, Cash. But it's *not what you think it is!*"

Startled, the irascible man jerked upright in his chair. "What are you talking about? What is it, if not money?"

"You need," answered Lou choosing his words carefully, "to be turned inside out and upside down by the Spirit of the Living God, and *cleaned*, thoroughly. You need to get off your chest all the lies and deceit that you've been using all these years to fool yourself and everybody else. You worship the Lord, yes, and serve other gods, like Israel of old. But *I* won't tell on you, Cash. Certainly not. It's not my business. It's yours. Now let me tell you this. I haven't twenty-five thousand dollars. I haven't even a hundred. How I have used it is between God and me. But if I had it I would not give or even lend it to you. It wouldn't be right. Because, Cash, money is *not* what you need."

With a whining snarl like a wounded animal at bay, Cash sprang up and stood over Lou, his hands spread like a vulture's claws. Nancy took a silent step forward. He mustn't hurt Uncle Lou. Suddenly, like a maniac, Cash seized a wooden chair. Raising it high above his head he crashed it in splinters on the floor. Nancy screamed. Cash rushed to her corner. He tore the flimsy green curtains aside.

"You!" His eyes glared. The hiss of his voice was like a cobra. "I thought we were rid of you. You have turned this man against me. He was my friend. You got fired and so you came whining about it down here! You little devil! I'll ruin you for this. I'll run you out of town." He was raving now in a high strident voice. Suddenly the door opened and the policeman on the beat walked in.

"What goes on here?" he demanded.

Cash turned on Nancy. "You called the police. You dirty little cheat."

Nancy protested. "I didn't call anyone, Mr. Cash."

"Naw, the lady didn't call me. You were yellin' and I heard the crash. I come in to see what the ruckus was about. I knew Lou here couldn't do much to help hisself. You better come on home with me. You've had just a drop too much, I guess."

Cash sputtered and drew himself up to his small height. "*Me?* Drink? Maybe you don't know who I am; I *never touch* the stuff."

The officer laughed sneeringly. "Well, maybe that's what you need then." He looked from Lou to Nancy. "Anybody want to make any charges? No? Well, let's get on, then."

He shoved Cash out the door and after a few words on the sidewalk, he saw him into his car and stood looking after him. Then he shrugged and went back on his beat.

Nancy and Lou stared at each other.

"Why didn't you tell me who it was, in Burma, Uncle Lou?"

"I couldn't bear to. I thought I'd give him a break. Besides, I knew it would be twice as hard for you, living there, to know it."

"I'm glad I'm out of there. It's been horrible."

Nancy suddenly glanced at her watch.

"I have to go now, Uncle Lou." She gave him a long, long look, then she flung her arms about him and kissed him, choking back a sob. "Thank you for everything, for always, Uncle Lou. Good bye."

Before he could answer she was gone. It was not until the next day when he had occasion to go carefully over the details of that evening that he remembered she was carrying a small suitcase.

Jack drove home thoughtfully from the Sunday evening service. He hoped that it was not only his imagination that Nancy Lansing had been deeply moved that morning. He had called several times during the day, but the Cashes always reported her out. He longed to have a talk with her. Already the day between Saturday and Monday seemed long without her presence nearby in the next office. He had hoped she would be there at church that evening.

"Well, Lord, You know all about this," he said aloud as he drove through the quiet dark streets. "You made woman in the beginning. I don't know why they're so full of whims and humors, nor why a man can't understand them. You know what I think of this girl Nancy, Lord. You know I—*love* her. You know I've waited for You to tell me when or whether to make a move. Am I too sudden?" He was silent for several blocks, struggling with himself.

"I want it all Your way, Lord, not mine. I feel as if she's in some kind of trouble. If she is, comfort her, and work it out, all in Your own wonderful way."

He put his car away and went up to brush a good night kiss on Cindy's soft hair, and give Teddy a little loving pat.

Then his doorbell rang. Because she was on his mind, he had a wild idea that it might be Nancy. Instead of Nancy, there was Tom Martin, pacing up and down like a caged animal waiting for him.

"Jack," Tom began, taking a seat with a condescending air, "I don't know how much you realize of what has been going on, and how the whole church has been talking about your secretary. We aren't blaming you, for we all noticed before you came how worldly she was and how much she went for the men. I've been talking with some of the best members. They do not think she is an asset. We all feel that we ought to get rid of her."

A sudden flare leaped in Jack's eyes. For a moment he did not trust himself to answer.

A long moment he was silent. Then with stern self-control he replied pointedly, "You speak of the 'whole church' and 'some of the best members.' I would like first of all to know *exactly* who you mean, by name, please."

"Well, ah—" began Tom, squirming.

"Please be specific. A charge like this is serious and requires a definite proof by actual facts."

"Well," began Tom once more, "frankly, I guess my wife can tell you more about the details than I can. She and Sue Immerman have been very much distressed over the whole matter. I promised them that I would go straight to you with it."

"I see. Then I should really talk to them about it. I assume that they can give me names, since those two women are certainly not 'the whole church.' But there is the other question. I want to know who you think are the 'best members,' and why they are best. I shall have to go to them also."

"Oh, you know the main ones." Tom missed Jack's sarcasm entirely. "Uh—Cash, for instance."

"He is one? And the others?"

"Well, I haven't actually talked to others, but I understand that the whole board is somewhat of the same opinion."

"You make an accusation which can ruin a girl's reputation and her whole life, and worse than that, hinder her from coming in touch with the Lord through Christians here in the church, and yet you only 'understand' that it is so. You have not traced the rumors to their source? Does Blount concur in this? Or Flemming Elder? How about Mr. Manton?"

"Well, it's a rather delicate subject, you can see. I haven't talked to them. I didn't want to stir up a hornets' nest."

Tom was more and more uncomfortable. Jack was pinning him with his steady relentless gaze.

"Then you are likening the 'best members' to hornets? Perhaps I may agree with that before this is over, Tom. Because I intend to get to the root of it. I am well aware that there is a great deal of jealousy and intrigue in many a church. If it exists here, I would say that what we need is a thorough housecleaning. May the Spirit of the Lord do just that among us. I shall get busy on this immediately. Good night, Tom."

Jack stood up. Tom stood also, too dumbfounded to demur. He stalked down the front walk and into his car.

Jack slept very little that night.

Dawn was just breaking when the phone at his bedside rang, insistently.

It was Meta Cash. Her voice was high and harsh.

"Jack!" she demanded. "You'll have to come over here right away. Mother wants you. Something has happened to Dad, and Nancy has disappeared."

twenty-eight

Dunn Cash was dead.

When Jack arrived Alice was weeping weakly, helplessly, sometimes hysterically. Ellenelle was crying alone in a corner. Meta was rattling dishes, still resentfully, in the kitchen. Elbert was talking to the undertaker.

But Nancy was nowhere to be found.

The undertaker insisted that the coroner must be called. Until he passed his decision, rumors were sure to fly. Alice Cash was sure that her husband's big bottle of sleeping pills had been more than half full the night before. Now it was empty. Nevertheless, the police discovered that Nancy had been there the night before, alone in the house with Cash, and now she had vanished. It was rumored, too, that they had quarreled.

Jack went about with a drawn face, his heart wrung out in prayer for the girl who had become so very precious to him. What deep dark places they had passed through together! Wherever she was, whatever she had done, she needed him.

As soon as he could slip away from Cashes' house, he checked the airport, the railroad stations and the bus terminal. There was nothing definite to go on. Nobody seemed to remember a girl that fitted his description of her. Finally he discovered that Elbert had her home address. He called her father. She was not there, and the last letter from her, just delivered that morning, gave no hint that she was coming. Mr. Lansing agreed to call if she turned up. If she did not, he would fly down himself.

The Pine City papers carried an ominous story Tuesday morning.

Jack was desperate. If Nancy had taken a train north on Sunday night she should have reached home by late Monday evening. Surely she would not have gone by bus.

His daughter Cindy studied him at the breakfast table. "I guess even God doesn't know where she is, does He?" she remarked, startling Jack out of his reverie.

"Oh, yes, He knows, dear. Nobody is ever lost out of His sight, you know."

"Well then, why are you so worried? Is it because you think she isn't saved, Daddy? Because she is. I'm sure she is."

Jack stared at her. "What makes you think so, honey?"

"I watched her yesterday in church. We were sitting across the aisle with Emma. She was crying when you talked." Jack was continually amazed at his child's perspicacity. "I suppose you know she loves you, don't you, Daddy?"

Jack caught his breath. "Why, no, I don't, child. What makes you think so?"

"Oh," she shrugged enigmatically, "I don't know. I just know so. I've seen her look at you. Do you love her?"

Teddy saved Jack's equilibrium by putting in, "I do. I think she's swell. We always have a good time with her. You do love her, don't you, Daddy?"

Jack paused. Should he take his children into his confidence? The truth might affect their lives as much as his own. Young as they were, it was only fair to tell them.

"Yes, I do. I love her very much."

Cindy nodded wisely. "I knew you did," she said confidently. "She will be our mother when she comes back, won't she?"

The child was uncanny!

"Come here, young 'uns," said Jack gently, putting one on each knee. He hugged them up to him. "Do you think it would be nice to have her live here and be your mother?"

"Yes," they chorused. "We like Emma, but we want a mommie, just as soon as she comes back."

His heart gave a lurch; she might be coming back, but—to what?

"Let's ask Jesus to find her for us," suggested Jack.

The children bowed their heads with his and prayed, each in his own words.

Then the telephone rang.

"There she is," shouted Teddy gleefully. "I knew God would do it."

"Mr. Warder?" sounded a man's voice.

Jack paused, trying to identify it.

"Yes?" he replied eagerly.

"This is Lou Johns. You don't know me. I'm a friend of Nancy Lansing. I saw the story in the morning paper and I have some information that may help to find her."

With thankful heart Jack hurried down to Fourth Street. In less than two hours he was on his way to New York by jet plane.

Over and over the glad story that Lou Johns had told him kept singing in his heart. He did not know that Lou Johns was thanking God at the same moment for a man like Jack to look after his precious Nancy.

Back at the Cash house all was still turmoil. The board of directors of the bank had hastily called a meeting, to which both Chuck Immerman and Mrs. Cash were required to come. Elbert pleaded ignorance and kept his thoughts to himself.

For the most part, friends and neighbors stayed away from the Cash house, lest they too become involved in matters of law: there were more of those than a mere suicide—or murder—called for. The honor of the great god Money was at stake. It began to look as though the Cashes would lose every cent, including their lovely home.

Mrs. Cash was prostrated. What would they do? She was well aware that her son Elbert had no notion of taking on his family as a liability. If he managed for himself alone he would do well. What could she do? Meta was not trained to work. The future looked worse than dismal. She longed to be lying beside her husband, earthly cares over and done with. All she could do was weep. She did flounderingly pray to the One whom she had been trained to worship. He was still her God; she trusted vaguely that sometime He would show a reason for all this. But to her He was actually an unknowable being, without a shoulder to weep on, or arms to hold her close. Yet if anyone had asked her if she believed Him to be a loving Father, she would have readily said, "Yes."

The only persons who came to help were JoAnne and Evelyn Donaldson. They stood by every day, one or the other of them, quietly doing the little things that were too much trouble for the rest to see to, like washing out a few clothes; starching and ironing Elbert's white shirts ready for work every day; fixing something especially attractive to eat; washing up all the odds and ends of dishes that collect when one or another is continually coming to the kitchen for a makeshift snack.

At first Alice Cash resented them. But the sympathy and tenderness of the woman who had so recently been in public disgrace melted her own pride. Even Meta welcomed JoAnne's cheery visits.

Flowers came from others, a great formal spray from the Immermans, another from the Martins. Mr. Manton saw to it that the church sent a huge white cross of flowers. Beautiful as they were, however, the flowers could not understand nor comfort like human beings who had themselves suffered sorrow and shame.

Tuesday afternoon the coroner was to give his verdict.

An extra edition of the paper was to cover all the gossip of the double tragedy. It was a reporter's heyday in Pine City.

The papers were already printed and on their way to the newsstands when Jack Warder called Mrs. Cash from New York.

No jet plane had ever traveled as slowly as the one on which Jack took passage to New York. His thoughts traveled the distance scores of times like flashing radar waves. In spite of the tragedy and uncertainty of the case of Dunn Cash's death, Jack's only concern at the moment was Nancy. Never once did he consider the possibility that she had had anything to do with his uncle's death. He wondered how she would look when she saw him come in. Would she be startled, or alarmed? Would she resent his coming? Or would she be pleased? Would she even be there at all?

Jack was well aware of the chatter and surmises to which a young unmarried minister is always subject, and he assumed that Nancy had also been aware of the gossip. But she had so well succeeded in hiding her real feelings that he actually did not know whether she would welcome his arrival or not—unless, of course, he could rely on his small daughter's intuition.

When at last he reached the house, he was as nervous as a boy on his first date. He rang the bell and waited, trembling and praying. It seemed years before anyone answered his ring. Oh, that it might be Nancy herself, and nobody else.

The door opened at last and there she was. Her lovely eyes leaped to his in delight and surprise. They told him all he wanted to know. In one sweeping motion he closed the door behind him and took her in his arms. A long, long moment he held her close; her soft hands stole up about his neck warmly, clingingly. Then he held her off to make sure he had really seen that light in her eyes that was just for him. It was still there, deeper than ever, burnished bright with tears of joy. Slowly, reverently, he laid his lips on hers. That kiss told all the unspoken thoughts of all the weeks past.

At last Jack took a long delightful breath and smiled, the smile that Nancy had learned to watch for and to love.

An ecstasy came into her face. "Oh, it *is!*" she whispered. "Isn't it?"

"What is, dearest?" he murmured, touching her cheek and hair and eyes with his lips again.

"That smile. It *is* for me? Oh, I have *loved* it so!"

With that he smiled again. "All for you, darling," he whispered and kissed her once more.

They laughed together for very joy.

"But tell me why you are here," she cried, drawing him down on the couch beside her. "How did you know where I was?"

He gave her a tender, serious look. Taking both her hands he turned to face her.

"I'm here because of you, dear, because I love you with all my heart. But there is a reason why it has happened this way. It's not going to be easy to tell or easy for you to hear. Can you bear it? I know you can. I've seen you take the darts of those scandal mongers with never a bat of your eye. I have been ready to tear them limb from limb sometimes."

She hid her head in relief and laughter on his shoulder. He put both arms around her again and held her very close.

"There will be no more of that sort of thing, I assure you," he said vehemently. "I had such a talk with Betty Martin yesterday that I think she will never open her mouth in my presence again. I settled a few others, too."

"Oh, Jack!" cried Nancy, aghast. "They will throw you out of the church!"

"Let them." He shrugged. "If *they* brought me there, I don't want to stay. If I'm there because the Lord wants me there, they can't put me out."

An adoring, worshipful look came into Nancy's eyes.

"Of course," she said. "And Jack—" she halted, fumbling for the right words, "I want you to know that—that I—" He waited. Suddenly she looked up at him pitifully, like a little child. "I don't know how you say it, but—"

"Yes?" he breathed eagerly.

"I know now that I'm a child of God—just a very little one, but I'm born!"

"Oh, my darling!" He drew her to him again. "I am so glad."

"So am I," she said in a small voice. "I have been such a

251

conceited little fool, thinking I could get along without God! JoAnne taught me a lot, and of course you did too—you most of all. Jack, I want you to meet Lou Johns sometime."

"I have." He chuckled. "That's why I'm here. He is the one who thought you must have come up here. You see, everybody is looking for you because of what happened. Nancy, Dunn Cash died the night you disappeared."

Nancy caught her breath and her eyes grew wide with horror.

Gradually the implications dawned upon her. "Oh, Jack! They didn't think I—" She gave a wail. "Oh, Jack!"

"They didn't really think so, I hope, but of course it wasn't the best time to vanish." He smiled at her whimsically. "Lou Johns—what a wonderful man he is!—has told me a little of what happened that night. I wouldn't blame you for wanting to leave. Cash had no business to fire you. He took too much on himself. He always did. There should have been a board meeting before he said a word to you. I should have been told of it. The whole thing was outrageous. The kindest thing we can say about my poor uncle is that he was not quite sane when he did it. I think he deliberately took too many sleeping pills, for it has come out that he actually did 'borrow' funds from the bank. Oh, it's all a mess. I'm most sorry that it happened because of the disgrace to the name of the Lord. Cash was so well known as a leader in church affairs. But the Lord is able to bring some good out of even this, some time."

"I didn't use to believe that possible, but He has, already, hasn't He?—for us, at least," said Nancy shyly, wonderingly, her hand stealing up his sleeve to touch his face.

Jack grabbed her again and kissed her. "He sure has, my darling. Isn't He good to us! I firmly believe He will be able to give us enough love—His own love—for even the Martins; it will take all the bitterness out of what has passed. Now, tell me, when will you marry me, dear?"

She gave a little catch of her breath again and turned a beautiful pink. In playful severity she said, "You don't realize, Mr. Warder, that I decided Sunday night that I would never set foot in Pine City again, twenty-five thousand dollars, or not."

"No? But *you* don't realize that a woman does have a right to change her mind!"

"Oh, Jack!" she exulted. "I can't wait to get back, now that it's with you. But what about those precious children of yours —ours?" she corrected herself. "They may not like this new deal."

"Just wait till you hear!"

Jack related Cindy's observations.

"You see, the Lord always has things worked out for us, if we'll only wait and trust Him." He beamed. "Now when shall it be? Make it soon. They need a mommie, as they said, and I need you, and we'll stop the mouths of all those cats."

"Well, give me a month or two to get ready. I won't have any dowry for you if I don't wait until my do-re-mi comes in." She laughed. "Perhaps my running away will make me forfeit that, after all, but I don't care! In fact," she added soberly, "I'm afraid of money."

"Thank the Lord for that!" exclaimed Jack. "I am too. I guess we've both seen what the love of it can do. My heart aches for those relatives of mine. I should get back and try to help them. I had to find you first, though. My darling! I can't believe it!"

Suddenly Nancy grew thoughtful. Her eyes sought the far distant horizon beyond the skyline of the city.

Jack watched her, reveling in her loveliness. She was vivid with sudden inspiration.

Finally she turned to him, her dream hovering in her eyes.

"Darling, did you say that Mrs. Cash is really going to lose her house?"

"Yes." He nodded. "It will have to be sold for perhaps half of its value, the boat and everything else. She will get nothing out of it. I don't know what they will do. Elbert isn't much help. He won't try to look after much more than Elbert, if I do say it about my own cousin."

"Jack," she began eagerly, "could we buy it with the twenty-five thousand?"

He looked a little puzzled, almost disappointed. "Do you think we need such a fine house, dear?"

"Oh, no, I didn't mean that. Maybe we'd live there, too, for a while. But I'd rather have a little cottage for us at the edge of the grounds. No, but for Alice to live there always and take care of it. And it would be wonderful for your school! That big Florida room would make a marvelous kindergarten, and there's plenty of lawn to add more rooms sometime for more grades. I want to see you start that. I'd like to see kids learn some of the things I wish I had learned when I was little. Maybe I wouldn't have been so foolish and bitter against the Lord if I had known Him then."

Jack gazed at her in amazement.

"Darling! Do you mean that?" He seized her and looked her squarely in the face.

"I do," she said solemnly. "And could we have Uncle Lou come and be sort of clerk or keep the books or something, when it gets so large that we need him?"

"Darling, you're speeding. Look out. You have me out of breath keeping up with you. What am I marrying, a jet bomber? Darling," he paused, looking troubled.

"Oh, I know what you're going to say," she broke in, "that we are going back to a lot of problems. I know that there are some, *right in me*. But Jack, I've seen these last weeks how God has been working things out. Won't He handle all the rest just as well?"

Jack's face shone. "Of course He will, dear." He drew her to him once more.

"Well, there's just one more thing I want. I would like to put in my application to teach for you, at least for a while. You know, I majored in early childhood education at one of our nation's best schools." She dimpled and laughed at his astonishment.

Just then the front door opened and Mr. and Mrs. Lansing appeared.

Nancy arose, radiant in her joy.

"Mother, Dad, I would like to present my future husband, the Reverend Jonathan Warder. Jack, here are my folks. You'll *have* to like them. Now as soon as you all get a little bit acquainted, Jack and I are going over to see Mr. Laidlaw. We want to let him know that Uncle Harry's will really carried a punch. Yikes! What if he hadn't made me go south?"

HARVEST HOUSE PUBLISHERS

For The Best In Inspirational Fiction

RUTH LIVINGSTON HILL
CLASSICS

Bright Conquest
The Homecoming
The Jeweled Sword
Morning Is For Joy
This Side of Tomorrow
The South Wind Blew Softly

JUNE MASTERS BACHER
PIONEER ROMANCE NOVELS

Series 1
Love Is a Gentle Stranger
Love's Silent Song
Diary of a Loving Heart
Love Leads Home

Series 2
Journey To Love
Dreams Beyond Tomorrow
Seasons of Love
My Heart's Desire

Series 3
Love's Soft Whisper
Love's Beautiful Dream
When Hearts Awaken
Another Spring

MYSTERY/ROMANCE NOVELS

Echoes From the Past, *Bacher*
Mist Over Morro Bay, *Page/Fell*
Secret of the East Wind, *Page/Fell*
Storm Clouds Over Paradise, *Page/Fell*
The Legacy of Lillian Parker, *Holden*
The Compton Connection, *Holden*
The Caribbean Conspiracy, *Holden*

PIONEER ROMANCE NOVELS

Sweetbriar, *Wilbee*
The Sweetbriar Bride, *Wilbee*
The Tender Summer, *Johnson*

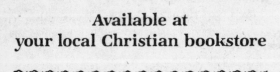

**Available at
your local Christian bookstore**

Dear Reader:

We would appreciate hearing from you regarding the **Ruth Livingston Hill Classics**. It will enable us to continue to give you the best in inspirational romance fiction.

Mail to: Ruth Livingston Hill Romance Editors
Harvest House Publishers, 1075 Arrowsmith
Eugene, OR 97402

1. What most influenced you to purchase **The South Wind Blew Softly**?
   - ☐ The Christian story
   - ☐ Cover
   - ☐ Backcover copy
   - ☐ _____
   - ☐ Recommendations
   - ☐ Other **Ruth Livingston Hill** Classic Romances you've read

2. Where did you purchase **The South Wind Blew Softly**?
   - ☐ Christian bookstore
   - ☐ General bookstore
   - ☐ Other
   - ☐ Grocery store
   - ☐ Department store

3. Your overall rating of this book:
   - ☐ Excellent ☐ Very good ☐ Good ☐ Fair ☐ Poor

4. How many **Ruth Livingston Hill Romances** have you read altogether?
   (Choose one) ☐ 1 ☐ 2 ☐ 3 ☐ Over 3

5. How likely would you be to purchase other **Ruth Livingston Hill Romances**?
   - ☐ Very likely
   - ☐ Somewhat likely
   - ☐ Not very likely
   - ☐ Not at all

6. Please check the box next to your age group.
   - ☐ Under 18
   - ☐ 18-24
   - ☐ 25-34
   - ☐ 35-39
   - ☐ 40-54
   - ☐ Over 55

Name _____

Address _____

City _____ State _____ Zip _____